AN OCEAN OF COURAGE AND FEAR

Other Books by Jerry Borrowman

*Compassionate Soldier: Remarkable True Stories of
Mercy, Heroism, and Honor from the Battlefield*

*Invisible Heroes of World War II: Extraordinary
Wartime Stories of Ordinary People*

*Catastrophes and Heroes: True Stories of
Man-Made Disasters*

*Why We Fought: Inspiring Stories of Resisting
Hitler and Defending Freedom*

By Bernard Fisher and Jerry Borrowman

*Beyond the Call of Duty: The Story of
an American Hero in Vietnam*

AN OCEAN OF COURAGE AND FEAR

JERRY BORROWMAN

SHADOW
MOUNTAIN
PUBLISHING

Photographs of Al Jowdy and Sandy Oppenheimer on pages 244 and 245 are courtesy of Al Jowdy and Sandy Oppenheimer, respectively. All other images are in the public domain.

Visit us at shadowmountain.com

Library of Congress Cataloging-in-Publication Data

Names: Borrowman, Jerry, author.
Title: An ocean of courage and fear Jerry Borrowman.
Description: Salt Lake City Shadow Mountain, [2024] | Includes bibliographical references. | Summary: "This gripping novel opens days after the attack on Pearl Harbor and details three years of sea battles that spanned the Pacific from the Aleutian Islands to Hawaii and Okinawa with the crew of one of the most decorated ships of the Pacific War, the heavy cruiser USS Salt Lake City."—Provided by publisher.
Identifiers: LCCN 2023049888 (print) | LCCN 2023049889 (ebook) | ISBN 9781639932368 (hardback) | ISBN 9781649332530 (ebook)
Subjects: LCSH: Salt Lake City (Heavy cruiser)—Fiction. | United States. Navy—History—World War, 1939–1945—Fiction. | Pearl Harbor (Hawaii), Attack on, 1941—Fiction. | Sailors—United States—History—20th century—Fiction. | BISAC: FICTION Historical 20th Century World War II | LCGFT: Historical fiction. | Novels.
Classification: LCC PS3602.0779 024 2024 (print) | LCC PS3602.0779 (ebook) | DDC 813/.6—dc23/eng/20231215
LC record available at https://lccn.loc.gov/2023049888
LC ebook record available at https://lccn.loc.gov/2023049889

Printed in the United States of America
Publishers Printing

10   9   8   7   6   5   4   3   2   1

CONTENTS

CONTENTS

DEDICATION AND THANKS

This book is dedicated to the thousands of men who served on the USS *Salt Lake City* in World War II.

My special thanks to Derk Koldewyn and Chris Schoebinger, my Shadow Mountain editors, for their superlative skill in polishing and finishing my story and to Senior Chief Petty Officer Jonathan Koldewyn, USN, for his insights into military etiquette and protocol. I am grateful to Al Jowdy and Sandy Oppenheimer, who served on the USS *Salt Lake City* in World War II and who appear as themselves in the book, and to their family members Louise Jowdy and Randy Oppenheimer for their review of the book. Bill Gallagher read the manuscript during its development and offered helpful insights and suggestions.

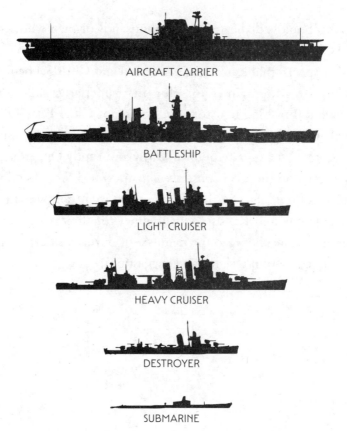

AIRCRAFT CARRIER

BATTLESHIP

LIGHT CRUISER

HEAVY CRUISER

DESTROYER

SUBMARINE

CHARACTER LIST

FICTIONAL CHARACTERS

Lieutenant Commander Justin Collier

Heidi Collier

Verla Collier

Emery Collier

Lieutenant Commander John Branson

Lieutenant Riley Bracken

Machinist's Mate First Class Stuart Appelle

Lieutenant Ross Allen

Seaman Jules Foreman

Signalman Third Class Lloyd Kartchner

Dr. Kawikani "Kani" Caro

Kailani Ikaika

Koa Ikaika Sr.

Koa Ikaika Jr.

Ensign Bud Miller

Audrey Miller

Mrs. Matsui

Seaman Arkin

Chief Pettinger
Ensign Oliver
Seaman First Class John Boyle
Seaman Boulter
Dr. John Ferguson
Angela Millburn

HISTORICAL CHARACTERS

US NAVY
Vice Admiral William Halsey
Vice Admiral Thomas C. Kinkaid
Vice Admiral Charles H. McMorris
Vice Admiral U. S. Grant Sharp Jr.
Rear Admiral Husband E. Kimmel
Rear Admiral Norman Scott
Captain Leroy W. Busbey
Captain Marc Mitscher
Captain Bertram Rodgers
Captain Ernest Small
Captain Ellis Zacharias
Commander Worthington Bitler
Lieutenant Paul G. Dimmeck
Lieutenant Dan Rowan
Boatswain's Mate First Class Alex Mihalka
Gunner's Mate First Class Elmer Breeze
Fireman First Class Vito Bommarito
Water Tender Third Class Walter Freysinger
Stores Assistant Third Class Sandy Oppenheimer
Seaman Albert "Al" Jowdy

US ARMY AND ARMY AIR FORCES
Major General Albert Brown
Major General Douglas MacArthur
Lieutenant Colonel James Doolittle
Captain William Willoughby

BRITISH NAVY
Captain William Patrick McCarthy

JAPANESE NAVY
Marshal Admiral Isoroku Yamamoto
Vice Admiral Boshirō Hosogaya
Rear Admiral Aritoma Gota

CIVILIANS
President Franklin Delano Roosevelt
Marlene Dietrich, USO

USS Salt Lake City

Chapter 1

AT SEA

December 7, 1941
Carrier Task Force 8,
230 miles west of Pearl Harbor, Oahu

"Sir—the communications officer sends his regards and says this message is marked urgent!" The messenger's voice was tinged with anxiety, not because he knew the contents of the message, but because he had seen the look on the face of the radio operator who'd decoded it and then handed it to him to deliver to the bridge. The messenger was glad to hand it off to the officer of the deck.

Lieutenant Commander Justin Collier, third in command of the heavy cruiser USS *Salt Lake City*, sensed the young man's concern and immediately stepped away from the conversation he'd been having with the navigator to accept the message. "Thank you. Please stand by." Though pretending not to look, the bridge complement near Collier glanced at him as he unfolded the message and read it silently—it was unusual to receive an urgent message in the peacetime Navy, so this was a matter of curiosity.

Now on their way back to Pearl Harbor after taking part in a secret mission escorting the carrier USS *Enterprise* as she ferried combat aircraft to Wake Island, the heavy cruisers USS *Salt Lake City*, USS *Northampton*, and USS *Chester* had been joined by nine destroyers, all under the command of Vice Admiral William Halsey, to protect the *Enterprise*. The cruise had seemed routine until now.

Still wondering what was in the message, the bridge crew were startled when Lieutenant Commander Collier exclaimed, "This can't be right!"

For his part, Collier blushed as soon as he realized that he'd expressed his thoughts out loud—a foolish thing for an officer to do. But there was no time to explain, and he raced to the interphone on the back bulkhead of the bridge. Picking up the line that connected directly to the captain's cabin, Collier unconsciously licked his lips while waiting for the captain to pick up. It took two rings before Captain Ellis Zacharias responded with a terse, "Yes, what is it?"

"Captain, this is Collier—we've received an urgent message from the task force commander that I think you should read on the bridge."

"Be right there," Zacharias said, and slammed his phone back into its cradle. Collier hung up the handset and stepped forward on the bridge, aware the bridge crew were watching him. He tried to think of something to say but decided against it. In a matter of moments Zacharias burst onto the bridge and went straight for Collier, who handed him the paper. The men—now watching the captain instead of Collier—saw Zacharias nod several times as he worked his way through the message. Then he dropped his hands to the side. Turning to the bridge crew he said, "Gentlemen, it seems as if the Empire of Japan has decided to start a war."

This was not entirely unexpected, as tension between the

United States and Japan had been ratcheting up for more than a year, but it was a shock that what just moments before had been a possibility had actually happened. And they had no idea *how* Japan had begun the war. Most of the ten men on the bridge thought they would hear that Japan had attacked the Philippine Islands, the most logical place to attack. Now there was an expectant silence as they waited to learn more.

But instead of continuing, Captain Zacharias turned to Lieutenant Commander Collier, still officer of the deck, and said, "Bring us to full ahead and maintain current heading to Pearl. Adjustments may follow from the flagship, but for now we're heading home."

"Aye, sir. Full ahead, maintain current heading."

"Also, inform all lookouts to be on heightened watch for enemy aircraft. I'll go down to radar to speak with them personally after making a general announcement."

"Aye, sir. Right away." Collier gave the order to the lee helmsman, who signaled the desired speed to the engine room, and then motioned for both the talker and the messenger to move closer. The talker was responsible to relay orders over the interphone system to members of the bridge watch who weren't physically on the bridge; the messenger was responsible to carry messages and orders anywhere on the ship from the officer of the deck. When the two young men stood before him, he said to the talker, "Alert the aft lookout and aft steering to be on heightened alert for enemy aircraft." Then to the messenger, "Take the same order to the bridge lookouts atop the pilot house."

"Aye, sir," both men replied. "Be on heightened alert for enemy aircraft." Ship's protocol was to repeat all orders to ensure they were properly understood.

Meanwhile, the captain, who'd stopped to talk briefly with

the gunnery officer, raised his voice again and said, "Now I'll speak to the crew." The signalman stepped to the audio control panel, cleared his throat, activated the microphone that broadcast throughout the ship, and said forcefully, "Now hear this, now hear this! Captain Zacharias to address the crew." He was as curious as everyone else to hear what the message would be.

December 7, 1941
San Diego Naval Air Station

"Say again?" Lieutenant Commander John Branson shook his head, sure he'd misunderstood one of his best dive-bomber pilots as they walked toward the mess hall.

"I said, sir, I'd like to request a transfer to Hawaii to fly a float-plane on a capital ship." As the one who'd been misunderstood, Lieutenant Riley Bracken, US Navy Pilot Corps, did his best to keep his voice steady, realizing this was just the first of many exasperating conversations he'd have as news of his request made its way around the flight crew.

"So a fellow who can take off and land on an aircraft carrier, bring a state-of-the-art Dauntless dive-bomber into a controlled dive at 250 knots, the skin on your face stretched back to your ears from the acceleration—you want to trade that in for launching an awkward little Kingfisher from a slingshot, buzzing around looking for trouble, then landing on an oil slick in the ship's wake and getting picked up by a crane to get back on the ship?" Branson looked at Bracken like he'd lost his mind.

"I know, I know. All that amazing talent wasted."

Lieutenant Commander Branson shook his head. "How does this make sense to your brain?"

"It's a lot harder to miss the ocean than a carrier deck?" Bracken regretted this as soon as he said it. He was being sardonic, but Lieutenant Commander Branson was being serious. "Sorry, sir. I know you're concerned for me. I do have my reasons."

Branson shook his head and then stopped to look directly at Bracken, who stopped walking too. "Tell me your reasons. Because you're going to have to make a pretty convincing case to get me to sign off. We have every reason to think we're going to war—we'll need the best precision bombing ever, and as one of our best Dauntless pilots, you want to back out of the program? That's a load of nonsense."

"Sir, I have three reasons. First, the sentimental one: I grew up loving books about ocean warfare, couldn't get enough of it. All those books were stories of battleships and cruisers, frigates and destroyers—great big guns firing salvo after salvo. You know, the dreadnaughts and all. So for me the Navy is all about capital ships, not the air corps. Now that my daydreams are real, and we're likely to go to war, I'd like to serve on a cruiser or a battleship." He hurried to continue when he saw Branson inhale. "I know, I know—naval warfare is changing, naval airpower is as important as artillery now. I mean, that's why I decided to become a pilot when I tested well for aviation. But that brings me to reason number two: The floatplanes. While I do well enough in dive-bombing practice, it's not really my strength. I think you'll agree that my scouting skills are the keenest—and I can do that just as well in a Kingfisher as in a Dauntless—probably better, in fact, because they're specifically for both at-sea scouting and land scouting, which I think will be crucial if we're going to engage in island warfare where capital ships would support beach landings. And if I can protect a capital ship, even more vulnerable than a carrier—because it's out there to escort the carriers—well, it seems like that's important too."

Branson was quiet for a moment. "You said there was a third reason."

Bracken hesitated.

"Well?"

"You'll hate this one, sir. It's just that I have a cousin who's third in command of a heavy cruiser, and he's aggravated that I chose to become a pilot instead of serving in a line position. But since I *am* a pilot, he thinks a request to transfer to his ship would be a great thing. We were best friends growing up—and my mother puts a lot of pressure on him to watch out for me."

"You need watching out for?"

"My mother seems to think so. Part of it has to do with a couple of times I crashed our car—once directly in front of the police precinct in Queens where we grew up. Justin was always the sane one in our family, and my mother's drilled it into his head that anything that happens to me would be his fault."

Branson laughed. "Sounds to me like you had all the hallmarks of a future fighter pilot."

"One last thing, Commander Branson. I guess it's a fourth reason. In a Kingfisher, you can rescue downed flyers by landing right on the water where they went down. I guess I'd like to be the guy who saves your guys when they crash. For what it's worth."

Branson started walking again. "Okay, that last one's a good reason. And while I don't see the difference between scouting in a Dauntless or in a Kingfisher, I guess they both serve the same purpose." He walked away before stopping and turning back. "Fine. I'll sign off on your request. But you ought to get your story straight if you're going to go through this with anyone else—and there will be plenty of people with questions."

"Sir?"

"You can't be both the guy who only knows his limits—in a car or a plane—when he exceeds them *and* the guy deliberately flying a search grid at 150 knots per hour at 3,000 feet. You can't be both." Branson sounded a bit triumphant in having worked this out.

"Yes, sir. I see your point." What Riley didn't say is that he did, in fact, love the dive-bombing, pushing the limits of himself and his aircraft—the adrenaline rush was amazing. And he did believe he *could* be both of those guys at the same time. But the real reason for the transfer request was that lately he'd had a few terrifying seconds of vertigo as he pulled out of a high-speed dive—which put both his aircraft and his tail-gunner's life at risk. Better to fly a clunky, slow floatplane with little risk than to chance both his life *and* the life of a comrade. But a pilot, regardless of what plane he flew, could *never* confess to vertigo, or he'd find himself sitting behind a desk or in a control tower for the rest of his career. Riley knew he had to stick with the excuses he'd come up with rather than exposing the real reason. He was not ready to give up flying. Not this soon.

When Branson didn't ask any more questions, though obviously still irritated to lose one of his pilots, Lieutenant Bracken said, as lightly as he could, "Besides, what could be more fun than getting launched from a slingshot, landing in the ocean, and getting cranked back up to the deck in rolling seas? It's a slow-motion adventure every time."

Branson smiled, which meant that things were okay between them again. "Maybe so, but that's not for me. I'll take a carrier landing in a typhoon before I ride a *crane* back aboard. I hope you save a capital ship or two, though. I have a brother serving on the *Pensacola*—take special care if you're operating in her area."

Lieutenant Riley Bracken quietly drew in a breath—the worst was over. With the transfer approved, he could now face up to the guff he'd get from the other pilots.

Branson and Bracken were about to enter the mess hall when the general alarm sounded to alert everyone on base to prepare for an announcement. Both stopped in their tracks. "Now hear this, now hear this! Stand by for an announcement from the commander." They looked at each other, wondering if this was the announcement of war everyone had speculated would come.

December 7, 1941
In the engine room

In the engine room of the USS *Salt Lake City*, Machinist's Mate First Class Stuart Appelle paused from his inspection tour to marvel (as he did nearly daily) at the twelve White-Forster oil-fired boilers which provided the enormous amount of steam needed to power the 9,200-ton heavy cruiser through the ocean, including the incredible 107,000 horsepower produced by four high-pressure Parsons steam turbines that drove each of the four propellers needed to move the ship at up to 32.7 nautical miles per hour. With 280,000 pounds of fuel oil on board, the ship had a maximum range of 12,000 miles at fifteen nmph, but far less range at higher speeds. The boilers were a marvel in themselves. For example, some were dedicated to distilling salt water into fresh water, both to meet the needs of the human crew and to provide clean water to the main boilers. Others generated electricity to operate thousands of motors, turning everything from the clocks on the bulkheads to the massive gun turrets. And heat from the boilers warmed the ship in cold weather and turned the fans that ventilated it in hot weather. The engineering department was the essential element of the ship, and when Stuart Appelle was there, he was in his element.

For reasons he could not explain, Appelle loved the sounds and smells of an engine room, from the deep guttural roar of the superheated control boilers blazing away at up to 875 degrees Fahrenheit to the high-pitched hiss of the steam as it entered the turbines at 600 pounds per square inch. The whine of the turbines lowered in pitch as the steam pressure dropped while working its way from the small blades at the high-pressure center of each turbine to the huge fan blades that captured the last possible bit of thrust near the exhaust port at the end. And finally, there was the sound of the great shafts connected to the screws outside the ship making a throbbing sound as the giant propeller blades churned the water to give the ship thrust. It was like standing in the middle of a huge symphony orchestra, and Appelle was its conductor. Though often hot and miserable in the engine room, he was grateful the Navy had provided him the chance to transfer to a heavy cruiser which, in his mind, was the perfect ship in terms of size, speed, and mission. A third the size of a battleship but three times the size of a destroyer, a heavy cruiser was just the right combination of maneuverability and speed that Appelle thought ideal.

So far, his inspection had showed all was well with the boilers, but he stopped to listen when he heard the words, "Now hear this, now hear this! Captain Zacharias to address the crew." Since taking command of the *Salt Lake City*, Captain Zacharias had used the public address system sparingly, so this must be important.

"Men of the USS *Salt Lake City*. We have just received word from *Enterprise* that this morning, Sunday, December 7, at 0748, the Japanese commenced an attack on the naval base at Pearl Harbor from a large contingent of aircraft carriers that appear to have come from the north of the Hawaiian Islands. While information is sketchy, preliminary reports indicate that all—repeat all—battleships have been damaged or sunk while at anchor.

Nevada managed to get underway but was thereafter struck by a torpedo. Her crew decided to intentionally ground her on a coral reef rather than sink in the channel where she'd obstruct passage."

Captain Zacharias paused while men all over the ship gasped, then groaned and cursed at the news. Like Lieutenant Commander Collier when he had read the message a few minutes earlier, many declared that it couldn't possibly be true—not *all* battleships damaged or destroyed! Such a catastrophe meant a complete failure on the part of the ships to defend themselves against the unprovoked aerial attack. Most of the men on the *Salt Lake City* had friends on other ships or in the dockyards. Some, like Lieutenant Commander Collier, had family living on the islands.

How could our fighters have failed so completely? Appelle wondered. And what about the antiaircraft batteries on each ship? Those should have sent up an impenetrable barrier of flak to keep the Japanese dive-bombers and torpedo planes from getting close. It seemed impossible that an entire Japanese battle fleet could come that close to Hawaii without being detected—it made no sense!

Captain Zacharias continued. "I understand this news is incredible, but it has been confirmed by multiple reports, including those intercepted by our own communications staff. While no word has been received as to the political response from Washington, we must now consider ourselves engaged against a hostile enemy. Time will tell if this leads to war, but for now we are authorized to engage the enemy if we encounter them." This led to a cheer as the men recovered their equilibrium and used the cheer to burn off some of the anger that had surged with news of the attack. "Our first response is to launch scout planes to see if we can find any straggling enemy aircraft. If they do, we will turn to follow their aircraft back to their carriers and mount a counterattack!" This led to a second round of cheers, which was critical at this moment when the crew needed to come together in accepting a new reality. "I expect that each of you will do your duty and face the future with courage and resolve. We will not let this challenge go unanswered! That is all."

On the bridge, Lieutenant Commander Collier joined in the cheering but acknowledged the fear that tightened the muscles in his stomach. He and the men were not frightened at the thought of going to war—they'd been preparing for it their entire adult lives. But this attack in Hawaii put many of their families at risk. Most of the men in the Pacific Fleet had thought the attack would come against the Philippines, but Captain Zacharias had been a naval attaché to Japan, spoke fluent Japanese, and on this knowledge had predicted that the attack would be against Pearl Harbor. Unfortunately, senior command had ignored his warnings, and so the attack had succeeded because of a surprise element that should have been no surprise. Collier's wife, Heidi, and his two children came to mind, and he found himself saying a subdued mental prayer, *Dear Lord, please protect my family. Keep them safe.* He then tried to reassure himself. *I'm sure they're okay—the house is far enough from the harbor that it would be a waste of bombs to attack there.* But who could say for sure? It was impossible to escape the anxiety that everyone with family in Hawaii was feeling. Usually it was Heidi who worried if Justin was safe. Now he was in the dark—and it was an unexpected feeling. More than anything, Justin wanted to get back to Oahu to see how they were.

But this moment of personal reflection was short-lived. Captain Zacharias stepped over to Collier. "Sound General Quarters. I doubt that we're in the flight path of the Japanese fighters and bombers, but a burst of adrenaline will do the crew good. I'm going below to the plot room to communicate with *Enterprise* to see if we can figure out how this happened and what we should do next. Also, issue orders to the Kingfishers to implement a search pattern."

"Aye, sir. Move to General Quarters and launch the Kingfishers."

With that, Captain Zacharias left the bridge, and Lieutenant Commander Collier moved to the microphone. "Now hear this, now hear this, General Quarters, General Quarters. All hands man your battle stations. The route of travel is forward and up to starboard. Set material condition Zebra throughout the ship. Reason for General Quarters is potential incoming hostile aircraft."

All eighty-seven officers and 576 enlisted men aboard the heavy cruiser USS *Salt Lake City* immediately scrambled from their current assignment or from their bunks if they'd been sleeping to take up their assigned battle station. A heavy cruiser was nearly the size of a battleship, but with lighter armor and smaller guns which allowed for greater maneuverability. Everyone was on combat duty during General Quarters. "Material condition Zebra" meant that all watertight doors were sealed to prevent water and fire spreading in the event of an attack, even though it made it more difficult for men to move around the ship. While not yet declared in Washington, DC, the *Salt Lake City* was at war.

December 7, 1941, 0745
Honolulu, Hawaii

Heidi Collier felt a pang of regret as she flipped pancakes in a cast iron skillet. When he was in port, Justin would cook Sunday morning breakfast—a ritual the whole family enjoyed. She'd been curt with him when he left on his most recent deployment, not able to suppress the feeling of abandonment that often accompanied his military career. Yet she knew that as a senior officer on the *Salt Lake City*, Justin had to go to sea with the ship—even in peacetime. She wanted him to succeed and knew that his assignment as third officer was the best path for him to advance in his career, but she also wished he had a desk job where he left for the office in the morning and returned home at the same time every evening. Now he was out to sea, upset with the way they parted, and she was frustrated that it was an issue between them. She sighed.

"Morning, Mom," her eleven-year-old son, Emery, said as he entered the kitchen. His thirteen-year-old sister, Verla, was already setting the table.

"Morning, Mr. Sleepyhead—nice to see your smiling face." Emery hadn't been smiling, but he did when his mom drew attention to it.

"The airplanes woke me up," Emery said. "It sounds like a carrier's back in port." Emery's favorite thing to do with his father was to watch from the street outside their house as a returning carrier's aircraft would launch from the ship and land at the airfield on Ford Island.

"The airplanes?" Heidi stopped for a moment, and realized that she had unconsciously dismissed the drone of airplanes just a few moments earlier. But as she thought about it, she realized that Emery was right—there was a steady sound of far more airplanes than would be expected even for a carrier returning, and more chaotic. As she started to reply, there was a rumble of dull thuds off in the distance.

"They must be target practicing again," Verla said. Having grown up on military bases, she and her brother were used to the sound of military maneuvers, including airplanes dropping bombs on target sites, or heavy guns firing at practice targets on shore.

Heidi listened intently as a rapid succession of concussions hit the house, rattling the windows—not that the explosions were close to them, but forceful enough to tell that they were larger than usual. The frequency was disconcerting. She unconsciously turned off the burner on the stove and was moving toward the door when the air raid sirens started whining—a rising shriek that caused the hair on the back of her neck to stand up. She and the children raced out the front door and into the street, where they saw great clouds of black oily smoke rising up from Pearl Harbor, four miles away. From their vantage point in the Aiea Heights neighborhood, they saw the magnificent harbor stretching out before them, marred by the horrifying sight of torpedoes and bombs raining down on the great battleships in the harbor from aircraft with red spots on the fuselage and the top of each wing.

"They're attacking the base!" Verla shouted. "They're attacking our ships!"

Heidi was momentarily speechless—there had been so many false alarms in the past few months about Japanese attacks supposed to be coming at any moment that the sight of an actual attack seemed unreal.

Heidi noticed other neighbors reacting as she had. Their next-door neighbors, the Millers, clutched each other in their driveway. Bud Miller, an ensign on Admiral Kimmel's staff, had hastily pulled on some trousers and a white sleeveless undershirt. He was holding onto Audrey, clad in a housecoat. His hair still mussed from sleep, he kept saying, "I've gotta get down there, Audrey." And she was trying to keep him with her.

Her neighborhood friend Kailani Ikaika was kneeling in the street, crossing herself continuously as her toddler, Koa Jr., clung to her. Koa Sr. owned a restaurant just outside the base and was, Heidi thought, probably there prepping for the Sunday lunch crowd. She squinted, trying to see if she could see the area where his restaurant was, and was relieved to see that there wasn't any smoke rising from there—yet. Other areas nearby did have damage.

"Are they going to attack us?" Emery asked anxiously. "Are they going to kill everybody?"

That brought Heidi back, and she reached down and drew the children close to her. "No, they're not going to attack us up here—they wouldn't waste their ammunition. But we need to move inside just in case." That was the sensible thing, but no one moved, still too transfixed by the spectacle before them. But that changed instantly when the forward magazine of the USS *Arizona* exploded in a gigantic fireball that was momentarily brighter than the morning sun. Even though they were too far away to feel the heat of the explosion, seconds later the blast wave tore through the neighborhood, so powerful it pushed Heidi and the kids back a step. They instinctively recoiled as the blast shattered a small building on the pier next to the ship. "We need to get inside right now!" Heidi shouted, and she and the kids returned to the kitchen, where she made them huddle under the table. She held them close and could feel both of their hearts beating quickly. She wondered if they could feel her heart doing the same. The sound of bombs and torpedoes exploding, of constant airplanes circling and swooping, and of air raid and fire engine sirens continued—urgent, but diminished by distance. They were witnesses to the horror but removed from the full effects of the injury.

After what seemed like an eternity, Verla looked up into Heidi's face, her lip trembling a little. "Do you think Daddy's all right?" she asked.

Heidi was startled that it was her daughter who had first thought of Justin. Heidi searched her feelings, but didn't feel anxiety for her husband. "I believe he's all right," Heidi replied. "I'm so glad his ship is out to sea." She felt a simultaneous wave of relief and guilt that the very thing that she'd been resenting had likely saved Justin's life. She pulled her children closer. "We'll say a prayer for him."

She had begun to pray when the roaring whine of aircraft got suddenly louder. Airplanes were flying directly over their neighborhood. *From Kaneohe*, Heidi thought. *And heading down to Pearl.* She clambered out from under the table and looked out the kitchen window. Just as she'd thought, more planes—so many planes—were coming over the mountains between their home and Kaneohe to the east. She rejoined the children under the table, hearing another round of explosions starting up. "We'll stay here until we hear the all-clear sirens," she reassured them.

She paused and then drew her children in again. "And then I'm going to ask you to be brave while I go to the base hospital to see if I can help. I'll see if Kailani or Mrs. Matsui can keep an eye out for you. Kailani might need you, Verla, to help keep an eye on Koa Jr. The hospital is going to need as many nurses as they can get. Even though it's been a while since I worked in a hospital, they'll need my help. Will you be okay while I'm gone?"

"Of course," Verla said. Emery nodded and assured her he would be as well.

Heidi steeled herself and took a few moments to look deep into each of her children's eyes. "I know you're scared," she said. "I am too, but if we can help, we should help. I don't think that there will be any more planes after this group, but if they return, go back under the table and stay there until the all-clear signal has sounded. Will you promise me you'll do that?"

"We promise," they said, almost in unison.

"When your father returns, we'll learn more about what's happening." She decided to state his return as a fact rather than a hope, and it seemed to have the calming effect she'd hoped for.

Just then the air raid sirens began sounding the all-clear, and Heidi pulled herself up from under the table and then helped Verla and Emery up.

"Let's go see if we can find Kailani," she said, and led her children back out into a world that had been irreversibly changed. The sky over Pearl was dark with smoke; countless fires raged both on land and on the ocean along Battleship Row. What was left of the *Arizona* stuck up out of the fiery sea, bent and twisted beyond recognition.

And then what Heidi saw made her gasp—people, hundreds of them, making their way up the roads toward their neighborhood, refugees from the devastation below.

"The hospital might have to wait a little while," she said. "Let's find Kailani and see what we can do here."

Heidi and Kailani (and Koa Sr., one of the first to arrive back home), went to work, arranging shelter for the stunned (and in some cases injured) people who had fled to higher ground. Most ended up huddled together on lawns, staring at the destruction and fires as they burned out of control. When Heidi finally felt like she could leave, she pulled the family Chevrolet out onto the road and headed downhill, anxious to go volunteer at the base hospital.

"Sir, the scout planes are all recovered—no enemy ships sighted."

"Very well." Lieutenant Commander Collier rubbed his eyes. They'd been at battle stations for more than six hours, extending his shift and leaving him fatigued. With no Japanese aircraft spotted, the adrenaline was beginning to wear off for the crew. Now they felt an emotional letdown that earlier had been fueled by anger. "I'll report to the captain." When Collier did call the captain, who had used the time since being notified of the attack to check in on the key departments of the ship, including radar, sonar, gunnery, damage control, and the engine room, Captain Zacharias told him to let the crew stand down from General Quarters. That meant the crew could return to their normal on-and-off duty pattern. It also meant that Justin Collier could get a couple of hours of sleep. He made his way to the audio panel and sounded the order, "All hands, stand down from General Quarters. Repeat, stand down from General Quarters." He thought standing down would bring relief from the tension. Instead, it simply left a feeling of emptiness. Pearl Harbor had been destroyed.

Chapter 2

A FUTILE SEARCH

December 9, 1941, 0200
Pearl Harbor

Dr. Kawikani Caro turned to Heidi Collier and said, "I've applied tannic acid to the burn on this patient's legs and face, which should soon start to form a leathery coating over the skin. Administer morphine as needed so the patient doesn't disturb the injured areas." Fortunately, the young seaman was asleep at the time, having been burned over more than a third of his body. The charred skin and scarlet wounds were gruesome, but Heidi Collier was not put off by it. All she could think of was the agony he'd suffered while being brought to the hospital and the painful recovery awaiting him.

"Yes, doctor. I'll watch it very carefully. I worked in the burn unit at Johns Hopkins." Heidi adjusted the flow of the IV drip line providing badly needed fluid to the patient's body.

The doctor looked at Heidi Collier with new appreciation. "I see. Then you know how poor this man's chances of recovery are. So much fluid lost through the damaged tissue. The next twenty-four hours will decide."

"I know that tannic acid is effective with small wounds, but these areas are so large." She shook her head.

"I don't have any other treatment options at this point. I can't bandage the area, or the fabric would adhere to the skin and guarantee an infection." The doctor's frustration was evident.

"Of course—I know you're doing the right thing. I'll make sure he lies still." Heidi hesitated as she recalled the moment when this sailor was brought in. He'd cried out in pain, but had reached out his hand when he saw that she had tears on her face. "I'll be all right," he had said. "Others have it worse than me." The thought that *he'd* comforted *her* was very moving.

"If I were the type to wager, I'd bet that he survives," she said.

"I hope you're right." The doctor started to move off.

"One more thing, doctor. May I use restraints on his wrists if he becomes agitated? I'd hate for him to touch the affected areas. They're still so exposed."

"Yes, you have authority to do so, Nurse . . . sorry, I don't remember your name."

"Collier—Heidi Collier. I'm a nurse volunteer here—my husband is at sea on the *Salt Lake City*. I came here after the attack hoping I could help. I haven't worked as a nurse since our daughter was born, but it all comes back quickly."

"I'm Kawikani Caro, but everyone calls me Kani. I'm sorry we haven't had time to get acquainted yet. You've been here for hours."

"I came down after the attack on Sunday and worked through the night, but I had to go home yesterday to check on my children and arrange for them to stay with a neighbor the next few nights while I work here. I did get a few hours of sleep." She yawned. "I've noticed it's the night shift that has the greatest need."

The doctor looked around at the hundreds of patients scattered about the naval hospital; some in hospital beds inside the open-air building surrounded by palm trees, many more still lying on stretchers and cots in the courtyard, where tiny blue-tailed skinks crawled up and over their bodies. The lizards were mostly harmless, but would frighten patients who were drugged and in agony from their pain, so the nurses did their best to shoo them away. The casualty list seemed endless, broken bones and burned bodies everywhere. The burn victims were the worst off because of the intensity of their pain. There were even a few heart attack patients whose bodies had succumbed to the chaos of the attack when they tried to respond beyond their capability.

The doctors and nurses had been working since the first patients had begun arriving on Sunday morning, and it was now 0200 on Tuesday, December 9. Dr. Caro shook his head. "So many have died, and many more are yet to die. My only hope is that the Japanese are racing back to Japan as fast as they can. I don't see how we could survive another attack."

"I don't know what more they could destroy," Heidi replied. Caro nodded.

"Well, it's a welcome miracle that a burn-trained nurse showed up. Thank you for volunteering."

"Mrs. Collier?" Heidi turned to the young woman who had approached from behind.

"Yes, what is it?" she asked.

"There's a phone call for you at the front desk."

She turned to Dr. Caro, but he waved her away with a simple "Go!"

Heidi raced to the front desk and snatched up the handset. "Verla, is that you? Are you okay?"

"It's Justin. I really can't say much. I'm fine; we're fine. I just spoke with Verla, and she told me you were at the hospital. I'm glad you're there to help."

"Oh, Justin, I'm so happy to hear your voice. I thought you were probably safe, but I had no way of knowing, and I felt like it was all right to leave the kids, but then this call came, and I worried that something was wrong." She choked back a tear. "It is such a horror here at the hospital—injured men everywhere. Kani . . . I mean, Dr. Caro . . . and the rest of the staff have been working nonstop since Sunday. We're doing the best we can—"

"I hope you can get some rest at some point. I've been talking with some folks here who were in the middle of it, and it kills me that you and the kids had to live through . . ." He stopped, trying to collect himself. Neither of them said anything for a moment. "I want more than anything to come see all of you, but I'm afraid I can't." His voice tightened. "I'm sorry I left under— "

"I'm sorry I was impatient with you when you left."

"I know. I'm sorry I let it get to me. It's going to be even harder now. I don't know how long we'll be away."

Heidi took a breath to steady herself and said, "It'll be all right. I know what it's like, you know. My father was away for so long. It won't be easy for us, but I won't make it any harder for you. You have to do your duty—this madness must be stopped before the mainland is attacked. You're trained to do it. We'll be glad to see you as often as we can, but I don't want you worrying about us while you're away." She swallowed to stifle a quiver in her voice.

"Thank you, dear. I was so worried about you and the kids—I never expected you'd be at risk instead of me. It made me realize . . . it made me realize just how much I love you and Verla and Emery. I had this crushing sensation thinking you could have been hurt. It was hard to breathe."

Heidi nodded. This is why she had fallen in love with Justin Collier, despite her girlhood vow to never marry into the military. He was so cool and collected on the outside, but inside he was sentimental and loving, and once she had discovered that, her heart took control. Having lived on seemingly countless Army bases as her father moved around on assignment, she'd yearned for stability. But after meeting Justin, she decided that love was what mattered most—and she loved Justin. But now she had to let him go.

"I'm okay, Justin. We'll be fine. You'll protect us from afar."

He'd do everything in his power to make that true. "I need to free up this line," she said. "And I'm sure you need to get back to work. So do your best to stay in touch, and we'll be here for you when you come back." She felt her throat tighten. "Just do your best to come back—I know you can't control that, but do your best."

There was silence. Finally he spoke, his voice as tight as hers. "I promise to try. I love you with all my heart."

Wednesday, December 10, 1941
North of Lihue, Hawaii

A cheer broke out on the bridge of the *Salt Lake City*. It was exhilarating to watch an enemy hunter turned into prey. Just half an hour before, the *Salt Lake City* had made an emergency turn to port at flank speed to evade a Japanese torpedo. Now they watched in anticipation as a Dauntless dive-bomber came streaking out of the sky at 250 miles per hour, releasing its bomb at the last moment toward a submerging enemy submarine. The sub must have been lingering just under the surface in order to get a line of sight on the *Salt Lake City*. But in the clear waters of the Pacific, that meant it could be spotted from the air, and the

Dauntless had acted the moment the ship was spotted. It was likely the captain of the submarine had spied the aircraft and was executing an emergency dive, but it was too late. The first explosion was expected—the bomb from the Dauntless exploding under the water. The second explosion is what caused the cheer as a massive waterspout burst up into the sky, telling them that the sub's hull had been breached. In a matter of moments their adversary was burning in the distance. Collier watched, knowing that there would be no survivors. The explosion would have created a shock wave that almost certainly killed everyone inside the sub. "Quite a sight, isn't it, Justin?" Captain Ellis Zacharias said.

"They deserved it," Justin said quietly. It was their first kill of the war, and it took just moments for the remnants of the submarine to slip under the surface, but that didn't quench the fire burning on the water. The fuel oil that powered the diesel engines could burn for up to an hour. *A funeral pyre for those who would have killed us first if they could.*

"We needed that one," Zacharias said to Justin, but loud enough that others on the bridge could hear. Collier nodded.

"Yes, sir!" He grinned widely, another signal to the bridge crew that it was all right to savor this small victory.

"Now, return to our zigzag pattern, and let's see if we can find another one."

"Aye, sir. Return to zigzag pattern—eyes and ears to search for enemy subs so we can get our own kill!"

Zacharias smiled—the second part of Collier's repeat of his order was unnecessary, but it was a morale booster. It was too easy to become gun-shy when trying to escape from an enemy sub attack. He appreciated his third officer's sense of the situation. Collier issued the appropriate orders to the lee helmsman and the lookouts, and then returned to his watch station next to the captain. Normally the captain would withdraw until a new sighting or order from the fleet, but Zacharias seemed content to linger.

"When I was at the academy in 1912, we learned all about how to shoot at other surface ships—it was all we had to think about. The only risk to our ship was incoming fire from an enemy capital ship and you could figure out fast whether they had bigger or smaller guns than you. Smaller, and you'd pound them from a distance. Larger, and you'd beat your way out of there as fast as you could pour on the steam. But the introduction of submarines and aircraft into naval warfare means that a ship like ours is vulnerable from everywhere—aircraft above, battleships firing over the horizon, and submarines lurking below the waves looking for a clear line to launch a torpedo. Now we have to think in three dimensions."

"Aye, sir."

"Those *Enterprise* birds—they're really something. If I had time to use my slide rule, I'd try to figure out how much sheer force is exerted on the wings at the beginning of the pullout. It must be enormous! It's hard to see how those wings can take the stress, but they do. There's a lot of engineering in that aircraft."

Collier laughed. "I have a cousin who could tell you that—he's a Dauntless pilot. He knows every single statistic about his aircraft, its maximum performance under stress. And he's always happy to tell anyone about it, even when they might not care. It's always puzzled me how he could be so mathematically precise *and* such a careless daredevil at the same time."

"I'd like to meet him if we're ever in port at the same time. I like math puzzles."

"Of course, sir. I'd be happy to introduce you. Right now, he's in San Diego, likely assigned to whatever aircraft carrier is coming here next."

"Very well." Zacharias hesitated, then sighed. "You have the bridge, Mr. Collier."

"Aye, sir." Then loud enough for all to hear, "I have the conn!"

"I know that you know to be watchful, Mr. Collier. But I can sense that there are other submarines out there—and they'll want their revenge. Keep everyone alert."

"Aye, sir."

Captain Zacharias left the bridge to return to his cabin to work on paperwork and maybe catch a quick nap. Collier was pleased at their conversation—it was the first time Zacharias had talked to him in such a conversational way. He didn't know why it should matter that the captain had confided in him, but it did. He glanced at his watch and then walked over and consulted the chart. "Helm, prepare to execute our next turn on my mark."

"Aye, sir. Turn plotted and ready to execute."

When traveling as an escort, it was essential that all the ships in the group act in concert with each other to avoid collisions. And the patterns were designed to provide maximum protection to the aircraft carrier, making it difficult for an enemy boat to ever get a clear shot at the carrier—something like a ballet, but choreographed to save lives.

Thursday, December 11, 1941
North of Oahu

The *Salt Lake City*'s next chance at war came the following day. The executive officer was officer of the deck, so Collier had gone to his assigned battle station in the fire control center, where the chief gunnery officer, Ross Allen, was directing fire against an enemy submarine. The *Salt Lake City* had been in the vanguard of the task force and was first to spot the enemy sub on the horizon, most likely charging its batteries and refreshing the air.

Allen had acted immediately as soon as the coordinates had been relayed from the lookouts to the control center. The window for firing on a sub was short—just the amount of time it took for them to initiate a crash dive, an emergency maneuver in which the ship floods all its tanks to reduce buoyancy and alters the angle of its steering fins to force the sub into as steep a dive as possible. It was always dangerous, since the dive had to be stopped in time to avoid having the hull crushed by the increasing water pressure.

"Fire!" Allen shouted to his gun crew, and Collier was pleased to hear the five-inch guns begin to fire their high-explosive shells in a steady rhythm.

Looking through his field glasses, Collier saw a puff of smoke and said confidently, "I'm sure that was a hit!" A submarine was most vulnerable on the surface, since guns could be sighted with a high degree of accuracy very quickly, as opposed to depth charges, which were nothing more than informed guesses.

Allen studied the horizon with his binoculars. "I think so too—but I'm not sure. Could have been a splash in the water." He changed the coordinates and gave the order to fire again. As he looked through his glasses, Collier saw splashes near the now-disappearing submarine but could not say for sure that any of their shells had landed. In this case there had been no secondary explosions to indicate the sub was hit.

"Cease fire!"

Lieutenant Allen turned to Collier and said, "I think we punched some holes, but I can't be sure. For better or worse the sub is gone." He shook his head. "Now it's up to the destroyers." Collier could sense the frustration in Allen's voice at the thought that they'd had an enemy submarine in firing range and couldn't confirm a kill.

"This will be good practice for the destroyers. They need some experience placing depth charges." Collier watched as destroyers from the task force swarmed around and ahead of the *Salt Lake City* to start laying down a pattern of depth charges. If you didn't kill a sub with surface fire, you had to try to crush it with high explosives underwater.

"For us it's like basketball—you either hit the target or you don't. You don't get points for a near miss. For the destroyers it's more like horseshoes," Allen said.

Justin raised a puzzled eye, so Allen explained himself. "You don't need a direct hit with depth charges to win the game—a near hit is enough to crack all the pressure seals on the sub and doom it to sink. Just get close and you make life a living hell for the men on board the submarine—the sound of those explosions is deafening. And if the explosions do get close enough, the submarine is doomed. I think it's a terrible way to die."

Collier nodded. "I agree. I'm glad we're on the surface. I wouldn't have done well on the submariner tests."

Allen laughed. "Test or no test, you'd never make it in the submarine service—you're six foot two, right? They'd never take you. You'd likely crack your skull your first day at sea."

Collier returned the laugh and gathered up his things. "You did a fine job today, Mr. Allen. You reacted quickly and accurately. Your crew knew their routine and completed it in record time. If we'd have spotted that sub even two minutes earlier, you'd have had them for sure. Please convey my congratulations."

"Thank you, sir. I wish we could confirm a kill, but we'll get them next time for sure."

Thursday, December 11, 1941
Pearl Harbor

"Nurse Collier." Heidi was aware of her name being called but didn't want to respond. Then a little more forcefully: "Nurse Collier. Heidi!" She was startled by a hand on her shoulder. She must have dozed off, because she was no longer in the dream that just a moment before had seemed so real.

"Yes, what is it?"

"Your patient, the burn victim. He's asking for you."

"He's asking for me—so he's regained consciousness?"

Dr. Caro smiled. "Against all odds, I think he's going to make it. His skin has formed the protective shell, and he's no longer losing fluid."

"Oh, Kani, that's such good news." Heidi immediately went to the young man's cot, who looked up and smiled. *How can he smile after all he's been through?* She decided the human spirit was the single most amazing thing in the universe. "Hello, there. I'm glad to see you're awake."

"Thank you, ma'am. I'm not thinking very clearly, but I wanted to thank you."

"Thank me?"

"I'm not sure how, but somehow, I heard you and the doctor talking while I was lying there. I think you both thought I was unconscious. At any rate, you stood up for me and it gave me hope." He swallowed, prompting Heidi to ask if he'd like some water, to which he nodded. After giving him a drink, Heidi sat down next to him. "Tell me your name—I know it's hard to talk, so just your first name."

"Jules. Jules Foreman." She knew this from his chart, but it was a way to start a conversation.

"Well, Jules Foreman, I'm pleased to meet you again. And

29

you're the one who gave *me* courage, so I'm glad it came back to you." She took his hand. "And I believe every word I said—you can do this." Then her voice softened. "But it will be much harder than you can imagine. Your body has suffered a great shock, and it will take time for it to heal itself. So don't be afraid to ask for help and don't get discouraged when it takes longer than you think it should. Everyone here wants to help, so please let us."

"You'll be here?"

Heidi smiled. "I will." All the tired nights she had been through were suddenly worth it.

As she walked away, she noticed Kani had been silently observing, and he gave her a thumbs-up and smiled. She smiled back. Sometimes this job was worth it.

Chapter 3

OPERATION TOKYO

February 1942
The Marshall Islands

"Fire!"

Justin Collier winced *before* the eight-inch gun fired. *Pavlov was right!* Then he recoiled a second time as orange flames shot more than thirty feet out of the barrel, accompanied by the physical impact of the shock wave striking his body. He was careful to cover his ears with his hands, since the Navy didn't provide any ear protection for the gunners or others near the guns when they fired. Even so, the sound was still painful. An eight-inch shell weighed 260 pounds—either armor-piercing or high-explosive—and could travel up to seventeen miles. It took a lot of gunpowder to launch it that far.

"Fire!"

And again, he winced before the second gun in the turret fired its round. There was no urgency to the firing pattern since the *Salt Lake City* was shooting at an enemy airfield on the island of Wotje in the Marshall Islands. He pictured the havoc their guns were causing on the island—ten large guns firing in a coordinated pattern to destroy any aircraft on the ground and to make it impossible for any planes in the air to land. *Our first chance for revenge on Admiral Yamamoto for Pearl Harbor.* In fact, it was reported that the *Salt Lake City* was the first American ship to fire on Japanese-held territory in the war. Even though it was hardly proportional, firing their guns in an offensive action felt terrific.

While the Japanese victory at Pearl Harbor had been astonishing, with eight 35,000-ton battleships and eleven other ships left smoldering in the water, Admiral Yamamoto had discovered his goal of eliminating the US Pacific Fleet as a threat to Japan's war aims in the Far East had *not* been achieved because its aircraft carriers and escorts were out to sea during the Pearl Harbor attack. Destroying the carriers had been a crucial part of the Japanese plan and had failed—now they were available to harass and destroy Japanese shipping and wage war against the Imperial Navy and air service. And that's what the *Salt Lake City's* mission was about.

"Kingfisher SOC reports two direct hits on the runway. Pilot says the metal grid is torn to shreds."

"Thank you," Collier said to the young messenger. For his part, Justin felt like he had the greatest observation point in the world—the outdoor bridge, situated just above the second large gun turret. The turrets were a terrific innovation in naval guns in that they allowed the eight-inch guns to swivel to a desired firing position without having to reposition the ship. It was thrilling to see the blast shoot out from the guns and watch as the guns recoiled from the blast. *No desk job in the world can match this!* He smiled. The smell of burned cordite in the air, the sound of the aft guns firing behind him; it really was heady stuff. Then he unconsciously pursed his lips. Thinking 'no desk job can match this' was a frequent reaction when something positive happened in the Navy, and Justin was ashamed to think it was a continuing reaction to his father telling him a career in the Navy would be a stupid waste of time—he could have gone to Yale to become a high-powered attorney like his father, with a desk job in Washington during the war. But instead, Justin had accepted "an inferior income with no social status." *Just one of the many times I disappointed you, Dad.* The problem was that every time he compared his life at sea to a desk job back home, he was giving his father power—as if Justin could finally win the argument with just one more piece of evidence against a man who would never admit he was wrong.

"Sir—enemy aircraft at ten o'clock coming in low!"

Justin simultaneously raised his binoculars and swung to the indicated position. The lookout had sharp eyes, for Justin could barely see two tiny dark flecks just above the horizon getting larger. But the lookout was right, and Justin immediately moved to the interphone to alert the bridge and fire control center. He was gratified to see the forty-millimeter and twenty-five–millimeter antiaircraft guns swing their turrets in the appropriate direction and waited for them to open fire as the aircraft came into range. There was a master fire-control center for the ship, as well as a director for each gun, and this was the very moment they had all trained for.

The number of lookouts had been doubled during the attack on the islands, so Justin moved quickly to each of the assigned positions to make sure they were aware of the new threat, both to protect themselves from enemy fire and to watch for new attacks from other directions. The *Salt Lake City* was particularly vulnerable while firing on an island target since the ship was moving very slowly in the water—nothing more than a firing platform for the guns. Traveling at such a slow speed made it a very large and easy target for enemy aircraft like these, which must have flown in from bases on nearby islands to join the battle.

"Take cover!" he shouted as the enemy fighters approached, and he moved behind a protective cowling that offered at least a little protection from the rapid-fire machine guns mounted in the wings of the fighters. The sound of the battle had changed in both tone and intensity; the high-pitched staccato of twenty-mm machine guns firing at the planes as they flew over the ship, the deep concussions of the eight-inch guns continuing to fire on the island, and the *pom pom pom* sound of five-inch guns firing at the fighters as they approached and receded.

"Sir, they're turning for a new attack, and they've been joined by a torpedo plane!"

"Signal the bridge—I'm going down to confirm this with operations!"

"Aye, signal bridge."

For his part, Justin raced to the steep stairwell—hardly more than a ladder—and slid down using the handrails. He raced onto the bridge in time to hear the captain order full ahead at flank speed.

"Recommendation?" the captain asked Justin evenly.

Justin looked out the window and replied, "Starboard turn to reduce our profile!"

"Make it so," the captain said to the helmsman, and the order was immediately confirmed.

Justin knew that the captain would have made the same order if Justin hadn't shown up, but Captain Zacharias could use this moment to test his bridge crew and educate them if necessary.

"All hands prepare for impact!" the captain said, which the talker repeated into the ship-wide loudspeaker system.

Justin couldn't help but lick his lips as they watched the enemy planes head straight for them, obscured occasionally by the furious puffs of black smoke put up by the *Salt Lake City*'s guns, now forced to adjust their fire pattern continually as the ship churned the water while accelerating and turning. Justin's heart was pounding as the enemy fighters adjusted their approach. And then, just moments before releasing the torpedo that was almost certain to hit the *Salt Lake City*, the torpedo plane suddenly disappeared in a great cloud of fire and smoke. Even in the daylight, the brightness of the explosion hurt his eyes as the aircraft was erased as if by magic.

"We hit him! We hit him!" the port bridge lookout shouted in astonishment. "We hit the torpedo plane!" It was highly unusual for a firing party to hit an enemy warplane, even while shooting thousands of rounds at it; the primary goal was to force the aircraft off their approach so they couldn't accurately drop a bomb or launch a torpedo. To hit one—just moments before it launched its torpedo—was unheard of, but that's what had happened.

"That was too close for comfort!" Zacharias said to Justin, relief evident in the captain's voice.

"Yes, sir! Permission to go down and congratulate Mr. Allen directly?" Justin asked tentatively.

"Good idea. My compliments—and tell him I'll have something special for him at dinner tonight!" Captains would often supplement the usual fare with premium cuts out of their own pocket to reward their officers.

"Yes, sir!" Justin wasn't the only one to smile at this. The lookouts confirmed that the enemy fighters had broken off their attack—it didn't make sense for them to continue without the torpedo plane since they couldn't do any real damage to the ship on their own. The *Salt Lake City* had enjoyed a very successful day—a ruined airfield *and* an enemy aircraft destroyed, with no friendly injuries. As he made his way down to the fire control center, Justin Collier felt terrific. *Sorry, Dad—there really is no desk job that compares.*

March 1942
Honolulu

The driver had a puzzled look on his face. He looked down at the address a second time, then up at Lieutenant Commander Collier, then back down at the slip of paper Justin had given him.

"Something wrong?"

"Um, it's just that I took an officer to this address yesterday. And when we got there, a doctor was just getting out of a taxi." The seaman looked expectantly at Collier.

"Are you sure? What was the officer's name?"

"Sorry, I don't remember, sir. Said he was finally coming home to visit his wife and two kids."

"*What?*" Collier shook his head. This made no sense. "And the doctor?"

"Looked Hawaiian. He was holding a Liberty House shopping bag, if that matters."

"Just take me to my house."

"Yes, sir." The seaman held the door as Justin got in the back and then lifted Justin's seabag into the trunk of the '38 Ford, an official sedan painted navy blue with the US Navy insignia in gold lettering on the side doors. Justin felt a headache coming on.

As they drove past a grove of coconut trees, Justin decided to try again. "Did this other officer tell you where he serves?"

"Yes, sir. He was very chatty. Most officers prefer to be left alone when I drive them, but some are talkative. This officer loved to talk." The young man caught himself, realizing that he was carrying on. "The officer said he was the operations officer on a heavy cruiser—third in command. Been out to sea since before the attack on Pearl."

Justin scowled. "And what uniform was this 'operations officer' wearing?"

"That was the funny part. He was dressed in an aloha shirt and dungarees—said he needed a break. But his orders were good, so I took him."

Justin caught his breath, then shook his head. "Riley Bracken! What a jerk!"

"Yessir. That was his name—Bracken. Why's he a jerk?"

"It's nothing, Seaman—just get me there as fast as you can." Justin Collier bit his lip to suppress a smile. He'd have to act offended when he saw Riley, but he couldn't have been happier. Riley was Justin's cousin and a practical joker—and he couldn't wait to see him. But he'd have to ask Heidi why Dr. Caro had come round. He had an uneasy feeling about that.

April 13, 1942
At sea, steaming toward Japan

"Lieutenant Riley Bracken to the bridge. Lieutenant Bracken to the bridge!" The announcement sounded all over the ship, easier than sending a runner to find the newest member of the crew, who was tending to his SOC Kingfisher.

"Why are you smiling, Mr. Collier?"

Startled by the captain's voice, Justin shook his head and quickly dropped anything resembling a smile. "Sorry, sir. Didn't know I was."

"You were. Why?"

"It's just . . . Lieutenant Bracken's my cousin—my rather

incorrigible cousin—and I'm sure a summons to the bridge will throw him off. He's the one I told you could help you figure out the stress on a Dauntless's wings during a dive."

Zacharias nodded. "Ah, well, I look forward to meeting him, then. He must be an excellent pilot to be requested on the *Enterprise*." Zacharias paused. "Incorrigible, you say?"

"Inveterate practical joker would be closer," Justin replied.

"I see." When the captain turned away, Justin breathed a quiet sigh of relief and returned to the map table. Being part of a top-secret mission was exciting but nerve-wracking. Since joining Task Force 16 to protect the carrier USS *Hornet* with its unusual cargo, the *Salt Lake City* had been required to maintain radio silence to make sure the enemy had no inkling of what was coming their way.

Justin glanced up as Riley stepped onto the bridge. He enjoyed seeing his confusion as to whom he should report to. "Lieutenant Bracken?" the captain asked crisply.

"Yes, sir! Lieutenant Riley Bracken reporting as ordered."

Captain Zacharias motioned for Bracken to move to the outer bridge, signaling Justin to join them. Riley looked to Justin for some sort of clue but received a small shrug in return, which was returned with a quick scowl to show his displeasure.

"Mr. Bracken, I know it seems incredible in an operation this size, including the *Enterprise* and the *Hornet*, three heavy cruisers, a light cruiser, and eight destroyers, but somehow, with more than 10,000 men to choose from, the air boss on the *Enterprise* decided you're indispensable to the mission and has requested that you temporarily transfer there to help prep for this top-secret raid." Zacharias narrowed his eyes. "You've been on the ship for just a matter of days, and now you're to leave?"

Justin turned away to hide his smile. It was obvious that the captain had decided to give Riley a hard time, even though the assignment was assuredly temporary.

Bracken straightened up. "Sorry, sir! I haven't heard anything about this. It's a surprise to me. I'd never do anything without your permission."

The captain shook his head. "Pilots." Zacharias then turned and nodded to Justin with the slightest hint of a smile. It was clear that it was now Justin's responsibility to follow through in his role as operations officer.

"I'll take care of it, sir." Justin liked the way that sounded—the "it" in his sentence being Riley Bracken.

"Very well." Zacharias looked at Bracken and added, "Just remember we need you back, Lieutenant. They have all the pilots they need on the *Enterprise*, while we have just a few." He paused. "And Mr. Collier tells me you can help me solve a math problem—so I anxiously await your return."

"Aye, sir!" Riley thought about adding "I shall return," the already-famous phrase General Douglas MacArthur had spoken as he left the Philippines just a month earlier, but he decided against it. Captains weren't to be trifled with.

As soon as Zacharias had left the outer bridge, Bracken turned quickly to Justin and asked "What's this all about? I didn't ask for any kind of temporary assignment."

"Not sure. We received a coded message by signal lamp indicating that you're needed there. I can only guess why."

Riley Bracken rubbed his chin. "What can you tell me about this mission that we're all part of? And how am I supposed to get to the *Enterprise*, anyway? We're moving fast, and there's no way to land a Kingfisher on a carrier!"

"I can answer the second question. Lieutenant Smith will fly you over in the Kingfisher and land near the carrier. They'll have a raft ready to pick you up, and then he'll fly back to us."

Riley was perplexed. "I really don't know why they would want me on the *Enterprise*. The captain's right—they have plenty of pilots. And who would be making the request? It doesn't make sense. I told them I wanted out of flying dive-bombers."

"I don't know either, but it must be important. Go over there and find out what they're looking for, and then let me know if you can. In the end it doesn't matter why they're asking or who's doing the asking—you've been requested, the captain's approved, so you're about to slow down a couple of thousand men while you fly over to the *Enterprise*." He should have left it at that, but couldn't help but add, "Seems normal for you."

Riley resisted the temptation to punch him—Justin outranked him, after all. "What about the mission?"

"I guess I can tell you about that, since Admiral Halsey is going to make an announcement shortly on the *Enterprise*. We received a briefing just after setting sail from Pearl, but were instructed to wait until hearing from the admiral to make an announcement to the crew." He paused.

"Well?"

"You saw the sixteen B-25 bombers on the *Hornet?*"

"They're hard to miss. I assume they're being taken to air bases in the Aleutians?"

"A good guess, but wrong. They're going to launch an attack on Tokyo."

"Tokyo? That's not possible! Can they even launch from a carrier?"

"Apparently so, although I understand that not one of the sixteen pilots has ever actually done it. Their first time will be their only time. They'll make a bombing run on Tokyo and then fly west to airfields in China."

Riley bit his lip, a sign that he was calculating in his head. "It can be done, I guess. There's just barely enough runway for the bombers to take off, particularly if they've lightened them up, but no way for them to land back on a carrier when the mission is over." When he saw Justin's puzzled look he added, "They're not maneuverable enough to match the rolling action of the ship. Dang! This is really something."

"A way of responding after what happened at Pearl Harbor. Apparently, it was ordered by President Roosevelt himself—and he wouldn't take no for an answer. The hope is that we'll demoralize the opposition, who right now think they're indestructible."

"And force Yamamoto and his navy to change their tactics to protect the home islands."

"So that's what's happening on the *Hornet*. I'm still not certain why they want you on the *Enterprise*. It's the flagship and all, sent to protect the task force in case of enemy air attack since the *Hornet's* aircraft can't launch while those bombers are on the flight deck."

Riley Bracken shrugged. "I honestly don't know, sir." Calling Justin "sir" was Riley's way of saying he was tired of talking and ready to get at it.

Justin bit his lip. "I'll walk down to the catapult with you. No one's told Lieutenant Smith about this yet, so I'll brief him directly."

"And you just can't stand to be without me?"

"Yeah, yeah, that's the real reason, for sure."

April 18, 1942
650 nautical miles east of Japan

"Sir! Message marked urgent!"

"What is it, Mr. Kartchner?" Signalman Third Class Lloyd Kartchner handed the message to Lieutenant Commander Collier.

"A Japanese patrol boat spotted at distance." He returned it to Kartchner. "Send this by semaphore to the *Enterprise*. Mark it urgent. I'll notify the captain."

"Aye, sir! Relay message to the *Enterprise*."

"Very good." Justin moved quickly to the interphone. They were still nearly 200 miles short of their preferred launching point for the B-25s. But if the task force had been spotted by an enemy boat, the risk to both the mission and rest of the task force had increased dramatically.

April 18, 1942, 0738
On board the USS *Hornet*

Captain Marc Mitscher summoned Lieutenant Colonel James Doolittle to the bridge.

"We have two reports of an enemy picket boat at maximum visual range. The *Salt Lake City* just messaged us by semaphore that their lookouts spotted the enemy boat, and one of our scout planes flew low over the flight deck and dropped a packet detailing the same information."

"And what of the boat now?

"Captain Zacharias of the *Salt Lake City* ordered the nearest ship, the USS *Nashville*, to fire on them, hopefully before they got a radio message off to Tokyo."

Doolittle was about to say something when the chief communications officer stepped forward. "Sir, my men have confirmed that the enemy boat did broadcast a message just before they were sunk. It will take some time for us to decode it—"

Captain Mitscher scowled. "It doesn't matter—they've clearly warned Tokyo that we're in the area. Hopefully the full extent of the task force wasn't obvious, but they'll know it's something."

Mitscher motioned for the navigator to step forward. "How far out are we?"

"650 nautical miles from the target, sir, and 170 nautical miles short of our preferred launching point."

"And ten hours earlier than we expected to launch." Mitscher turned to Doolittle, who had been selected to lead the mission because of his extensive experience as an aeronautical engineer and test pilot before the war. His experience had enabled him to grapple with the requirements to be placed on long-range bombers launching from an aircraft carrier. It was a difficult raid to plan, given that they had to increase the aircrafts' range to 2,000 nautical miles while carrying four 500-pound bombs each—and they had to take off from the flight deck of an aircraft carrier, even though they'd been designed for longer, ground-based runways. Doolittle had considered four combat aircraft, including the Martin B-26 Marauder and the Douglas B-18 Bolo and B-23 Dragon, but each of these aircraft had characteristics that made them undesirable.

He'd finally settled on the North American Mitchell B-25, even though it had a range of just 1,300 nautical miles. To extend the range so they could make it all the way to Russia or China, they stripped the plane down to the bare minimum so it could double its usual fuel load. Two test pilots performed successful takeoffs from a carrier in reconfigured B-25s, and so the decision had been made. Volunteer crews were selected and trained on short takeoffs (although they didn't practice carrier takeoffs since it was feared that the unusual nature of the drills could leak to the Japanese). The sixteen aircraft were loaded onto the new carrier *Hornet* on the East Coast, and now they were at risk of the entire mission failing because of a single enemy patrol boat.

Mitscher was about to ask Doolittle his opinion when a communications specialist raced onto the bridge. "Sir! Message from the admiral."

Mitscher took the paper from the young man's hand and read aloud: "To Mitscher—launch planes. To Col. Doolittle and Gallant Command: good luck and God bless you! Halsey."

"I guess that settles it. The admiral doesn't want to risk the ships in the task force by staying this close to the home islands."

"It's the right decision," Doolittle said calmly. "It'll make things dicey trying to make our landing fields in China, but we have to get to Tokyo before they can mount a defense—we're flying in naked."

Mitscher nodded. "Not a single fighter plane in the world could go that far to protect you and your men." He paused. "Okay, let's make it happen!" He gave the orders to turn the ship into the wind so the B-25s could get as much lift as possible, while Doolittle made his way to the flight deck where his men would assemble. Mitscher issued the order for the men of the 17th Bombardment Group to scramble to their aircraft for what could turn into a suicide mission. They were the best pilots available—all had volunteered, even before knowing the target. Once they did know the target, they were all in. In just a few minutes everyone would know whether it was possible to launch sixteen heavy bombers from an aircraft carrier in the western Pacific to bring the fight directly to the Japanese home islands.

Meanwhile, a Dauntless dive-bomber landed on the deck of the *Enterprise* and Lieutenant Riley Bracken scrambled out of the cockpit just as soon as the arresting wire brought the aircraft to a stop. Riley's transfer added him as a scout using the Dauntless for long-range, high-speed surveillance as the task force drew closer to the Japanese home islands. Which is why, just as soon as his feet hit the flight deck, Bracken ran toward Lieutenant Commander Branson—the officer who had requested his transfer to the *Enterprise*, and said urgently, "I saw the *Nashville* fire on a Japanese patrol boat. Has command been notified?"

Branson replied, "They have. Looks like they're going to launch the B-25s immediately. They're a long way out from Tokyo." Branson drew close. "I know you've been out on patrol, but are you up for another run? The admiral just sent word down that he wants us to launch all available aircraft to engage any enemy ships in the area and to scan for any signs of a larger fleet moving our way."

"Yes, sir. Glad to. But my aircraft is low on fuel."

"We'll take care of it. Go down to the wardroom and grab a sandwich and splash some water on your face. Be back here as quick as you can."

"Yes, sir." He hesitated. "And thank you, sir. For requesting me. This is pretty darn exciting!"

"You're welcome to stay if you like. I'm sure I can arrange a permanent transfer."

Riley Bracken smiled. "We'll see. Now I've got to hurry. I want to be in the air when those B-25s take off. I'll either watch them waddle their way into the sky or crash into the sea. That still seems pretty crazy to me."

"See you in a few minutes." Branson sighed. Riley was the best scout pilot he had, and after two of his men had come down with flu-like symptoms, he'd quarantined them. That's why he'd needed Bracken.

Riley was airborne just in time to see the first B-25, Colonel Doolittle's plane, start accelerating down the *Hornet's* flight deck. As the heavy aircraft reached the end of the runway, its engines were at full power and Doolittle struggled to get it into the air. The aircraft needed to reach a speed of sixty-eight miles per hour by the end of the deck. Fortunately, there was a forty-five miles per hour headwind, so the aircraft needed to gain just twenty-three miles per hour to achieve takeoff velocity. Unlike on the ground, where running out of runway isn't necessarily disastrous, when the bomber reached the end of the deck, it simply disappeared below the prow of the ship. Everyone on the flight deck and bridge held their breath, waiting to see if it would rise—or if it would crash into the drink. After what seemed an interminable interval, the huge aircraft swept up into view, a great cloud of exhaust fumes causing the image to blur as it started climbing into the sky. A cheer went up from the flight deck, but it was short-lived as the second of sixteen aircraft came lumbering down the deck. Like the first, it dropped below the front of the ship, then rose like a phoenix up into the sky. At thirty-second intervals, it took just eight minutes to get all the aircraft into the air. Surprisingly, the only aircraft that had a close call was the lead plane piloted by Colonel Doolittle.

In the air, Riley Bracken flew his assigned pattern, watching as the ships in the task force made an elegant U-turn to begin their return to safer waters. The location of the enemy carrier fleet was unknown, so the threat to the two US carriers, four cruisers, and their destroyer escorts was real and dangerous. But Bracken was concerned for the crews of the B-25s, who had a long and unprotected flight to what would certainly be a hostile reception by a very angry Japanese military. He hoped they could do their work and make their escape to China.

"Okay," Riley said to himself, "time to head for home." He banked the Dauntless into a turn and then had a thought: *What if I don't have vertigo anymore?* He pondered this for a moment—it would certainly give him more choices if the condition had cleared up. *Only one way to find out.* With no one in his assigned scouting area to watch him, Riley pulled the Dauntless into a steep ascent under full power to gain as much height as needed for a practice dive. He thrilled to the sound of the engine as it pulled the aircraft confidently higher. *All right, we're in the right position—let's find out.* With that, Riley eased up on the throttle, allowing the weight of the engine to pull it out of the climb and start to point it down toward the ocean below. *Just like reaching the top of the roller coaster at Coney Island*, Riley thought. With the aircraft starting to fall, he applied a little power to bring it into a controlled dive, and then increased the power to the speed required of a bombing run. The pressure against his body increased exponentially until he powered back to maintain just the right speed. *So far, so good!* Then, as the ocean loomed ever larger, he pulled back on the yoke to pull the nose up. The aircraft responded smoothly, just as it should have, but Riley felt his stomach come up into his throat, and he was overwhelmed by a wave of nausea. "Not this! Not still!" he cried plaintively while trying to avoid throwing up in the cockpit. He shook his head in despair. Still not a go for combat. He realized with a sigh that his destiny was as a scout, and the best place to be a scout would be back on the *Salt Lake City*. It was a bittersweet thought.

April 18, 1942
On the bridge of the *Salt Lake City*

"I wish it had been a little lighter so I could've had a better view of those bombers taking off," Captain Zacharias said to Lieutenant Commander Collier. Both had watched as the *Hornet* launched the aircraft and then executed their orders to withdraw the *Salt Lake City*. Withdrawing was complicated by having to keep to radio silence, but they were able to use radar, so the risk of collision was reduced.

"I think it's a miracle—and I hope it sobers the Japanese people up to the predicament their leaders have created for them. They're a powerful nation, but they're not even close to matching the industrial output of the United States." Justin was surprised that he had been so candid with the captain.

"You're right, of course. But it's the Chinese people I'm worried about right now."

"Sir?"

Zacharias's intimate knowledge of Japan, based on his years living there as a naval attaché, informed his thinking. "The occupation of Manchuria was a brutal massacre. One-on-one, the Japanese are a polite and solicitous people who are concerned for your welfare and comfort. But when it comes to others that they deem inferior, like the Chinese and Koreans, they are brutal. Colonel Doolittle and his men are going to drop their bombs on Tokyo, which will be a stinging embarrassment to the military leadership, and then keep flying to China where the locals will help them land their aircraft. Once the Japanese high command figures that out, I believe they'll be brutal in punishing the Chinese military—and not just those who help the raiders. They'll likely carry out reprisals against thousands—maybe tens of thousands—just to show that they're in control. That's been their standard protocol for controlling populations larger than their own. At least that's what I believe will happen."

In a subdued, unconvinced tone, Justin asked, "If that's true, is this raid worth it? Is this a good idea?"

"Absolutely. The Japanese had their victory at Pearl Harbor— now the United States needs a victory to bolster our morale. This war will not end quickly, and we need the people back home behind us." He was quiet. "But the cost will be high—I fear it will be high."

Chapter 4

A LONG WAY FROM TEXAS

August 1942

On the pier in Pearl Harbor

"You, there! Seaman! What's your name?"

"Jowdy, sir!"

"How old are you, Jowdy? Ten? Eleven?"

"Uh, seventeen, sir!"

"Right, and I'm an admiral." The chief petty officer shook his head. "They'll be drafting newborns soon, and I'll have to order diapers."

Jowdy, who was really fifteen years old but had misstated the year of his birth to match his older sister's, had lied to get into the Navy. Coming from a family of nine children, he thought it was a good way to support his family. Plus it seemed like a good way to see the world outside of Texas.

"What ship are you assigned to, Jowdy?"

"No ship, sir! I just arrived here." Jowdy looked around, still captivated by the palm trees and mountains. The part of Texas where he came from had hills, at best, and the dense foliage on the jagged peaks of the Koʻolau mountain range north of Pearl Harbor fascinated him.

"Well, you're on the *Hendrox* now. We need an extra deck-hand. I'll make it right with Personnel."

"Will I be part of the ship's company?" This was important, as it meant a permanent assignment to a crew.

"No, you will *not* be part of the ship's company—you'll have to earn that! Now get your things and get on board."

Jowdy turned to an older enlisted man close by and whispered, "Is this legitimate? Can he do that?" Jowdy had imagined himself on an aircraft carrier or a battleship, and the ungainly ship moored in front of him was anything but that. He had no idea what this ship was for.

"Let's see—you're a seaman, lower than the underside of anything on the bottom of the sea. A chief petty officer is the highest-ranking noncommissioned officer in the Navy, and the guy who really runs the ship. You want something done on a ship, even the captain goes to a petty officer to get it done. So, yes—he *can* do that, and you better shut up about it."

"What will they call me?"

"You'll be in the deck division, with one stripe. If you stick with it, you can become a bosun's mate—but right now you're still just a seaman, and you'll do whatever job they tell you to do."

A lot of people would be nervous, but Al Jowdy was not the type to be intimidated by something new. "Remind me what to say when I go on board?" He knew he was pushing his luck with his new friend, but he'd been shipped out to the Pacific with very little time spent in training—such was the nature of a wartime navy.

"You walk to the top of the gangplank, turn to face the stern—the back of the ship—and you salute the ensign. Then

51

you turn to the officer of the deck, salute him, and say, 'Seaman Jowdy. Request permission to come aboard.' He'll return your salute and say, 'Permission granted.' Then you'll move forward and out of the way until you see somebody who looks like he knows what he's doing. Then you'll tell that person you're a new deckhand who needs to know where to go to get started . . . and he may choose to help you, or he may ignore you." The older fellow looked at him, "Do you think you can remember that?"

"Remind me, what's the ensign?"

"Oh, for the love . . . it's the star field on the flag at the back of the ship—just face the back of the ship and salute."

Jowdy piped up, "And then I say, 'Seaman Jowdy. Request permission to come aboard.'"

"You're a genius. Now get to it!"

August 1942
Honolulu

"So what's the new captain like?" Riley Bracken asked. Riley and Justin were on leave from the *Salt Lake City* while repairs were being made and were sitting in the Colliers' living room in Oahu.

"Ernest Small? I know him from my academy days. He oversaw the ordnance and gunnery department when I was a midshipman. Of course, he wouldn't remember me, but he was a good instructor. He spoke in the main foyer of Bancroft Hall several times, and I went to his lectures. I also like that he commanded a couple of submarines before coming to the *Salt Lake City*, so he knows how a submariner thinks—that may give us an advantage with the enemy. He's very competent, particularly in conning the ship."

Verla, Justin's now-fourteen-year-old daughter, asked, "What does *conning* mean?'"

She and her brother Emery were sitting with their mother, but hadn't acted like they were paying attention to what the adults were saying. Her question reminded Justin that in fact, children are almost always listening.

"*Conning* means telling the helmsman where to steer the ship," Riley said.

"And how fast," Justin added.

"I want to be a helmsman when I join the Navy," Emery said. "That's got to be the best job ever—actually steering a giant ship."

Justin caught Heidi's sideways glance. It was inevitable that their son would think of joining the Navy, but he knew that Heidi would be happy if her children found their way outside the military life.

"Not me," Riley said easily. "You stand behind the wheel for hours at a time, never steering where you want to go, or telling the lee helmsman how fast you want to do it. Seems boring to me. I like being on an airplane where *I'm* the one deciding where and when to turn."

"I think I'd like that too," Verla said.

Heidi ended their questions with "I think right now the two of you should think about school that starts in two weeks. Once you get your education you can decide on what you want to do when you grow up."

Verla sat down next to her mother. "I'd also like to be a nurse. Mom has helped a lot of hurt people. Or maybe a doctor. Dr. Kani's really good at his job too."

Heidi stroked her daughter's hair. "You'd be a very good nurse—my patients always like it when you come down and help me at the hospital. I'm glad Dr. Kani's been understanding about that." Heidi didn't work there as often now that the base hospital was fully staffed. But she did substitute when needed and enjoyed bringing Verla along to shadow her occasionally. Emery stayed at a friend's house when she was working.

Justin frowned a bit at the mention of Dr. Kani. He had some doubts about that guy. He seemed nice enough, but the more Verla and Heidi talked about him, the more he decided he didn't like him.

"Back to Captain Small," Riley said. "I like that he relies on the SOCs—I've never been so busy. Seems like he's always watching the field around him."

"What's an SOC?" This time the question came from Emery.

"Scout Observation Craft—my floatplane."

"Your uncle's really good at scouting for us," Justin said. Then he said to Riley, "I'm glad you came back to the *Salt Lake City* after the Doolittle raid. I figured they'd try to keep you on the *Enterprise*."

"They did. But I like where I am better." What Riley did *not* say was his experiment with vertigo flying from the *Enterprise* had cemented his decision to stay on the *Salt Lake City*. "Aircraft and pilots are their full-time business on an aircraft carrier, so I'm nothing special there. But on a cruiser, we're in a class by ourselves, and no one really knows what to do with us. That suits me better."

Justin laughed. "You've made a reputation for yourself. The cooks love your stories, so you eat better than we do in the officers' mess, the petty officers indulge you guys because you stand apart from the regular crew they boss around; and the captain thinks you're indispensable. So, yes, I can see why you like it."

"And all the time you're up there running the ship. I have just one person to worry about—me. You worry about hundreds of men."

"Yes, I do. You're probably the smart one."

"But Justin's natural for command," Heidi said. "So it worked out just the way it should." Before either Justin or Riley could keep this line of conversation going, she changed the subject. "Have either of you heard any more about the Doolittle Raiders? The newspapers have been full of the bombing of Tokyo, but it's still not clear what happened to all of them."

"Well, here's what we know so far," Justin said. "The Russians have interned the crew that was forced to land in Vladivostok because of their non-aggression treaty with the Japanese. But the scuttlebutt is that the Russians will find a way to let them escape. Thirteen crews crash-landed in various places in China, but no one was hurt or seriously injured. And one aircraft landed intact. Fortunately, all the men in those fourteen crews have made it out of China, back to the States or back to their regular service assignments. The tough story is the sixteenth plane. They crashed on the Chinese coast where the Japanese could get to them. Radio reports out of Japan indicate that they took eight prisoners, three of whom have been executed already."

Heidi shook her head as Riley added, "And I feel for the five who are still prisoners—I wouldn't want to be held as a prisoner of war by the Japanese—everything we hear is that it's brutal."

Justin continued, "Captain Zacharias told me back when the raid was about to launch that he expected the Japanese to punish the Chinese people for this, and he was right. The reprisals have been atrocious—at least 10,000 citizens lined up and killed directly, plus an entire city that sheltered some of the crews burned to the ground. We'll probably never know the total, but in one briefing I heard an estimate of nearly a quarter of a million people killed because of Japan locking down the country to prevent a repeat of an aerial attack like that."

"So many innocent people killed. I wonder if it was worth it," said Heidi.

"It's hard to say. The effect on our morale has been terrific. And many in the Navy believe it was because of the raid that the Japanese decided to attack Midway Island—they wanted to keep us as far away from mainland Japan as possible."

"And that turned into an unmitigated disaster for the Japanese," Heidi said. Justin nodded. "Four aircraft carriers sunk, 300 Japanese aircraft shot out of the sky, and a heavy cruiser destroyed. If Doolittle's Raiders prompted that, it had a positive side."

"This is all too gloomy," Riley said. "I think we should take the kids swimming—I've been thinking I should try that surfing thing."

Heidi and Justin laughed. He'd probably be great at it.

"Can I try surfing too?" Emery asked enthusiastically.

"No, you can't. It's fine for Uncle Riley, but those boards are way too long for a child—so don't get any ideas."

"Ah, Mom," he said, "my friends are trying to learn. Can't Uncle Riley teach me?"

"We can go to the beach—but don't let your uncle talk you into anything out there."

"You should listen to your mother, Emery—she's far more sensible than I am," Riley said with a wink.

September 1942
Returning from Guadalcanal on the *Hendrox*

"It's a lot easier to keep the deck clean now that those 500 marines have landed on Guadalcanal," Seaman Al Jowdy said as he swabbed the deck. "I had no idea so many people could throw up at the same time."

The USS *Hendrox* had encountered rough seas on the trip from Pearl Harbor to the island of Guadalcanal. It turned out that the ungainly ship was a troop carrier, and many of the marines got seasick on the voyage. "I'd heard people say that you turn green when you get seasick, but I didn't take it literally until I saw those guys staggering back from the ship's railing—the ones who made it that far. I've never seen human skin that color."

"How is it that *you* didn't get seasick, Jowdy? It's not like you grew up on the ocean."

Seaman Jowdy was talking with his friend, Seaman Arkin. A gregarious extrovert, Al Jowdy made friends wherever he went. "I don't know—it just doesn't bother me. Maybe it's the food." He took a bite out of a greasy dinner roll that a friend on the mess crew had given him. "Food was scarce in my family, so I eat what I can when I can." He grinned.

Arkin was about to say something when the sirens for General Quarters sounded. Startled, both men jumped at the sound. "What's that mean?" Al asked. His question was answered when the loudspeaker crackled to life. "Now hear this! Now hear this! Torpedo running—torpedo running—brace for impact!"

"A torpedo?" Jowdy's eyes widened as he searched the water. His legs felt heavy when he saw a white trail streaking toward the ship. He stood stock still, knowing in his head he should run; but his feet weren't listening.

"We're gonna get hit!" Arkin shouted, and then the air exploded around them in a blast of noise and searing heat that blew a nearby bulkhead into nothingness.

"Abandon ship! Abandon ship!" It was harder to hear the public address system since many of the speakers had been blasted to smithereens by the explosion. But this message was easy to understand.

Nothing in his fifteen years of life could have prepared Al for that moment, since the ship was already tilting to the side as it started to sink. Yet in the moment, he knew exactly what to do. Noticing he was covered in oil, he threw his Mae West into the ocean and then jumped in after it. After struggling to the surface, he retrieved his Mae West and slipped it on, then began vigorously scrubbing his face and exposed skin with salt water to get the oil off. As he put his hands to the top of his head, he realized his hair had been burned by the blast. He turned to listen to the ship making loud groaning sounds as metal twisted and separated, and an odd whooshing noise as air inside the ship forced its way out through ventilation shafts and open hatches. In disbelief he watched the ship he'd been standing on just moments before sinking right before his eyes. A large spray of water ejected by the escaping air cascaded down on him, forcing him to turn away for a moment. When he looked back, the ship was gone, lost in a pool of air bubbles burbling to the surface. Al Jowdy was adrift in the water.

"Okay, Jowdy, stay calm!" The water was far colder than he thought it should be in the South Pacific, but he did his best to steady his breathing. "There are a lot of ships in this area, so somebody's going to rescue you." He wasn't sure about that, but it was better than thinking he was going to die. "You know how to swim, you have a life preserver, so you don't need to panic." And he didn't panic until he felt something brush against his back. When he turned to see what it was, he let out a holler. A body was floating silently in the water, the man's eyes staring up at the sun. Jowdy flailed about, simultaneously wanting to get away and concerned that the fellow might still be alive and needing his help. "Are you all right? Are you okay?" he shouted, but there was no response. The man's face was covered in blood, and his cheeks were sunken. "You were probably killed by the explosion," Al said quietly, still disturbed as the waves kept sending the body in his direction. Finally, gathering his courage, he dog-paddled his way to the body and grabbed the man's shoulder, which he gave a firm shake. His voice trembled as he tried to rouse the victim, but to no avail. "Okay. You're dead." Even though he knew that the corpse presented no threat to him, it was disturbing, and so he used his favorite swimming stroke, the elementary backstroke, to move away.

After moving perhaps a hundred feet, he noticed that the waves were moving the body away from him. He'd moved into a different current, which presented a new problem, since he was moving away from where the ship went down. "Something better happen pretty fast, Jowdy!" Still, as time passed, he stopped being as agitated.

After his nerves settled a bit, Al realized that he had to conserve his strength in the cold water, so he began treading water lightly, allowing his life vest to keep his head out of the water. After twenty minutes or so, he spotted a group of men in a life raft nearby, which released a burst of adrenaline. He shouted to them and waved his arms until he saw the boat change direction, the men inside paddling toward him. He had never been so relieved as when the boat drew close. The leader on the rubber raft told him to face away from the boat, and then strong arms reached down and grabbed him by his Mae West and swiftly pulled him up and into the boat, where he landed with a great splash in the middle. Rolling to his knees, he raised himself up to see the men who had rescued him.

"Are you hurt?" the young ensign in command of the rescue boat asked.

"I think I have some burns." Al coughed to expel some salt water and then felt his legs and arms. "But I don't think anything's broken."

An enlisted man at the back of the boat spoke up and said, "Okay, you sit on the port side of the raft—we need to keep the wounded men in the middle."

"Aye, sir."

"I'm not a sir—just do your best to help us."

"May I ask your name?"

"Chief Pettinger, but Mr. Oliver here is in charge," he said, pointing toward the young ensign. Even though he was brand new to the Navy, Al figured out that Pettinger was the most senior man in the life raft and would make all the major decisions, even though the ensign was an officer. Pettinger would phrase his orders in such a way that Ensign Oliver would almost certainly confirm, since it was Pettinger's skill that would keep them alive.

Al Jowdy nodded and moved to his assigned spot. Al wondered if Seaman Arkin had survived, but there was no way to know. As he adjusted to his new circumstance—safely in a lifeboat instead of drifting in the Pacific—he pondered the fact that his first ship had just sunk. It was a lot to take in. He was surprised to find that he was shivering, even though the day was hot. "We're not far from the islands, so they should pick us up soon, right?" he asked no one in particular.

"Sure," the fellow next to him said. "Except, maybe, for the sub that just sank us—if I were captain of any ship in the area, I might not want to slow down to pick up survivors just now."

"So what do we do?"

Ensign Oliver answered. "They know we're here, so they won't forget us. You're safe. We'll just have to go light on the emergency rations and water. They'll have to clear the water of enemy subs and aircraft before they can get to us."

The men in the lifeboat thought it might be a day or two before they were rescued—but they were wrong. Amidst the battles being fought, no ship dared stop long enough to pull them from the water, so the days passed endlessly in the sun. As the lifeboats gave up on finding any other men to rescue, they paddled their way to a common spot where they could talk to each other while making a bigger group for rescue crafts to find them. At one point someone got the good idea to lash all the rafts together so they could more easily grab the food and water that was parachuted down, and so their rescue would be quicker.

One of the most disturbing incidents was when one of the wounded men died. Pettinger suggested they put him over the side immediately, but this time Ensign Oliver asserted his authority. "We should leave him so he can be treated properly when we're rescued." Pettinger shook his head, but deferred. Mr. Oliver's order didn't last long though. In the intense heat the body began to swell, and so the ensign soon agreed that they should release him to the water.

"Does anyone know this man?" Oliver asked. The men just shrugged. "All right, let me see his dog tags. His name is John Boyle, and it says he's Protestant."

"Are you going to say some words before we put him over?"

Oliver nodded and reached inside his vest, where he found a small guide for officers that he always carried with him—a guide he studied frequently as he tried to learn the essence of his job.

Someone suggested he might want to hurry as it could be bad luck to keep a dead body on board.

"Well, I don't believe that," Oliver said, "but we do need to hurry so that he doesn't become more disfigured—that would be disrespectful." The others in the boat nodded, their respect for Oliver increased. "I have a prayer suggested for such an occasion. Would you please remove your hats?" Those who had them did so and assumed a solemn expression, realizing that it could have been any one of them who'd died instead of John Boyle. Then Ensign Oliver read in a reverent but firm voice:

"Having died while in service to his country, we now therefore commit the earthly remains of John Boyle to the deep, looking for the general Resurrection in the last day, and the life of the world to come, through our Lord Jesus Christ; at whose second coming in glorious majesty to judge the world, the sea shall give up her dead; and the corruptible bodies of those who sleep in him shall be changed, and made like unto his glorious body; according to the mighty working whereby he is able to subdue all things unto himself. Amen."

The men echoed the amen, and Ensign Oliver carefully removed then stowed Boyle's dog tags in his pocket so that Boyle's family would know what happened to him. After scrounging in the boat, they decided that they wouldn't need the small anchor and so tied it to Boyle's feet before slipping him over the side of the boat. Even though no one knew the deceased personally, they all felt the loss of a comrade.

On the tenth day, one of the men said, "You're awfully quiet, Jowdy." Quiet was an unnatural condition for Al, whose naturally cheerful temperament kept him chatting much of the time.

Al looked up and shrugged his shoulders. "Just waiting for our delivery. Kind of the only thing to look forward to lately."

The second day after the sinking, a scout plane had circled overhead, acknowledged the flare that they'd sent up, and then disappeared. That had been disappointing, but about two hours later the aircraft returned and parachuted a package filled with food and water to keep both their bodies and their hopes alive. At first there was celebration, but then Pettinger said, "This means that they're in no hurry to rescue us." That subdued their spirits, but there was nothing to be done about it. After that, a plane appeared faithfully every third day. Al Jowdy was right that it was the only thing to look forward to. They were still confined to the overcrowded raft floating listlessly in the water. Their airborne guardians were thoughtful enough to send a canvas canopy in their second drop that they pulled over the boat to shade them from the sun during the long, hot days.

The most harrowing experience came one afternoon when someone shouted to Al to pull his leg into the raft. He'd fired back, "What difference is it to you where I put my leg!" But his blood ran cold when the fellow pointed out a fin moving slowly in the water. Sharks were apparently hoping to get to the miserable men in the boat before they could be rescued.

On the fourteenth day Pettinger sat up suddenly and called for someone to pass him the field glasses. "What is it?" Ensign Oliver asked. The risk of the enemy coming after them was still very real in everyone's minds, and they started moving about restlessly while waiting on him.

"Here, Mr. Oliver, you take a look."

"What is it? What do you see?" Al asked Pettinger. Everyone was anxious.

Ensign Oliver pulled the binoculars away from his eyes and looked directly at Pettinger. "I think it's a US destroyer headed our way—is that what you saw?

Pettinger nodded. "I was pretty sure, but wanted to make sure I wasn't hallucinating!"

"A destroyer! A destroyer! We're being rescued?" Al didn't know for sure who said this, but it could have been any of them—or all of them.

The sound of men cheering on the other rafts confirmed the sighting, and soon everyone on their raft cheered as well. It was a glorious moment when the destroyer came steaming swiftly up to their position, slowing a couple hundred yards out to reduce the bow wave that otherwise might have swamped the rafts, and then dropped netting over the side so the men could climb up to safety. "What do you think, Jowdy?" Pettinger asked. He wasn't usually as excitable as Al, but it was about impossible not to be excited at this point.

"I think you and Mr. Oliver deserve a medal! You got us through this."

Pettinger nodded, and Ensign Oliver tipped his hat. Mr. Oliver would never be the young ensign again—he'd earned the respect of the men by remaining calm and seeking advice when he needed it. That's all an enlisted man needed—an officer more interested in getting it right than getting credit.

Once on board, each were given a blanket and a spot on the deck to wait while a medical officer or orderly examined them. Despite the provisions and water, most were emaciated from the experience. Al Jowdy and some of his raftmates were dropped off at Noumena in New Caledonia, where Al had just enough time to grow his eyelashes back before being assigned to a destroyer heading back to Guadalcanal.

Chapter 5

A VERY NEAR MISS IN THE SOLOMON ISLANDS

September 15, 1942
On the *Salt Lake City* near Guadalcanal
in the Solomon Islands

"Sir, I think you should listen to this." The communications officer motioned for Lieutenant Commander Collier to put on a headset.

"What've you got?"

"Lieutenant Bracken is reporting from his SOC he sees a shadow approaching the *Wasp* underwater. He expects a torpedo attack."

Justin ordered Signalman Kartchner to relay the information immediately to the USS *Wasp*, a light aircraft carrier in their task force, then he went straight to Captain Small, who was also on the bridge. "Sir, one of our SOCs reports a likely enemy submarine on an attack track for *Wasp*. The sub is submerged but near the surface." Justin then reported the coordinates.

Small didn't respond to Justin, instead issuing orders to immediately increase speed and move closer to the *Wasp*—some might say dangerously close for two capital ships. Then he said to everyone on the bridge, "*Wasp*'s aircraft have been invaluable. It's our job to protect her, even if we have to intercept the torpedo!" They were at General Quarters, but Small ordered Justin to warn all crew members to brace for impact.

Having already played cat and mouse with enemy aircraft and submarines for the last week while the fleet was landing troops on the island of Guadalcanal, everyone was tired and frustrated. The *Wasp* was the only carrier in the task force, which also included two battleships, two heavy cruisers, three light cruisers, and twelve destroyers. The *Wasp* was the Navy's smallest aircraft carrier, just 15,000 tons, built during the interwar period when treaties didn't allow for anything larger. Now she and the *Hornet* were the only two carriers in this part of the Pacific, and the *Wasp*'s lightweight design meant that she had practically no armor to protect her from bombs or torpedoes. The *Salt Lake City* had been doing its best to protect the carrier along with other task force vessels while also firing on the island in support of the landing troops. The *Salt Lake City*'s scout planes had been providing almost constant intelligence on the progress of the landings, as well as submarine threats standing nearly stationary in the water.

Guadalcanal, one of the largest islands in the Solomons, was a particularly miserable place to fight a war—thick jungle growth concealed the enemy, who also hid in caves where they could protect themselves from bombardment. For their part, they fought ferociously, showing that they understood the significance of this attack. If the Japanese lost the Solomons, northeast of Australia and due east of New Guinea, it would give the Allies a foothold in the western Pacific and prevent planned enemy occupation further south.

"Captain! Lookouts report torpedo tracks in the water—six of them!"

"Where?"

When he received the coordinates, Captain Small sighed. "We're too late—they're on a direct path to *Wasp*—there's nothing she can do to avoid getting hit."

"Brace for impact!" Justin shouted. Even though the torpedoes would likely miss the *Salt Lake City*, they were just 1,000 feet from the *Wasp,* so the *Salt Lake City* would feel the concussion of the explosions.

September 15, 1942
On board the USS *O'Brien*, near the *Wasp*

"This can't be happening!" Al Jowdy gaped in disbelief as a torpedo streaked straight for the USS *O'Brien*, the destroyer he'd been assigned to after being rescued from the sinking of the *Hendrox*. The destroyer was trailing in the wake of the *Wasp* to protect it from being hit from astern, but with a spread of six torpedoes, the *O'Brien* as well as the *Wasp* was in danger. He felt the dread in his stomach that he'd felt before—he couldn't move if he wanted to. But even if he could, where would he go? The hopelessness of his situation weighed on him.

As the world around him exploded, he shouted, "Oh, for pity's sake!" Knocked unconscious by the blast, he came to in the water, where for a few panicked minutes he flapped ineffectively. Finally, he was able to force himself to breathe normally and try to float. Fortunately, the action station he'd been at had required him to wear his Mae West. *Stay calm! Stay calm!* he thought. Then, *why does this keep happening? I can't go through that again.* His heart rate increased again. He shut his eyes and forced himself to slow down, to try to concentrate on anything other than the fact he'd been blown into the water again. He allowed himself to float and then looked around to see what was happening. From his vantage point astern of both ships, he saw the *Wasp* burning and listing, but not in danger of sinking right away. Even better was that the *O'Brien* was still afloat and sending out rescue boats to recover the crew. "Over here!" he shouted. "Over here!" Of course he wasn't alone in the water—other men were raising their arms and shouting, while others lay motionless. Al thought about all the ways there were to die in a sea battle. You could be killed instantly by a shell or torpedo; you could survive but be trapped belowdecks as your ship sank; you could survive but succumb to your injuries in the water; you could survive but attract sharks. And, as he had been before, you could be rescued by other comrades and live to fight another day. As Al called out and waved, he hoped there weren't any sharks around, but it was a risk he had to take to get the rescuers' attention.

September 15, 1942
The USS *Salt Lake City*

"This is going to be tough duty." Captain Small had assembled his entire leadership team on the outside bridge. "It's bad enough to see one of our ships injured by the enemy—but now we must put her down ourselves." He shook his head.

For the past six hours the *Salt Lake City* and other ships in the area had assisted in rescuing the crew of the *Wasp*, the *O'Brien,* and the battleship USS *North Carolina.* The *O'Brien* and the *North Carolina* had been struck by torpedoes aimed at the *Wasp*, which gave the stricken aircraft carrier some time to evacuate its crew. Fortunately, both the destroyer and battleship remained seaworthy, although the *North Carolina*'s forward turret was out of commission. Her crew had contained flooding from a hole beneath the waterline, but they had to counter-flood the opposite side of the ship to maintain trim. With all that water in the forward compartments, the ship was heavy in the bow, forcing the ship to steam more slowly, making it vulnerable to new attacks. During the extended rescue, the other ships in the escort had taken turns helping the rescue and patrolling for enemy subs, a dangerous dance since an enemy sub's best target was a surface ship stopped dead in the water to recover survivors.

The *Wasp's* injuries were simply too great for the ship to make it safely back to port. Three torpedoes had hit the small carrier, just one-third the displacement of the *North Carolina*, and fires at the bow were raging out of control. The water mains at that part of the ship had been severed, so there was no way to effectively douse the fires, and men were in constant danger of fuel explosions as they worked to gain control. Finally, after six hours, the order was given to abandon ship. It took forty minutes, mostly because the crew was reluctant to leave until all the wounded had been rescued. Now it was dark, and multiple explosions rocked the abandoned ship.

No action was taken to scuttle the ship until it was confirmed that 1,960 men had been rescued by the *Salt Lake City*, USS *Lansdowne*, USS *Helena*, and USS *Laffey*. Unfortunately, that meant that 193 men had been killed or were unaccounted for.

"Sir, the *Lansdowne* is in position."

"Attention on deck!" Small said, removing his hat. His officers did the same, as did the enlisted men watching from different vantage points on the ship. It was sobering to watch three torpedoes fired by a United States ship slam into the side of the carrier. The men braced for an explosion, but none came.

"I'm sure those were direct hits," Justin said.

"It's those infernal magnetic influence exploders!" Lieutenant Allen said. "They're totally worthless, just like the Mark 14 torpedoes they replaced. We've wasted so many opportunities because of defective torpedoes."

"What should they do?" Captain Small asked.

"They need to disable the influence exploders and set the depth at 10 feet. That will allow the impact to trigger the torpedoes."

Fire control on the *Lansdowne* must have agreed with this assessment, because a few minutes later three more tracks were seen running in the water, followed by three explosions. Justin shook his head. "That could have been us."

Captain Small stepped forward. "You're all dismissed to return to your duty station or your bunk. I think we're done for the night."

Despite the captain's order, several lingered, expecting to see the great ship go down. But it was not to be—at least not for another hour. Three Japanese torpedoes and three American torpedoes were still not enough to take the fight out of the *Wasp*. The carrier's rescued crewmen wept on the decks of their rescuers as they watched their former home struggle to stay afloat. At 1700, the *Wasp* finally slipped quietly beneath the waves.

"Do we have a report on casualties?" Captain Small asked Justin.

"The most recent report says it's likely that 200 men died, 366 wounded; of course, those are rough numbers based on the number rescued. It will take a while to figure out who's missing and presumed dead."

"And the number of aircraft saved?"

"I do have that, sir. Twenty-six aircraft were in the air when the *Wasp* was hit and have all landed safely on the *Hornet*, but that leaves forty-five that went down with the ship."

Captain Small shook his head. "That's a terrible toll. But we got the marines safely to the beaches, so on balance the Battle of the Eastern Solomons can be said to have gone our way." He turned to Justin. "I'm glad the *Salt Lake City* wasn't hit—we've lived to fight another day."

"Yes, sir." There was nothing more to say.

Chapter 6

THE ONE-SHIP FLEET— THE BATTLE OF CAPE ESPERANCE

October 11, 1942
With Task Force 64 near Guadalcanal
in the Solomon Islands

"Okay, Professor, so why are they called the Solomon Islands?" The boilers hissed in the background, but the snipes who worked in the engine rooms hardly noticed. The word *snipe* was neither derogatory nor complimentary—it was a term that the men who worked in the open gave to those who worked in the bowels of the ship, in the boiler and engine rooms. A snipe is a marsh bird with large eyes and brown plumage. The intense heat and dim lighting of the engine rooms caused the men who worked there to have perpetually red sweaty faces and large, dilated pupils whenever they made their way to the upper decks, and so they supposedly looked like snipes whenever they popped up out of the hatches into the sunlight.

"The Solomons got that name from the Spanish explorer Álvaro de Mendaña de Neira, who thought he'd found the source of King Solomon's gold when he explored this area of the South Pacific." The seaman who'd asked Machinist's Mate First Class

72

Stuart Appelle this question shook his head in disbelief that Appelle knew the answer.

"And had he found the gold?"

Appelle laughed. "Nope. No gold—just golden sand. But the name stuck."

"And what about the name Guadalcanal? What's an island got to do with a canal?"

"It has nothing to do with a canal," Appelle replied. "It's the largest of the Solomon Islands, and was named after the Spanish hometown of Pedro de Ortega Valencia, an assistant to de Mendaña. It's an Arabic word meaning 'river of the stalls,' since shopkeepers used to set up along the river where the Andalusian town of Guadalcanal sits in Spain."

The men in the small group who were huddled around Appelle laughed. "How do you know all this stuff? Nobody can know all this stuff!"

"Because I'm curious. When I found out that I was going to the South Pacific, I went to the San Francisco library and checked out as many books as I could about out here. I wanted to know the history of the place, who the people are who live here, and whether they're likely to support the enemy, resent them, or support us—or resent us." Appelle crunched a candy bar he'd purchased from Sandy Oppenheimer at the Pogey Bait earlier that morning. No one knew why it was called the Pogey Bait—the name given to both snacks and the store where they were sold—but that's what it was called on Navy ships. Ice cream and potato chips were sold at the Gedunk Stand. "Plus, I like history."

"But how do you *remember* it?"

Appelle got a little more serious. "I take notes. I know it's crazy, but it's just the way I study. When the captain announced that we were returning to Guadalcanal I looked it up in my notes. That's all."

Appelle was something of an oddity in the engine room—a college graduate who could have chosen to be an officer—but who requested the engine room instead. He'd majored in mechanical engineering at the prestigious Rensselaer Polytechnic Institute because he loved machines of all types. He'd planned to become either a naval architect, specializing in the design of efficient power plants, or take a job working in civilian transportation. But the war cut his education short before he'd received an advanced degree, so he thought he'd spend his time in the Navy working with his hands "in the grease." Because of his easygoing way and his seemingly encyclopedic command of arcane subjects, he was known as "Professor" in the lower decks.

"So, I have a question, Professor," one of the men in the group said.

"Fire away."

"Why fight in the Solomons? It's a big ocean—why are we taking a stand here?"

The others looked at Appelle expectantly. Enlisted men simply went wherever the ship took them, but every now and then it was nice to have some context.

"I don't know for sure—I'm not on the admiral's staff. But if you look at where everything is, I'm pretty sure we're trying to establish a protective line between Japan and our allies in Australia and New Zealand. Guadalcanal puts us northeast of Australia, northwest of New Zealand, as well as close to New Guinea and nearly due south of Japan. So to reach any Allied territory, the enemy has to pass through here first. If we keep the Solomons, we can protect our supply lines to Australia. That's why it was a big deal when we captured the enemy airbase at Lunga Point on

Guadalcanal back in August while it was still under construction. Now that we've finished it as Henderson Field, we can stop the enemy in their tracks during the daytime. They want it back, so we'll have to fight to keep it. Also, while our land-based aircraft can stop them during daylight, they still send ships at night down 'The Slot' on the inside strait from New Britain to Guadalcanal. They're sending so many ships it's called the 'Tokyo Express,' which doesn't look very good for our side. So that's another reason we're here—I think the task force is looking to shut down their transport and cargo ships."

"The captain's always up for a good fight, so we'll shove them right back up their slot to Japan!" Appelle and the others laughed with the man who said this. The chief engineer stuck his head through the door and told the men, "Break's over, boys. Get back to work!" Stuart Appelle nodded and made his way back to his duty station.

The interphone rang in the flight control center on the *Salt Lake City*. Even though it was 2200, two of the four floatplane pilots were on standby, anticipating an assignment. "Bracken here!" Lieutenant Riley Bracken said crisply.

"Lieutenant Bracken, the captain needs some eyes in the sky. Launch two SOCs to surveil the area."

"Aye, sir." Everyone knew very well what they were looking for—enemy warships working as troop transports and supply convoys. While the Japanese navy had operational control of the ocean during the night, when land-based fighters were grounded, they had to retreat to safe waters before sunrise. The ships the Japanese navy would usually use as transports and cargo ships were too slow to make it back to safety. So the enemy would have to use combat ships if they wanted to take back Guadalcanal.

Bracken hung up the interphone and signaled to Lieutenant Dan Rowan that it was time to go. Both men smiled since this is what they lived for—the chance to get into the air—if for no other reason than it was cooler up there. Plus, it was relatively safe—the Japanese weren't likely to fire on a floatplane in the dark, giving away their position by the blast from their guns, so the pilots could operate freely. Bracken knew two other planes would be launched from the other heavy cruiser in the area, the USS *San Francisco*. To avoid interference with each other, all four aircraft had specific zones to patrol.

As they reached the rotating catapults, Bracken did a final check of his flight uniform, then gave a thumbs-up to Rowan and mounted the catapult. They were flying without their rear-gunners, since the enemy wouldn't have any aircraft in the sky to harass them, and a lighter load provided greater range. Climbing the ladder from the catapult track to the cockpit, Bracken signaled to the flight controller that he was ready. Clearance was given and he revved the engine to full throttle, then leaned forward to put his head between his arms as he prepared for the incredible thrust of the gunpowder-fired catapult that would help him become airborne in less than two seconds. The roar of the engine was awesome as propeller wash buffeted the wings in anticipation of launch. Bracken bit his lip and then struggled to control himself from being thrown backwards as the catapult grabbed the huge center float under the fuselage and slung it forward with a mighty jolt. No land-based takeoff could compare to the near-instantaneous reaction of the aircraft to the wind now streaming around its wings, pushing it airborne in such a short distance. The Kingfisher's fabric-covered aluminum frame was light enough that it didn't even dip as it left the catapult track. In less time than it takes to say "one thousand-one, one thousand-two," Lieutenant Bracken's plane climbed steeply into the sky to make room for Lieutenant Rowan to launch his own SOC.

A few minutes later, circling above the *Salt Lake City*, Riley glanced down at Rowan's aircraft as it shuddered on its catapult. There was something off—a bright light flared in the rear-gunner's space. *This can't be good*, Riley thought, and then watched in horror as the catapult launched the SOC into the night sky, the glare from the cockpit burning a streak through the black sky in his eyes.

"Captain! Something's wrong over here!" Lieutenant Commander Collier motioned to Captain Small to come to the starboard side of the outside bridge. It was remarkable how fast the captain moved.

"Is that our aircraft?"

"Yes, sir, and it looks like it's exploded—or it's on fire!"

They heard the fire alarm sound at the rear of the ship but knew it would do nothing to help the aircraft that had already managed to launch, but looked as if its cockpit was on fire—a brilliant fire, brighter than expected. Captain Small narrowed his eyes. "His flares must have gone off inside the plane—nothing of the aircraft itself would burn that bright." They watched anxiously as the cockpit hatch opened, and the pilot threw himself out of the plane. A few moments later, the aircraft crashed into the sea, but light continued to glow from under the waves until the flares burned themselves out. It was an eerie and disconcerting sight.

"Man overboard!" they heard a deck watchman shout, but

both men knew that the pilot would have to fend for himself, at least for a time. With enemy ships so near there was no time in the dark to mount a rescue.

"There goes any hope of our surprising the Japanese," Captain Small said quietly. The flares had burned so brightly they could easily have been seen all the way to the horizon.

Small turned back toward the bridge, when Collier drew his attention a second time—again with disbelief in his voice. "Sir, there's a blinker light approximately four miles distant."

"What—a lamp signal? We're under orders to maintain silence!" The captain returned to the spot and lifted his binoculars in the direction that Collier had pointed. "That's a nonsense message—the pattern isn't forming any words."

Justin strained to understand it as well. Part of his duty assignment was to supervise the signals department, so he had learned to read and understand code and semaphore almost as well as the on-duty signalmen. "It isn't English, sir! It must be Japanese!"

"Japanese?" Small clicked his tongue several times, a sign he was deep in thought.

"Yes, sir. I'm sure of it."

"I bet I know what's happening—they think that flare fire was a signal from the troops on the island they're trying to resupply."

"Really?" Justin felt dumb for saying so, but it was a shocking conclusion for Small to reach.

Small turned toward the bridge. "I'm not completely convinced, but we know we have no ships at that heading—and it's where we'd expect the enemy to be. We need to act now!" Small stormed back onto the bridge and asked radar to confirm his suspicions. Radar was able to show that the ship in question had just come around the mountains on the north side of the island, which confirmed they were Japanese. This was all Captain Small needed, and he immediately issued new orders to the helm, ordering Lieutenant Allen to open fire on whatever ship was signaling, and then dictated a message to Rear Admiral Norman Scott, in command of Task Force 64, indicating that the enemy was sighted and that the *Salt Lake City* was engaging with its heavy guns. "It's going to get exciting now," Small said to those on the bridge.

Exciting was an understatement. While the *Salt Lake City* was first to spot the Japanese vessel, the light cruiser USS *Boise* was closest, and they began firing as well. For an incredible seven minutes the enemy ship continued to signal even as they came under fire from an increasing number of the ships in Task Force 64.

"What a fool!" Captain Small said to Collier. "They keep thinking they're being signaled from their shore deployment." Seven minutes is close to an eternity in battle, and the guns of the task force increasingly found their targets—the Americans were able to "cross the T" of the Japanese battle formation, giving the American task force a significant tactical advantage.

The first Japanese ship to be struck was the *Aoba*, a heavy cruiser and the flagship of Rear Admiral Aritoma Gota. "Another direct hit!" Collier shouted. At this point the *Aoba* was being fired on by the *Helena, Salt Lake City, San Francisco, Laffey,* and USS *Farenholt*—three cruisers and two destroyers—and the effect on the Japanese ship was devastating. The Americans wouldn't know until much later that a large-caliber shell smashing through the *Aoba*'s bridge killed Admiral Gota. He paid the ultimate price for his delay in assessing the situation.

When the *Aoba* started making smoke to slip out of the battle, the ships in the task force turned their fire on the heavy cruiser *Furutaka*, one shell hitting her torpedo tubes and starting a fire that made the ship completely visible to the Americans—and they responded immediately. The fusillade was devastating. At 2358, just two minutes short of midnight, a torpedo from the destroyer USS *Buchanan* hit the *Furutaka* in the forward engine rooms.

"*Boise* is moving to a new target," Justin Collier said coolly. "Lookouts report she's engaging a destroyer—most likely the *Fubuki*."

"Acknowledged," Small replied evenly. He gave orders for the *Salt Lake City* to advance on the *Fubuki*, and the *Salt Lake City*'s guns joined with others in raking the smaller ship with shells. In just a matter of minutes the *Fubuki* began to sink. Meanwhile, the *Kinugasa* and *Hatsuyuki* turned away to escape the Americans.

"You're not going to get away that easily!" Captain Small said, and he told the conn to pursue.

"Sir! Torpedo tracks in the water!"

Small ran to the outside bridge and gave orders to the helm to come hard to port at flank speed—a maneuver that would nearly swamp the left side of the ship and certainly throw men off balance all over the ship.

"It was *Kinugasa*, sir—they've also launched torpedoes at the *Boise*!"

Both men watched anxiously as the ship keeled over far enough to send great sprays of water up on the portside deck, but the torpedoes passed by without striking them.

"Good for you, sir!" Justin said with relief.

"Do you have a good bead on where the *Kinugasa* is?"

"No, sir. General direction only."

"Then order the searchlights to find them so we can return fire!"

Collier moved to the interphone, where he signaled the men in the crow's nest to fire up their arc lamps. In a matter of moments, the bright blue lights started to glow, adding yet another visual element to the battle now raging all around them. The flash of the guns was bright white, quickly fading to orange and red, the searchlights were blue-white, while the star shells hanging overhead added a ghostly glow that lit up the black ocean beneath. The men's eyes were dilating and constricting as they moved from light to dark and back again.

"We found it, sir!" The *Kinugasa* came into view as the spotlights from both the *Boise* and the *Salt Lake City* found their target.

"Signal Mr. Allen to fire at will!"

"Aye, sir! Fire at will!" The bridge party was almost in a frenzy—the *Salt Lake City* firing at targets on both sides of the ship, taking evasive action that could throw men off their feet, and the Japanese returning fire in a desperate attempt to avoid destruction. It was controlled chaos, with orders given in an artificially calm way, acknowledged in a flat reply, while inside the men were about to burst from the adrenaline flowing through their veins.

"Sir, the spotlights have given us the *Kinugasa*—but it's also given us to them!" Just then a shell from the Japanese ship exploded behind the bridge, temporarily deafening everyone in the area and sending a shower of paint flecks into the air.

"Evasive action—come to starboard twenty degrees!"

"Come to starboard, twenty degrees," the helmsman responded. The *Salt Lake City* was now both the hunter and the prey!

The engine room of the *Salt Lake City* felt like an inferno to Stuart Appelle and the rest of the men keeping the ship moving.

While the ship maneuvered at full speed ahead, the boilers operated at maximum temperature. Only occasionally did the firemen have to open the grates to check on the fires to make sure all the oil nozzles were open and firing, but when they did, the room was aglow. Appelle listened to the high-pitched hissing of the steam lines wending their way back to the turbines, which remained unchanged even as the ship made changes in direction. That was the key—constant pressure to the turbines to keep the propeller shafts turning at the speed required of battle.

Because the *Salt Lake City* had four propellers, the engine room played a crucial role in maneuvering the ship. While the rudder controlled a wide turn, the propellers could tighten the turn considerably by reducing the speed on the side to which they were turning, or even—at low speed—reversing those engines. But in battle, with all engines running at maximum speed, any kind of turn was problematic.

"Exciting, isn't it?" Appelle said to the man nearest to him, who glowered at him in return. Apparently not everyone shared his fascination with the dance the machinery was doing.

It's a paradox that the men at greatest risk of a torpedo or shell almost never know one is coming. Unless a hit was inevitable, the bridge had no reason to share the reasons for the ship's maneuvering with the men in the heart of the ship. Just as Appelle was leaning over to annoy his associate once more, he heard a new sound, one he had never heard before: a whistling kind of sound. Without prior experience, he should have had no idea what was coming, but it's the nature of intuition to connect many threads into a new pattern unconsciously. Which is why Appelle found himself diving for the battery-operated megaphone he seldom used and shouting to take cover before taking shelter himself. It was just a matter of seconds, but for some it was just enough time to save their lives. He shouted one last time, "Incoming!" then a crushing wave of air hurled him against the bulkhead, the result of a massive explosion above that also collapsed a massive steel beam onto the main boiler.

His ears ringing, his eyes burning, Appelle stepped forward as soon as he could wrap his mind around what was happening, and what he saw caused him to shudder—the room was strewn with fallen shipmates smashed against the bulkheads and floor, blood flowing from their wounds. His first instinct was to rush to their aid, but then he saw something that promised even greater horror. He rushed forward to the controls of the forward boiler— motioning for one of the men who'd managed to survive the blast to join him.

"We've got to shut this boiler down!" He pointed urgently to the pool of water forming at their feet, his mind working through what might happen if they failed. If the firetubes at the top of the boiler were exposed to air instead of water, the pressure in the boiler would drop, which would decrease the boiling point of the water, which would lead to an instantaneous increase in steam— and would blow the boiler to bits. "Help me shut down the valves to stop the fires!"

He wasn't sure that he'd been heard, even though he saw the man move his lips. He assumed the man's eardrums were likely ruptured. So he pointed at the valves and mimed closing them. His shipmate must have understood because he started closing the valves that would shut off the oil supply to the damaged boiler. Appelle moved toward the emergency release valve that would quickly draw down the steam, hoping to reduce the pressure so the boiler wouldn't flash. He was relieved to see the boiler's temperature gauge start to drop as the flames from the oil died away.

"Thanks!" he shouted. "Now let's take cover, just in case!"

It was disconcerting not to hear his own voice, but he felt the man grab his sleeve and start pulling him in the right direction. It was only then that Appelle had the presence of mind to put his hand up to his face, and recoiled a bit when it came back covered in blood. The fireman Appelle thought he was helping likely thought *he* was the one hurt and in need of help. As he stumbled forward, he thought that maybe the man was right. *Oh, dear Lord—what a mess. Please help my men who are injured!* he thought. He wasn't a particularly religious man, but a prayer seemed appropriate somehow.

"Sir, we're losing speed!" The lee helmsman was responsible for controlling the speed of the ship, so it was natural he'd be the first to notice.

"We took a hit from a shell right amidships—my guess is that it damaged the engine room." In making this report Justin did his best to control his voice.

"Sir! The *Boise*'s been hit!" Both Collier and Captain Small turned to where the lookout was pointing. Not far away they saw the *Boise* quickly losing speed as a fire engulfed the main superstructure.

"They must have hit one of her magazines for a blast like that. She's done for if we can't protect her!" Small clicked his tongue.

"Justin, I need you to go down to engineering and see how bad it is. I need all the speed I can get. We're going to surge ahead and continue to fire on the *Kinugasa*—it's us or them right now. Everything you can give me!"

"Yes, sir!" Collier sprinted off the bridge to make his way to the engine room.

"Full ahead—all available power!" Small said to the lee

helmsman. To the helmsman he said, "Put us between the *Boise* and the *Kinugasa*—I want to draw their fire."

"Aye, sir, moving to the gap between *Boise* and *Kinugasa*."

Every man's voice was excited. The battle had been raging for just twenty minutes, but it felt like twenty years. With all the eight-inch guns firing as well as the five-inchers, the *Salt Lake City* looked like a flamethrower, great arcs of fire blasting thirty to forty feet out from the barrels of the eight-inch guns. Moving to the interphone, the captain dialed down to the main fire control center and ordered Lieutenant Allen to concentrate all his fire on the *Kinugasa*. He didn't need to explain that at this close range either ship could kill the other, so it had to be the *Salt Lake City* that landed the decisive blows.

"Oh, dear Jeremiah!" Lieutenant Riley Bracken's father had taught him to say that so he wouldn't run afoul of his mother, who despised anyone who took the name of God in vain. Most of Riley's shipmates had graduated to far harsher words, but Riley Bracken was content to stick with those that had served him for so many years.

For the past twenty minutes Riley had watched in astonishment as the battle broke out beneath him. At the relatively leisurely speed of 150 miles per hour, he'd circled above the fight, providing radio intelligence on the positions of the enemy ships, confirming that three Japanese heavy cruisers and seven destroyers were matched against the Americans' two heavy cruisers, two light cruisers, and six destroyers. It was a fight of equals, but the enemy's delay in responding to the initial salvo after the flare incident had given the Americans an edge. Riley's greatest success of the night was warning the American fleet that the final ships in the Japanese group were coming into position to fire. Now, all twenty ships from both sides of the fight were after each other. The explosion on the *Boise* had led to his exclamation, and then he watched as the *Salt Lake City* surged ahead of the *Boise* and opened full broadsides on the *Kinugasa*. It was an even match— the *Salt Lake City* and *Kinugasa* both were firing as fast as their eight-inch guns could reload.

"Those barrels must be white-hot by now," Riley said to himself. "Their accuracy will fade as the metal fatigues." He sometimes wondered if talking to himself was a sign of psychological problems but decided that since he was alone no one cared.

"I need to do something!" But there was nothing he could do. It would be suicide to fly between the dueling ships pounding away at each other.

"A hit! A hit!" He cheered as the *Salt Lake City* landed a blow directly on the *Kinugasa* and then watched with relief as the enemy ship broke off the battle and steamed at full speed away from the *Salt Lake City*.

"Wonder why they're not pursuing." From his vantage in the air, he could see that the *Salt Lake City* had taken numerous direct hits but didn't know of the damage to the boiler. "Still, it's a win—they landed no troops or supplies, and we gave better than we got!" He radioed the *Salt Lake City* for instructions and was told to monitor the withdrawal as long as possible, and then notify them when he was ready to land.

"Can you hear me?"

"Yes, sir," Stuart Appelle replied, "but barely. The ringing in my ears is giving me quite a concert."

Lieutenant Commander Justin Collier bit his lip—he knew

from personal experience that the damage caused by guns firing and enemy shells exploding could cause permanent damage. He'd encountered the chief engineer earlier, who had reported that all boilers but one were still online. The chief, with Stuart Appelle and his crew's assistance, had helped push the remaining boilers beyond the red line to give Captain Small the extra burst of speed he needed to surge forward in the attack on the *Kinugasa*. But now word had come from above that the enemy was retreating, and the Task Force was regrouping to move south of Guadalcanal for safety. Although daylight was still three hours away, land-based aircraft could soon provide cover while the ships in the fleet assessed their damage and saw to the funeral parties of those killed. It was the chief engineer who suggested that Justin meet Stuart Appelle and his crew, given that their quick action had averted a far worse disaster in the engine room than that caused by the shell exploding. After reporting back to the captain on the bridge and receiving damage control reports, Justin had made his way back to the engine room to check on Appelle and the crew who'd been hurt in the attack.

"You shut down the lead boiler?"

"Yes, sir, it was dicey. I saw water leaking from it, and knew we had to get the heat down quickly or we'd have a flash explosion. We were able to shut down the fires before it exploded," he said, pointing to a man nearby. "Seaman Boulter had to interpret my sign language. He deserves a promotion, as far as I'm concerned."

"I'll look into that," Collier said. "And perhaps for you as well." He smiled. "Thank you for acting so quickly to save the ship." This made Appelle blush, though you couldn't see it on the always ruddy face of a snipe.

"What about your men?"

Appelle hesitated. "Not quite as well on that score. I have several injured and two were killed. I think they should be put up for awards."

"I'll see to it."

Collier was about to dismiss Appelle but was interrupted. Though Justin was a line officer, Appelle wasn't one to stand on formalities. "If I may ask, sir, how did things turn out?"

"You may ask. I'll tell you what I know so far. We have five men killed and twenty wounded. Our SOC pilot, whose fire started the battle, is somewhere in the water, as is his plane—we hope he'll be rescued soon. We suffered three serious hits, including the one in your engine room. We landed at least 150 eight-inch hits on enemy ships, which is a lot—our chief gunnery officer and his men all deserve medals as well. And the Japanese have withdrawn from the battle, not us. So I count it as a victory."

Appelle nodded. "That's good, sir. And the other ships in the fleet?"

"Not sure—I know the *Boise* was badly damaged and is likely to need repairs. The initial reports I've received suggest that we'll get a month or so in Hawaii while repairs are made. All in all, I'd say we came out of this as well as we could hope for—we did our duty."

Appelle nodded—no more words were needed.

"Oh, and one more thing," Collier said. "The admiral sent a message saying that from this point forward the USS *Salt Lake City* should be known as the 'One-Ship Fleet.' I guess we impressed people when we went in guns blazing to save the *Boise*." Justin Collier smiled. What greater honor could be bestowed on a ship than that? Both men felt a deep sense of pride in what they and the rest of the crew had accomplished.

Chapter 7

DRY DOCK, HONOLULU

January 1943
Pearl Harbor

"Jowdy, Albert!" the officer of the deck shouted.

First-Mate Striker Al Jowdy stepped forward.

Standing on the pier in front of one of the most awesome ships he'd ever seen, he was about to be accepted as a member of the ship's company on the USS *Salt Lake City*. After all he'd been through, it felt good to finally have a permanent assignment.

The officer who'd called his name read through the papers in front of him as Jowdy stood at attention. Al watched as the officer's eyes narrowed and he shook his head. "Is this all true? You've really been in the water twice?"

"Yes, sir." He decided to add, "And I've only been in the Pacific four months! Two of them in a rubber raft."

The officer laughed. "I'm not sure we want you, Jowdy— seems you're not very lucky."

"But it's just the opposite, sir! I'm a lucky charm. Think how much worse it would have been for those ships if I hadn't been on board?" He took a chance and grinned. It worked.

"Well, Jowdy, welcome to the *Salt Lake City*, I guess. Hope you'll never swim in salt water again."

"Thank you, sir."

"Normally I'd assign a seaman with such little time in the service to the deck crew to get acquainted with the ship, but I think you can skip that step given what you've been through." He looked at his papers, scanning for open assignments. "How would you like to be assigned to a gun crew?"

"That sounds good, sir. What kind of gun?"

"You can assist the gunner's mates in the fantail to service the new forty-mm guns that are being installed. Your full-time job will be to keep the guns clean and ready to fire at a moment's notice. During combat you'll assist in loading shells into the gun and keeping the casings orderly as they're ejected. Does that sound like something you can do?"

"Yes, sir. Beats swabbing the deck." He grinned again.

"Oh, there'll still be plenty of swabbing. Combat is messy and your gun turret must be spotless. Plus, you'll still do general shipboard duties when not in combat or drilling." The officer lifted his hand when it looked as if Jowdy was going to say something. "That's all, Jowdy. Boatswain's Mate First Class Mihalka here will be your supervisor for shipboard duties. Right now, he's the one to show you where to go. Your bunk will be three decks below the gun deck." Jowdy saluted and turned to follow.

As he and Alex Mihalka started to walk to the stern of the ship, Mihalka asked the inevitable question of all new arrivals on a ship, "So where you from?"

"San Antonio, Texas," Al replied. "It sure looks a lot different there than it does here."

"I'm from Aurora, Illinois. Beautiful, but not Hawaii. Of

course, there's no enemy trying to kill you there, so I suppose that works to its advantage." The two men laughed.

As they reached the ladders at the back of the ship, Al lugging his seabag, he said, "So I've got a good spot to sleep?"

Mihalka smiled. "If you call sleeping directly ahead of the propellers a good spot. It's noisy and hot as Hades—and you'll get the wonderful smell of burnt diesel oil from the smokestacks. But other than that, it's good."

Al Jowdy shook his head—even with all of that it wasn't so bad. He figured he'd find a better spot to sleep, given a little time. "So we really sleep *here*? Seems pretty stuffy."

Mihalka eyed him suspiciously for a few moments, then decided he was trustworthy. "Well, as long as you promise on your mother's name that you won't tell anyone, most of us have a 'summer cabin' in the lifeboats. We sleep down here if it's cold or rainy, but most nights we crawl into one of the lifeboats, where you get more air and less noise. There's one open, but you have to be quiet about it so no officers find out. Can you do that?"

Al nodded. "I'll be like the Shadow." Then he added the Shadow's famous opening line, "Who knows what evil lurks in the heart of men . . . the Shadow knows!" Al laughed the Shadow's ominous laugh and said, "I promise no one will see me—thanks for the tip!" And thus it was that Al Jowdy found a home.

January 1943
Oahu

"I can't thank you enough, Mrs. Collier. This sure beats the chow at the barracks." Lieutenant Rowan, the scout pilot who'd bailed out of his aircraft and spent the Battle of Cape Esperance in the water and then on an island, smiled. Justin had invited him to their home while they were on leave.

"I really insist you call me Heidi. And you're welcome—we're glad to have a hero share a meal with us."

"Mom—can he tell us about the fire and being in the ocean now?"

Emery Collier had sat quietly long enough. He was thrilled when his dad said that his Uncle Riley had invited the Kingfisher pilot to lunch, but his mother had made it clear she didn't want them talking about it while they were eating. Now lunch was over, with only crumbs left from the lemon cake, and Helen Matsui, their neighbor and part-time housekeeper, nanny, and cook, cleared the plates from the table while the family and their guest moved to the living room. Mrs. Matsui's family had been in Hawaii for decades, and while Japanese immigrants from the mainland were being sent to internment camps in remote areas of the West, the governor of the territory of Hawaii had made a direct appeal to President Roosevelt to allow those living in Hawaii to remain free. Not only did he and the civilian government have full confidence in these neighbors, many of whom had been, like Mrs. Matsui, in Hawaii for generations, but they also needed their services to keep the islands functioning. Heidi and Justin knew that their friendship and patronage of Mrs. Matsui was risky in their neighborhood—Heidi had already fended off several not-so-polite inquiries from Audrey Miller—but they felt it was the right thing to do.

"All right," Justin said, "Lieutenant Rowan, would you share the story of your time in the ocean with my son?"

Dan Rowan smiled. "I feel like mine's the least interesting story of the night. You guys got to fight the bad guys. I had a cockpit full of flares that scared the heebie-jeebies out of me." He smiled. "After Riley launched his SOC, I waited and then gave the signal to go. The signal flares were in a box in the rear gunner's compartment, just where they should be—I didn't think anything of them. I was alone on the flight because it was strictly recon. We weren't going to do any rescues that night, and we weren't thinking we'd see any Japanese fighters. When I brought the engine to full throttle, the plane started shaking—which is normal—but then I heard a noise in the back which I now know was the box of flares tipping over. They must not have been secured properly. I have no idea how one of them ignited, but my guess is that the movement of the box scraped one of the igniters, and voila—a flare was burning inside the cockpit at more than a thousand degrees Celsius. I knew something was wrong when I heard the pop that means a flare's ignited, followed by the smell. It was too late to abort the takeoff—in fact, the catapult launched at almost the same moment the flare popped, so I was thrown backwards by the force of the takeoff at the same instant my brain was sorting out what that noise in the back could be."

"So you light a flare like a match?" Emery asked. At thirteen years old he was even more fascinated by the military than he'd been at the beginning of the war.

"Depends on the type of flare," Riley answered. "The manual flares we carry use a friction head to start. The rear gunner drops those flares over the side to mark the spot of a rescue. It has a little parachute to hold it in the air as long as possible. We also use manual flares when we set down in the ocean to signal a submarine if we need help with a rescue. It still doesn't make sense to me that jostling in the cabin would just light one like that, but it did. Then the flame from the first lit the rest."

Justin responded, "From the ship the flares were so bright that it was like looking at the sun—we had to shield our eyes. Your SOC was the brightest thing in the ocean—it must have been terrible in the cockpit."

"I knew I was in trouble the second I smelled the smoke—it's really acrid. I guess instinct took over. I knew I had to get out of there, so I jettisoned the canopy and banked the airplane low to the surface so I could bail out. There was no time to gain altitude to use a parachute, so I got as close to the ocean as possible and essentially tipped myself out. Of course, I made sure the aircraft was headed away from the ship. The moment the tip of the wing touched the water I leaped out and prayed the tail fin wouldn't hit me."

"I could see it from the air," said Riley. "Letting the wing touch the water was exactly the right move, since it tipped the prop toward the water, lifting the tail up and away from you. The thing that was amazing is that the flares continued to burn even after the plane broke up in the water."

Dan Rowan smiled again. "So that was it—over in a minute. I was alone in the water, the *Salt Lake City* was steaming away from me at full speed, and then the big guns started firing. Now that was the real show!"

"Were you scared?" Emery asked.

"Heck, yes, I was scared. I knew the ship couldn't come back to rescue me, so I had a couple of moments of panic before my training asserted itself. I was glad I had my life vest on, and I allowed myself a minute to just lay back in the water with my head floating. It was dark out, but the moon was shining. When I looked around I saw an island not too far off, so I started swimming toward it."

"The ship couldn't rescue you?" Heidi asked.

"We would've had to use searchlights to find him in the water," said Justin, "and with ten Japanese combat ships in the area, we just couldn't risk it. We hated the thought of leaving a man behind, but there was no other choice. We hoped he could stay afloat in the water so we could start a rescue at daylight."

"Which is what happened," Riley said. "That morning at first light, I went looking for him in the water but figured out quickly he'd probably made for an island. There are dozens of uninhabited islets in the area, so I looked for the ones closest to where we were when he had to ditch. It took half a day, but we finally found him. I landed near the beach, he swam out to the plane, and just like that, we were back on board."

"Wow!" Emery said.

"I'm glad you're safe," Heidi said.

"It's pretty amazing that it happened. Now that it's over, I wish I would have laid back in the water for an extra twenty minutes to watch the battle, but I was too busy swimming. What I did see was the most awesome experience imaginable. At any given moment, up to two hundred big guns were firing in the dark, star shells were hanging in the sky, and later, two of the ships turned on their searchlights. It was certainly unforgettable. Though it did feel odd to be an observer with no role to play. I didn't like that."

"And tell me again why everyone says *you* started the whole thing?" Verla spoke up for the first time.

Justin replied, "He was so close to the island when he ditched his airplane that the Japanese thought their troops there had lit flares to show them where to drop supplies. When they returned what they thought was a signal, we knew right where they were. Captain Small figured it out first and ordered us to start firing."

"So maybe the accident was a good thing?" said Emery. "Maybe you're the reason we won?"

Dan Rowan nodded. "I hadn't thought of it like that—but maybe I did help after all."

February 1943
Repair dock, Pearl Harbor

"Jowdy—you can either chip paint or stand a welder's watch."

Al Jowdy had no idea what a welder's watch was, but standing watch sounded easier than chipping paint. *Anything* sounded better than chipping paint, since he'd been doing just that for the last two weeks. His mind wandered as he thought about those two weeks, and they weren't happy thoughts—with the ship tied up in port for repairs from the battle, the land-based crews, mostly civilians, had a great deal of work to do. But the Navy boys were given tasks to keep them busy and out of trouble. Chipping paint was an activity that would keep them busy for weeks. "But why chip paint? I don't see any rust," Al Jowdy asked the bosun's mate supervising his work crew.

"To minimize fires in combat. It's all 'spit and polish' in the peacetime Navy, so they paint the ships endlessly to keep them looking good. But all those layers of paint can catch fire in battle, sending off toxic fumes that can kill a man. So now we scrape it all off and replace it with a single layer."

"And they never thought about that during peacetime?" Jowdy asked, one eyebrow raised. "It never occurred to them that a battle cruiser might go into . . . battle?"

"Jowdy, you're wasting your time trying to figure out the Navy—in peacetime or in war. Your job is easy—chip paint if they tell you to chip paint and slap on new paint if they tell you to slap on new paint. It's the officers who figure all that out."

Jowdy said nothing in response to that—he'd learned a few things since his enlistment six months earlier, and one of them was to drop it when he was about to accuse the Navy of being stupid. This was one of those times.

"Jowdy!"

Al Jowdy jumped as he was brought back to the present.

"Yes, Boats?"

"Welder's watch or chipping paint—or I'll choose for you, if you like."

"Welder's watch!"

The bosun's mate looked at him suspiciously. "You *do* know what's required on a welder's watch, right?"

"Of course, Boats." Jowdy shifted his weight. Boats was the name given to bosun's mates for everyday use.

"Fine. Mihalka, you take care of Jowdy. I suspect he's not as well prepared as he suggests."

Alex Mihalka nodded. "Aye, Boats." Then very quietly to Al Jowdy, "My turn to babysit the new kid—again!" Jowdy bit his lower lip. He'd say thanks later.

"All right, then. Get out of here!"

The two men moved away. "So you know what you're supposed to do?"

"Um, I watch welders?"

Mihalka laughed. "Actually, that *is* the right answer, as stupid as it sounds. We have a bunch of civilians welding all over the ship as they remove the old guns, install the new ones, and repair the damage to the ship from the Battle of Cape Esperance. The problem is that with all the paint we have aboard, a stray spark could start a major fire. So every single welder is matched with a member of the crew who stands by to put out any accidental fires. It's boring—the biggest problem is staying alert. But God help the man who misses a spark that starts a fire because he was daydreaming." Mihalka looked at Jowdy, suspecting he was daydreaming right that second. "So come on. I need to get you a headgear and a fire extinguisher."

"A headgear—why? I'm not doing the welding."

"Because if you look at the arc, you'd burn your eyeballs out and spend the rest of your life blind. So you wear a helmet with a dark plate of glass so you can watch what the welder's doing."

Jowdy shook his head. *Maybe chipping paint wouldn't be so bad.* The thought of staring while a welder worked for four hours sounded like a recipe for a headache. He'd find out over the next week he wasn't wrong.

"Thanks for watching the kids," Heidi Collier said to Justin. "I don't get called in very often, but there were a lot of burn patients from this recent battle, and that's where I can be most helpful."

"Glad to. I see so little of them lately. Seems like they're both doing okay, given that they're living in a war zone with a dad who's out to sea most of the time."

"They are. They miss you . . . I miss you. But we're doing fine. I'm glad you got permission for us to stay in Hawaii."

"Me too." Justin scooted closer to Heidi on the couch. "One of the men you're helping was in our boiler room. How's he doing?"

"He's going to live. Your medical staff did a good job helping him until he got to port. But his face is disfigured, and I don't see that much can be done about that. It's hard to keep his spirits up. Kani . . . Dr. Caro's worried what will happen when he gets discharged."

"Would it help if I visited him?"

"It would—maybe we could do it together."

Justin nodded. That sounded good. With so much anxiety every time he left port and the letdown when he returned, it was hard to keep his relationship with his family on an even keel. It was like he lived in two different worlds—ship life for months at a time where concerns about the kids and their school and swimming lessons were never a thought, the danger and excitement of battle that kept adrenaline flowing almost to the point of addiction, and then the inevitable letdown when the ship returned home safe and those seemingly mundane things became his top priority. He was grateful that Heidi worked hard to find ways for him to reintegrate within the family when possible.

"What about a hike up to a waterfall tomorrow?" Heidi said brightly. "There's no school. We could take a picnic and go swimming at the base of the falls."

Justin inhaled. He was supposed to meet with a civilian contractor to discuss the logistics of replacing one of the *Salt Lake City*'s radar masts. He must have taken too long to reply because he felt Heidi stiffen.

What he should have said was that he couldn't make it, but he surprised himself as he heard himself say, "I think that's a great idea—I'll have to change my schedule, but I don't see why I can't do that. I'd love to go to a waterfall."

He turned to Heidi and smiled. She looked back at him with a puzzled look, but then snuggled in and rested her head on his shoulder.

Chapter 8

THE BATTLE OF THE KOMANDORSKI ISLANDS

March 27, 1943
Near the Komandorski Islands
0600 On the fantail

Al Jowdy shivered. "Tell me again why we're sailing to Russia when the war's being fought in the South Pacific?" A blast of arctic air forced him to close his eyes and pull his wool coat tighter around his neck. Al and his gunnery supervisor, Gunner's Mate First Class Elmer Breeze, looked up expectantly to hear the response from Al's deck boss, Alex Mihalka, a Bosun's Mate First Class who supervised Al when he wasn't needed on the forty-mm guns.

Mihalka replied, "We're not sailing *to* Russia; we're sailing *by* Russia." The team was cleaning their forty-mm gun to clear it of salt spray and corrosion—an essential task in the daily battle of steel versus the ocean.

"That doesn't answer my question."

Mihalka shrugged. Al Jowdy had an endless well of questions, and Mihalka suspected that if they could just parachute him into the Imperial Palace in Tokyo, he could talk Emperor Hirohito into surrendering just to escape the steady stream of chatter. "I'll answer, but first I have a question—have you ever once looked at a map?"

Jowdy laughed. "Not of Russia, that's for sure."

"Well, if you *had* looked at a map, you'd find that we've steamed northeast of Japan, and that we're heading to the Aleutian Islands, not Russia. You'd also see that the Japanese have built two bases on American islands in the Aleutians: Attu and Kiska. Not only is it US territory that they've stolen, but it gives them a good launching point against the troops and sailors we have stationed in the Territory of Alaska, as well as a good jumping-off point if they decide to attack the Pacific Northwest. So *we* want our islands back, and *they* want to resupply them so they can keep us occupied in the North Pacific as well as the South Pacific!"

Jowdy nodded. "I almost went to Seattle to transit back to Groton, Connecticut, for submarine training, but I had the good fortune to get pneumonia instead, so now I'm on the *Salt Lake City* working with you." He smiled.

It took a moment for Mihalka to reply. "Yes, that *is* good fortune, isn't it?"

0725 On the bridge

"Captain on the bridge!" Everyone stiffened, even though they were in good form already. Lieutenant Commander Justin Collier turned to the captain.

"Report, Mr. Collier?"

"Yes, sir. We're maintaining a base course of twenty degrees while zigzagging. Speed is fifteen knots, and we're maintaining six-mile intervals from the other ships in the task group. *Coghlan* and *Richmond* are in the lead. No reports of enemy activity so far."

Captain Bertram Rodgers was about to say something else, but was interrupted by a signals corpsman coming onto the bridge:

"With respect, sir, message marked urgent from Admiral McMorris." The *Salt Lake City* was part of Task Force 16, which included the light cruiser USS *Richmond* and four destroyers: the USS *Coghlan*, USS *Bailey*, USS *Dale*, and USS *Monaghan*. As the only heavy cruiser in the group, the *Salt Lake City* would take the lead should they engage the enemy in combat.

Captain Rodgers studied the message while Justin Collier stood by, unconsciously biting his lip while waiting to learn what the admiral had said.

"Come to course eighty degrees and increase speed to standard."

Captain Rodgers's order was confirmed. "Aye, sir—coming to course eighty degrees and increasing speed to standard."

Then Rodgers announced to the bridge, "Admiral reports that *Coghlan* and *Richmond* have made radar contact with two Japanese transports and a destroyer. There are undoubtedly more warships in the group. We'll maintain this speed and heading until we come within firing range. Sound the alarm for battle stations!"

It fell to Justin Collier to make the announcement. "Aye, sir, sound the alarm for battle stations." He moved to the microphone, flipped the appropriate switches to activate all loudspeakers throughout the ship, and then intoned, "Now hear this! Now hear this! General Quarters, General Quarters; all hands man your battle stations. The route of travel is forward and up to starboard. Set material condition Zebra throughout the ship. Reason for General Quarters: enemy ships sighted; enemy ships sighted. All hands man your battle stations!"

There was always something thrilling about making this announcement, and Justin knew that all over the ship more than 650 men were dropping what they'd been doing and were jumping out of hammocks, setting aside their food trays, and, for those who had outside battle assignments, rushing to dress in their foul weather gear. In the lower decks and at the gun turrets, the ammunition elevators were being loaded with shells, breeches were being opened, and the fire control platforms and control center were being manned to respond to whatever was required of them.

After receiving reports from each of the operational areas, Justin reported to the captain, "Ship is at battle stations."

"Very good." Captain Rodgers was thoughtful. "Initial intelligence suggests that the Japanese have the same complement as us; one heavy and one light cruiser and four destroyers. But I'm not betting on that. They have both troop transports and cargo ships to protect, so I'm expecting a bigger fight."

"Yes, sir." Like most men on the ship, Justin had an unsettled feeling in his stomach. At this spot in the North Pacific, they were out of range of all land-based aircraft, and there were no aircraft carriers in their group. There were also no submarines, so the surface ships were on their own for whatever was coming. This would be an old-fashioned naval battle—fought only with guns and torpedoes.

0750 In the engine room

Stuart Appelle responded to the command to slow the two port propellers and then listened for the metallic sound of the rudder being turned. He glanced at the compass mounted above his workstation and watched as the ship swung twenty degrees to port as it came to a new heading of zero degrees. "Due north!" he said to himself. That wasn't a heading they often followed. Once the turn was completed, he gave the order to bring the port propellers back up to the speed of the starboard engines.

He heard the repeater ring and looked up in expectation as the arrows first moved up to the top of the ring, then to the bottom, and then came back to "full ahead." He repeated this order to his engine room firemen, who controlled the oil flow to the boilers, and then confirmed the change to the bridge. "Full ahead" meant "maximum sustainable speed," but was still slower than flank speed, an emergency speed that consumed great gulps of fuel oil while putting an unsustainable strain on the engines and propellers.

Stuart walked over to his group and motioned for them to come together for a brief team meeting. There were new replacements since the Battle of Cape Esperance. "We'll be going into battle soon, so we'll have to be very fast to respond to bridge commands, particularly when we have to maneuver by changing the propellers' speed. So stay alert—your reactions may be the difference between victory and defeat. The only function of our ship in battle is to maneuver as a mobile firing platform, and the captain repositions us to the needs of ever-changing conditions. We're the ones who make that possible. I know I can count on you!" The men received this with a hurrah and then hurried back to their duty stations.

0811 On the fantail

"Jowdy!"

Al Jowdy looked up and caught his breath. He was surprised that he was perspiring given that it was below freezing on the fantail. His foul weather gear kept his torso hot, while his hands and face were chilled, and that made his work difficult.

"Aye, Chief!"

Elmer Breeze motioned for him to come close and then leaned his face up against Jowdy's ear. "Listen, Al, this is your first time in battle on the *Salt Lake City*, and I'd hoped to give you some experience on using these new forty-mm Bofors guns. But so far there aren't any enemy aircraft, so there's no reason to fire antiaircraft guns. We'll be assisting the eight-inch gun loaders by managing the canisters after they've been fired. Once back in port, we'll ship the empty shell casings back to the ammo factories to be reused. It's going to get hectic around here when we come into range, and we'll only have visibility for a minute or so before smoke from the shells puts us in a haze—after that, those of us working the guns are blind. That's why we have the fire control platform up behind us—hopefully they can see above the smoke to keep us on target. Our job is to keep the decks clear and the piles of spent shells orderly. They are *heavy*, so we'll always have two men per shell. Just follow my lead and you'll be fine. Any questions?"

Al Jowdy shook his head. "No, Chief. Thanks." He was nervous about going into battle. In a twisted way, it sounded exciting from a distance, but everybody on board assumed that the enemy wanted to kill them and sink their ship right out from under them, so it was a fight they wanted to win. And Al had a hard time shaking the memory of getting blown into the ocean twice. He wasn't sure he'd survive a third time, particularly in water this cold. He took a deep breath and shook himself to loosen up. The *Salt Lake City* currently held the fleet record for fastest firing time—a record they wanted to keep—so today they'd have to be at their very best to keep that tradition of excellence alive.

What that meant for Al and Elmer was that there would be lots of empty canisters to manage.

0835 On the bridge

"Sir! Lookouts report four new masts—two heavy cruisers and two light cruisers!"

Captain Rodgers acknowledged and then swung to Justin Collier. "Told you! The Japanese are serious about these bases—they've come loaded for bear!"

"Yes, sir!" Justin walked over to the communications panel and studied the messages received so far. "According to intelligence the two heavy cruisers are the *Nachi* and *Maya*, and the light cruisers are the *Tama* and *Abukuma*. They also have four destroyers. Eight ships to our six."

Rodgers inhaled. "We're badly outgunned. We'll have to make every shell count." He turned suddenly. "I'm going to the fire control center to consult with Mr. Allen. You have the bridge again—but I'll be back."

"Aye, sir." Then, "I have the bridge!"

Shortly after the captain left, one of the men said forcefully, "Sir, lookouts report that the enemy transports are turning to course 275 degrees."

"Transports turning away," Justin said evenly. "Steady as you go."

At 0840 they watched a massive flame shoot out from the Japanese heavy cruiser *Nachi* as it started the Battle of the Komandorski Islands. "They're firing on the *Richmond*," Justin said evenly for the benefit of the men on the bridge. A second sheet of flame leaped out from the side of the *Nachi*, followed by the *Richmond* returning fire on the Japanese ship. "Second and third salvos have straddled the *Richmond*." That was good—no hits yet, but both sides were finding their range.

At 0842, Justin braced as the *Salt Lake City*'s eight-inch guns joined the fight. The chief gunnery officer was firing in support of the *Richmond*, and his gun crew found their range on the second straddle.

Justin couldn't stop himself from yelling "Yes!" when one of *Richmond*'s six-inch guns landed a blow on the starboard side of the *Nachi*'s signal bridge. Then a second shell hit the *Nachi*'s mainmast, which destroyed its ability to communicate by radio.

"Status report, Mr. Collier?" Justin turned at the sound of the captain's voice, embarrassed that the captain may have heard his shout.

"*Richmond* has landed two blows on the *Nachi*—the bridge and their mainmast." He peered through his glasses and then pulled them away. "Make that three hits, sir! It looks to me like they just hit the *Nachi*'s torpedo compartment, given the extent of internal explosions. Good news to be sure!" After a moment, "It looks like the *Richmond* has ceased fire."

The captain nodded. At this point the *Salt Lake City* had pulled ahead of the enemy cruiser, and her stern turrets continued to fire on the stricken ship. "Notify Mr. Allen to continue for another three minutes and then cease fire." The captain wanted to make sure the enemy ship was permanently out of action—the fact that the *Nachi* was injured did not mean that its guns couldn't continue to inflict damage on the Americans, so he wanted to completely disable them. At this point the Americans were doing very well against the more powerful Japanese armada.

0900 Scout observation plane launching platform

"Things are heating up now!" Dan Rowan said to Riley Bracken as they watched, from near the *Salt Lake City*'s catapult, the blasts from the *Richmond*'s six-inch guns, as well as the *Nachi*'s and *Salt Lake City*'s eight-inch guns. Bracken laughed at the younger pilot's excitement.

"Hot indeed! I say we get the heck out of here and circle high and dry, safely away from all these people who are trying to kill us."

It was still dark at this early hour this far north of the equator. But the sky was lightening in the southeast, and it would be easy, in the air, to spot the ships in the battle by the blast of their guns, and by the trail of their wakes in the water. Knowing when the Japanese were turning and their relative positions to the American combatants could provide a crucial advantage in the battle, so Dan and Riley were completing their final checklists for launching.

"You go first," Riley said. "I'll follow." Then he repeated the flight pattern they should fly to avoid contact with other American scout planes and provide comprehensive cover for the battle scene. Dan confirmed his understanding of their orders.

"Okay, here's mud in your eye!" Dan said cheerfully. He and his rear-gunner boarded their SOC, then he pulled the canopy closed and brought the propeller to maximum revolutions. At the signal from the flight controller, the catapult whirred into action, and the little aircraft lurched forward and up into the air.

"All right," Riley said after an appropriate interval to his flight controller. "It's my turn!"

His mind registered the flash of a gun in the distance, although it didn't mean much since so many guns were firing on so many of the ships, but something was different this time. Riley turned his head just in time to hear a shrieking sound that caused his flight controller to shout frantically, "Hit the deck! Hit the deck! Incoming!" The 335-pound high-explosive shell fired by the *Maya* at the *Salt Lake City* traveled the four miles that separated the two ships in just over seven seconds—yet somehow the human brain could still register the sound as it approached the ship. With no time to think about it, Riley dove under the cowling of the launch platform, adrenaline flooding his body.

0912 On the bridge

"Captain, damage control reports a direct hit from the *Maya* on our port side aft. One of our Kingfishers is on fire, and they intend to jettison it over the side." Justin Collier did his best to keep his breathing steady as he said this. He knew that one of the SOCs had launched, and that the second should have been gearing up to when the ship was hit. Either his cousin or Dan Rowan were likely to have been injured.

"Any casualties?" asked the captain.

"Several wounded, sir. No dead to report currently."

"Very well." The captain's voice was calmer than Justin's since *his* cousin wasn't a scout plane pilot. The damage control party hadn't reported the names of the injured.

Before Justin could continue thinking about it, someone punched him in the head with a sledgehammer, and he found himself getting up off the floor and wiping debris out of his eyes. Another eight-inch shell from *Maya* had exploded just aft of the bridge, blowing out the back windows. After taking a moment to regain his balance, he looked around the room and asked, "Is anyone hurt?"

"I'm okay, sir!" the helmsman said in a shaky voice. The others said the same, even though one of the signalmen had blood dripping from one of his ears.

Justin walked over to the signalman, aware that he was likely in shock. Taking him by the shoulders he said gently, "You need to report to a medic." He could see that the man was struggling to understand him with his damaged eardrum. Justin leaned closer to his other ear and said, "Report to the infirmary. Have them check your ears." The signalman nodded, still somewhat dazed. As he started to move off, Justin motioned for a young ensign to accompany the injured man to the surgeon.

"Damage report?" The captain acted as if nothing had happened.

"Yes, sir. Just a moment." Justin walked to his station and began receiving reports from the areas affected by the hit. "Two men killed, sir. Damage to the ship is nominal."

At this point it was hard to keep it all straight—the *Salt Lake City* continued at full speed, still firing its eight-inch guns, and continued to take hits from the *Maya*. The control room was orderly, but tension was high.

The captain gave orders to come to a new heading that would reduce the ship's profile to the Japanese cruiser, while still allowing the aft turrets to fire. Meanwhile, Japanese destroyers were maneuvering to launch torpedoes. Having taken control of the conn, it was the captain's job to keep up with all these developments to make sure the *Salt Lake City* was in position to destroy the Japanese ships while protecting it from the threat of hostile guns and torpedoes. It was a complex game that required nerves of steel.

0940 Out of ammunition

"Jowdy! We've got a problem!"

Al Jowdy turned to Elmer Breeze, his supervisor, who continued, "The eight-inch guns are running out of ammo, and since the forward guns haven't fired a single shell, they want us to go forward and bring more shells back."

In fact, the eight-inch guns in the two turrets above the fantail had fired more than 300 rounds at this point in the battle. The barrels were red-hot, which made them less accurate, but they were the only ones positioned to attack the enemy on the *Salt Lake City*'s current course.

Jowdy's eyes widened. "Go forward?" That was strictly forbidden, and there was no procedure for such a transfer since it was anticipated that the forward and aft guns would fire at approximately the same rate, with their respective magazines stocked for the right amount of ammunition. "Won't we get written up?"

"Orders from the senior officers—the situation is desperate, and we need all guns available to fire from whatever angle is needed."

Al Jowdy whistled, then nodded, "Yes, Chief, but how?"

"We have to improvise." He motioned for Al to follow him. "The officers have given the orders, now it's up to us to figure out how to make it work. We'll need to move approximately fifty of the three-hundred-pound shells for the big guns."

Al Jowdy swallowed hard—15,000 pounds of shells to be moved by human muscles. And he'd never been forward of the mess hall at midships—it was forbidden for the enlisted men to move outside their assigned area. Breeze turned to their shipmate Alex Mihalka, the bosun's mate who supervised Al when he was performing deck duties. "Care to join us?" Mihalka nodded. "Good—then up the ladders to starboard," Breeze said, which was standard procedure for foot traffic on the ship. You always went forward on the starboard side, and to the stern on the port side—otherwise you'd get run over by oncoming traffic.

"Fifty eight-inch shells!" Al muttered. Elmer confirmed that with a "Wow!"

1103 On the bridge

"Mr. Bitler, you have the conn."

"Aye, sir." Then loudly, "I have the conn."

Commander Worthington Bitler, executive officer and second in command of the *Salt Lake City*, stepped forward confidently. He'd been off the bridge until a few minutes earlier checking on damage control, a particular skill of his. He motioned for Justin Collier to come over. "What's the status of the flooding in the damaged forward section?" Left unsaid were the navigation problems they'd have since the flooding was causing a noticeable list.

"The flooding is controlled, sir. I recommend we transfer fresh water from the starboard tanks to the port tanks to offset the list."

Commander Bitler nodded. "My thoughts exactly. Make it so."

"Aye, sir. Transfer water to port to offset the list." Justin turned to leave the bridge, but hesitated.

"Something else, Collier?"

"Just wondering if you'd heard anything about the damage to the scout plane—any injuries?"

Bitler looked puzzled, then understood. "Your cousin . . . my initial report said no one was killed, but that Lieutenant Bracken did suffer nonfatal injuries. I'm not sure to what extent. Would you like to go to the infirmary to find out?"

Justin shook his head. "No, sir, I need to get on this water transfer problem. But I'm glad to know he's alive." Bitler nodded, and Justin left the bridge. As he made his way to the outside stairwell that led to the affected section, he staggered as another shell from the *Maya* crashed into the *Salt Lake City* at midships, blasting a hole in the superstructure near the communications center. His instinct was to run to that site to render assistance, but he quickly resumed his original path—it was difficult enough to maneuver the ship in battle, but a list made it far more of a challenge, so he had to focus on the problem he was responsible for.

1120 Port side traffic

"Careful, Al. These dollies aren't well balanced." Al Jowdy thought the world of Alex Mihalka, but his ability to state the obvious was sometimes annoying.

"Wow. I wish I'd noticed that . . ."

"Careful what you say, Mr. Jowdy!"

"Yes, Boats. And I'll be careful with the dolly."

Mihalka, Jowdy, and Breeze had joined a small group of seamen assigned to the problem of transferring ammunition between the two magazines. They'd settled on two crews: While one was loading a dolly in the forward magazine and then moving aft down the port side of the ship, the other would be unloading in the aft magazine and then moving forward on the starboard side. It seemed like every time they thought they had a clear passageway, someone in a great hurry to follow urgent orders would appear, and Jowdy, Mihalka, and Breeze were always in their way.

"I thought it was hot working the guns!" Al said. Sweat was pouring down his face and neck from the strain, and he had to continually wipe it out of his eyes. This work was strenuous, even more so because it was such an emergency. It was a relief when they reached the aft magazine, and several other gunner's mates came to help them lift the shells from the dolly onto the automatic feeder mechanism that would send them up to one of the eight-inch guns. It was backbreaking work in the heat of battle, and just as soon as one load was emptied, they started forward up the starboard side for a new load. "And I thought submarines were stuffy!" he said under his breath.

"Submarines, Jowdy?" Breeze asked.

Al hadn't expected to be heard. "Yes, Chief. Before coming to the *Salt Lake City*, I was planning to go to sub school. But before I could get back to the States, a sub in Hawaii drafted me into service. I thought it would be exciting, but it was so boring. When we did get a chance to shoot at an enemy ship, our torpedoes were all duds. Worse, I came down with double pneumonia on our way back to Pearl Harbor. I was never so glad to get off a boat in my life. That's what brought me here."

"And what exactly does that have to do with now?"

Jowdy hesitated—"Just that, uh . . ."

"Just that what?"

"Just that this is kind of like being on that sub—that's all I'm saying. Stuffy and hot."

"In other words, Al's missing his submarine," Elmer Breeze said cheerfully. Al smiled as Elmer and Alex laughed.

1153 Flooding in a fuel tank

"Take cover!" Stuart Appelle was startled by the urgency of his own voice. But his reaction was not overblown, as a cascade of water came crashing through the ceiling of the engine room. The shell that had caused Lieutenant Commander Collier to stumble while on his way to transfer water had far more serious consequences in the engine room.

"Sir! Salt water's infiltrated the forward oil tank!"

Stuart Appelle blanched—then his face flushed. "Quick—shut off the valve to the main boilers!" He rushed to the spot where two of his staff were frantically turning the valve. But it was too late—the boilers were drawing maximum fuel from that specific tank when the shell struck and there was no way they could have stopped the salt water from mixing with the oil that was now on its way to the firebox. "Shut down the fires!" he shouted as he ran swiftly toward the boiler, but he could see that this was also too late as the orange glow of the fires began to sputter—first in one boiler, then the next, and then the next.

"Shut down all engines!" He looked around at the men, some of whom were in shock from the explosion that caused the problem, others from the realization that he was ordering them to put the ship dead in the water—the worst possible situation for a ship in battle. "*Now!*" he shouted. The men's training took over, and one by one the fires in the boilers went out. There was still steam pressure in the boilers, but it would quickly fall. "We've got to purge the lines," he said forcefully, then barked out orders to make that happen. "I'll notify the bridge," he said more quietly. Nothing like this had happened before. He was aware that the lives of every man on the ship was now in jeopardy, their only hope resting in the hands of his crew. And it was anything but certain that they would succeed in time.

1155 On the bridge

"Sir! We're losing speed!"

Captain Rodgers spun to the helmsman, who had made the report. "Say again?"

"We're losing speed—rapid fall-off."

Rodgers turned to the lee helmsman, the person responsible for communicating with the engine room. "What's happening?"

The lee helmsman was about to answer when the interphone rang. "Yes?" The helmsman listened, nodded, then asked a question while everyone on the bridge stood stiffly waiting for his report. Finally, he hung up the receiver. "Sir, engine room reports that salt water infiltrated an oil tank which was then drawn into the boilers. Some failed immediately; the others have been shut down."

"So we're dead in the water." Captain Rodgers considered this. "Raise a flag that says 'my speed zero' so that the rest of the task force know we're out of action!"

"Aye, sir," the signalman said.

The captain looked at Worthy Bitler and then reached a decision. "Give the order to abandon ship!"

Bitler's eyes widened. "Sir?"

"We're a sitting target—zero speed and already in the sights of the *Maya*!"

"Aye, sir. Abandon ship." He started to move to the public address station but was interrupted.

"Belay that order!" the captain said. When Bitler turned, he said quietly, "We won't abandon our friends—the *Salt Lake City* will go down fighting!"

Worthy Bitler nodded vigorously, "That's right! That's just what we *should* do, sir!"

The others on the bridge all nodded their assent, knowing that the end was near.

The lee helmsman said, "Sir, the engine room reports that they're working to purge the salt water and hope to restart the boilers."

"Did they give an estimate?"

"Best estimate is fifteen to twenty minutes, but they're working as fast as they can."

Rodgers nodded. "Thank you." He turned to his communications officer. "Radio the other ships in the fleet and tell them we've been hit and are temporarily dead in the water. Request smoke to help obscure our position."

"Aye, sir. Radio ships with our position and request smoke." Captain Rodgers then issued orders for the *Salt Lake City* to start making smoke. This was a process of burning a specifically formulated oil to make a thick, impenetrable smoke that resembled an artificial fog bank. Once surrounded by the smoke, a ship could maneuver to a new position while the enemy ships were blind to its position. In a closely fought battle like this it could make a difference, but in a world with radar arrays, its beneficial effect would only be temporary.

As the smoke billowed up around them, Rodgers gave new orders to the helmsman to change the profile of the *Salt Lake City* using the remaining forward speed they had from before the boiler shutoff. This would draw down any remaining steam, but it was their only hope.

Lieutenant Commander Collier entered the bridge and reported to Captain Rodgers, "Sir, the transfer of fresh water is complete, and the list is mostly corrected." He looked around, curious but not expecting an explanation for why the ship had stopped nor why they were now shrouded in a thick, foul-smelling haze of smoke.

But Rodgers motioned for him to come over. "Salt water fouled the oil lines to the boilers—they're purging them as we speak." Justin nodded, then moved to his communications station. He listened on his headset as the radio crackled to life. With the captain's permission he switched the radio to the overhead speakers so everyone on the bridge could hear.

"Sir, it's our SOC—he reports that *Richmond* and *Dale* have made heavy smoke and are now surging forward with guns blazing!" There was a positive murmur from the men on the bridge.

Then Justin broke into a startled smile. "And he reports that *Bailey*, *Coghlan*, and *Monaghan* are all heading straight for the Japanese cruisers to launch torpedo attacks!" This elicited a full-throated cheer from everyone but the captain.

"Three destroyers are heading straight against two heavy cruisers?" Rodgers was staggered. "It's almost a suicide mission—and they're doing it to protect us!"

When the impact of what they were doing sank in, Justin had to wipe his eyes with his sleeve. Losing engines in the heat of battle was almost certainly a death sentence, yet the courage of these other ships may have given them a chance. He glanced up at the clock on the bulkhead. It was exactly ten minutes since the last Japanese shell had hit the *Salt Lake City*—the one that caused this calamity.

"Sir! Engine room reports that the lines have been purged, and they're firing the boilers. With residual steam you should have power momentarily."

"Thank you," said the captain to the lee helmsman. He shook his head. "Unbelievable—ten minutes. If anything like this had ever happened before, ours would be a record." He gave new orders to the helm and waited to feel the trembling under his feet that would indicate the ship had forward motion again. It was perhaps another sixty or seventy seconds before the deck trembled ever so slightly. The captain turned and looked at Justin, who gave a thumbs-up. They noticed the navigator cross himself in a prayer of thanks. "Ahead at whatever speed she can give us." Everyone in the room glanced at the speed indicator and marveled as it slowly came up to fifteen knots. The *Salt Lake City* had maneuvering speed. The men in the engine room were miracle workers.

"Let's get out of this smoke and see what we can do to repay the enemy for this scare." The men smiled, relieved by their captain's confidence.

1210 Flooding in the fantail

Al Jowdy's eyes widened as water started seeping into the compartment. The sound of enemy shells smashing into the *Salt Lake City* a few minutes earlier had scared everyone. They hoped that the damage wasn't serious; but this looked serious. Al's first instinct was to rush toward the ladder to get up on deck—unlike everyone else on the *Salt Lake City*, he'd been in the water twice before and didn't want to experience that again, particularly in water as cold as this. But the thought of being trapped below-decks with water rushing in was far worse than the thought of jumping overboard if the ship was sinking. Just as he was about to make his move Alex Mihalka came sliding down the ladder. Speaking to all the seamen in the area he shouted, "Grab anything made of cloth and follow me—we've got to move fast!"

Jowdy looked around the room and saw his jacket, which he grabbed, as did the other men who now followed Mihalka down a series of passageways that took them to a room where water was pouring in through holes punched through the hull by enemy fire. "Stuff the holes with the jackets!" Mihalka shouted. Jowdy shook his head in disbelief—a 10,000-ton ship was to be saved by cloth jackets? But he went to work with the others and found that with a great deal of effort, it was possible to force the jacket into the hole and stop the flow of water. It was desperate work, and so the men worked desperately. "Wonder how many more holes there are?" he said to himself, surprised when Mihalka responded, "That's not our concern—we're responsible for *these* holes."

"Aye, Boats." Just then some new men appeared with bedding and Al started helping them stuff it into the remaining holes. It was hard to believe, but after ten minutes of frantic work they'd stopped the leaks. Much to his relief the water that had been lapping around their ankles drained down the passageway and into pipes that would carry it down to the bilge, where Eddy pumps would lift it up and over the side—assuming they weren't overwhelmed by too many holes letting in too much water.

"All right," Mihalka said, "why don't we go up to the deck and see what help they need there?"

"Aye, Boats. Right away, Boats!" As he and the others proceeded through the passageways and up the ladders topside, he found himself shaking with relief. When they reached the deck he waved to Elmer Breeze, who came over to talk to him. "We just stuffed jackets into holes in the side of the ship!" Al said in disbelief.

"That doesn't sound good," Elmer replied. "We've been keeping the shell transfer going so the eight-inch guns can keep firing." He looked at Al, who was still breathing very rapidly. He put his arm around the teenager's shoulders. "I don't know about you, but this is all pretty terrifying. A guy could lose it if he didn't learn how to stay calm."

Al nodded. The simple act of being touched by another person helped him slow his breathing. "Thanks." He took a long deep breath and held it, reminding himself that he was still just fifteen years old, despite what he'd written on his enlistment papers. His experience in war was enough to scare the wits out of anyone, he decided.

"Come on. If Mihalka doesn't need your help, I could use some help with the empty canisters."

"Sounds good, Chief. I'll follow you."

1213 In the engine room

"Twenty-two knots!" Stuart Appelle said this with a lump in his throat. The ship was now at the captain's desired speed. He shook his head in wonder, then motioned for the members of his team to come close. He tried to say something, but the words just wouldn't come. The lump in his throat simply hurt too much. He tried again, but nothing. Finally, he just stepped forward and started giving each of the men a bear hug. Each returned it with affection. Then, given the urgency, he asked the men to put their hands into the circle to give themselves a cheer. It was a rowdy one, and then everyone burst out laughing. Nothing like this had ever happened before—dead in the water, then fires restored, and in what must be record time. Then as quickly as they came together, they withdrew to their workstations. They had 10,000 tons of ship to keep moving.

1220 In the fantail

"That's it!" Elmer Breeze sat down heavily on a stack of eight-inch ammunition. "All the shells transferred, and the decks kept clear of spent shell casings. And you acting like the Dutch boy who put his finger in the dike to save Holland from flooding. Not a bad day so far, Al."

"I think I deserve a heart attack," Al Jowdy said as he sat down on a wood crate. It was a temporary break since the aft guns were still firing on the deck above them. Out on the open deck the concussion of the big guns was deafening, each man finding ways to put cotton in his ears or take other protective measures. But belowdecks it was deep thuds that shook the floor and bulkheads. Then they felt the impact of another shell smashing into the ship forward.

"How much more of this can we take?" Al asked.

"I don't know. We're clearly outgunned. I have no idea what caused us to lose speed for so long, but that can't be good. My guess is we're in pretty bad shape."

Al Jowdy nodded. There was a pit in his stomach that hurt. He wasn't one to worry, but this was really scary. He'd spent enough of his young life on a rubber raft awaiting rescue.

1225 In the air

"*Bailey* just launched torpedoes," Dan Rowan said into his headset. He was worried sick about the shell that had destroyed Riley Bracken's SOC. He'd seen the flash of the explosion from the air and was afraid that no one had survived the hit. But he had a job to do, so he'd been reporting continuously throughout the battle. "Torpedoes launched from the *Maya*—9,500 yards!" He circled high above the area, watching to see if any of the torpedoes would hit. The enemy had fired intermittently on the SOCs up to this point, so he had to continually change direction to avoid getting hit. Now Dan watched as the torpedo tracks of the Japanese-launched torpedoes closed in on the American ships, then let out a deep sigh of relief as he pushed the button on his radio. "All five torpedoes missed."

"Confirm that, SOC! All five misses?"

"Aye, sir—no hits." He banked into a turn and then winced as he watched two eight-inch shells smash into the *Bailey*. He then reported to the *Salt Lake City* that the *Bailey* had lost all forward speed. "*Bailey* has been hit twice and is dead in the water. *Coghlan* is also hit, but still has power." These reports were depressing. It was clear that the Japanese had suffered fewer hits and casualties and had far heavier armor to protect them.

As the *Salt Lake City* started firing again, he moved his plane to a new position. The *Salt Lake City* was using an unusual firing pattern where the shells followed a very high arc before raining down on the enemy flagship. When their shells hit, it was from high above and directly into the midships of the upper deck. "That's kind of cool," he said with a smile. "Wonder who thought of that?" Then he noticed a change in how the Japanese ships were maneuvering. "What the heck is *that* about?" His brow furrowed as he squinted to make sure he was really seeing what he thought he was seeing.

1230 On the bridge

"Sir!" Justin Collier sounded astonished, drawing everyone's attention. "Admiral reports the Japanese are withdrawing."

"Withdrawing?" Captain Rodgers shook his head. "Why would they? We have far more damage than they do."

Another bridge officer spoke up. "Sir, Lieutenant Rowan confirms that the Japanese are withdrawing. He has a crazy theory why."

Captain Rodgers raised an eyebrow. "And that theory is?"

"Rowan says our unusual firing pattern with the high arc trajectory made it appear that the Japanese were being bombed by land-based aircraft. His theory is they think we have air reinforcements."

"Well, that *is* crazy." The captain paused for a moment as he considered this. "But it's possible. We've kept up a steady stream of radio traffic with the SOCs in the air and with our land-based stations. It's likely difficult for the Japanese to keep track of all the aircraft above them. If Admiral Hosogaya thinks they're under fire from land bases, given the hundreds of shells they've fired, he may feel the only prudent course is to turn for home."

"Wow! If that's so, we're really lucky," Justin said under his breath.

"Yes, we are," the captain replied. Justin blushed.

"Sorry, sir."

"No, don't be sorry. We're almost out of ammunition, we've been hit multiple times, men have died, and we're low on fuel, particularly with one of our tanks fouled with sea water. They could have finished us off but have withdrawn instead. If that isn't good luck, I don't know what is."

"Yes, sir." Justin smiled, as did all the other men on the bridge. It would take months to tease out the details of the battle, including the Japanese reasons for withdrawing. But for now, it looked like they were safe. Justin took a deep breath. Then the words the captain had said struck fear in him—"men have died."

"Sir," he said, "request permission to go to the infirmary?"

"Permission granted." The look of dread that had come over his third officer's face was enough to tell him that Justin needed to go. Just then, Lieutenant Ross Allen stepped onto the bridge. "Ah, my chief gunnery officer—congratulations are in order," Captain Rodgers said. "Our SOC pilot thinks the Japanese mistook your last firing pattern for ground-based bombers."

"Really?" replied Ross. "I mean—really, sir?"

Captain Rodgers laughed. "No matter the reason, it looks like we'll live to fight another day. Now, tell me about our fire during the battle."

"Yes, sir. We fired 806 armor-piercing shells, then twenty-six of our high-capacity explosive shells when we ran out of armor-piercing shells. We fired thousands of small caliber shells at them. I'd have thrown firecrackers if I could have. The cupboards are pretty bare. But we landed our fair share of hits."

"Very good, Mr. Ross. Please convey my appreciation to your men for a job exceptionally well done."

"Yes, sir. Thank you, sir."

The captain then turned to his second in command, Commander Bitler. "Other damage to report?"

"Aye, sir. Our rudder stops were carried away, so we're limited to ten-degree course changes. We'd make a very tempting target if there were any enemy in the area."

Captain Rodgers nodded. "Thank you for your terrific work in managing damage control during the battle—you had a lot to contend with." He stepped forward to speak privately with Bitler. "And I intend to put you in for a commendation—no one could have handled it better than you!"

"Thank you, sir." Bitler was speechless.

"Sir," the signalman said, "the admiral sends his respects and says it's time to withdraw."

The Battle of the Commander ("Komandorski" in Russian) Islands was over. The Americans had received greater damage, but the Japanese withdrawal meant that they lost the battle. The Japanese garrisons in the Aleutians would not be reinforced or resupplied, and the threat of Japanese bases in the North Pacific had faded. And it was the USS *Salt Lake City* that had both received the greatest damage from and inflicted the greatest damage on the enemy—a truly heroic day in the history of the ship.

March 29, 1943
On the deck

Lieutenant Commander Justin Collier looked out at the sailors standing at attention on deck and then turned to the captain and said formally, "All assembled, sir." They were about to present an award to a seaman that neither Collier nor the captain had previously met—just one of the hundreds who labored at his job without recognition, until he was put in a position to do something heroic.

Captain Rodgers stepped forward and motioned for Fireman First Class Vito Bommarito to step forward. Bommarito saluted the captain, who returned his salute crisply, and then spoke loudly enough for the assembled crew to hear: "It is with deep appreciation from every member of the crew that I present the following citation: SF1/C US Navy Vito J. Bommarito—for service as set forth in the following citation is awarded a Letter of Commendation: 'For meritorious conduct during the engagement with a superior enemy force in a three and one half hour engagement off the Komandorski Islands. While patrolling his part of the ship, during the heaviest part of the action and while the ship was the objective of heavy enemy fire, he discovered a partially flooded compartment and with complete disregard to his own safety entered the darkened compartment, dogged down the hatch above him and proceeded to investigate and isolate the damage. By his fearlessness and prompt, courageous action in entering the flooded compartment, without assistance and protection, further flooding of the larger compartment was prevented. Later during the action, he traced out and repaired a damaged compressed air line to the smoke generator. His conduct throughout was in keeping with the highest traditions of the naval service.' /signed T. C. Kinkaid, Vice Admiral, US Navy—Permanent Citation."

The captain stepped forward and handed the official citation to Bommarito, who accepted it gingerly. The captain leaned close to Bommarito and whispered something that made him smile, and then stepped back. "That is all, Mr. Collier."

"Aye, sir." Justin stepped forward and issued a loud and crisp "Dismissed!" and the crowd quickly dispersed. Then he offered his personal congratulations to Bommarito, as did the men in Bommarito's crew.

Chapter 9

SAN FRANCISCO AND NEW YORK

April 1943
Mare Island Naval Yard Hospital,
northeast of San Francisco

"How's he doing, Doc?" Justin Collier asked.

The *Salt Lake City*'s chief medical officer shook his head. "Physically, Lieutenant Bracken is doing as well as can be expected. The onboard amputation we performed was good and clean, and the wound has healed as it should. Normally, he could be fitted with a prosthetic leg in another two weeks." The surgeon turned to face Lieutenant Commander Collier directly. "Some of the best orthopedic surgeons in the world are stationed here at Mare Island—they're starting to build out the Pacific Orthopedic Center, which should be fully operational by August. But even now they have the resources and expertise to fit him just as soon as he's ready."

"You said 'normally.' His case isn't normal?"

"Part of learning to walk with a prosthesis is having enough upper body strength to use crutches for a time while making the transition. It isn't just his leg that he lost. Lieutenant Bracken's right arm and shoulder were crushed by the blast, and he's quite helpless on that side—his dominant side. If he'll be patient, they can do more surgeries to repair his shoulder, but I don't see how he'll ever get back the full use of his arm. So it's a double trauma. In time, he should get to the point where he can manage crutches, which will allow him to get used to the prosthesis. But it's going to be a long journey. And right now, he's struggling mentally. I'm not sure he has the motivation to make it all work."

Justin nodded. "On the one hand, it's a miracle we did as well as we did in the battle—the Japanese had us outnumbered two-to-one. If they hadn't withdrawn, they could have kept on pounding us until we sank. But they did withdraw. We had two of our men killed—a great loss, but not nearly as bad as it could have been. On the other hand, there are the wounded like Riley whose lives are turned upside down." He hesitated for a moment. "Is it okay if I go in and see him?"

"Sure. It will be good for him. But don't take it personally if he isn't very responsive."

"I understand." Justin started to move toward the door, then hesitated. "I have one more question, Doc. Since he's in between surgeries and prosthetics anyway, is he up to travel to the East Coast? I'd like to take him home to see our families—that might cheer him up."

The doctor glanced up, then looked back down to Justin. "Normally, I'd say no—better to keep him here under care. But as you said earlier, this isn't normal. He doesn't have any wounds to tend, and if you used a wheelchair, I don't see why not. It will be taxing on both of you physically, though."

"I'm up to that. The ship's going to be here for six weeks. If we took the train, we could have maybe ten days in New York City—our families live in Queens. Or he could stay there, I assume, if he wanted to use East Coast doctors, and then I'd come back to join the ship."

"He *could* stay back there—he's not flying any more airplanes in this war. But I really think he'd get the best care here in San Francisco. I'd encourage you to bring him back, but it's up to him." The doctor was thoughtful. "Plus, I don't see why you need to take the train—he can travel by air if you can find military transport. I'll draft a letter clearing him medically to travel."

"Thank you. I'm not sure he'll go along with it, but I'm sure Captain Rodgers will give us permission if Riley agrees."

A few minutes later Justin had his answer.

"No! I'm not going to Queens or anywhere else. Just drop it!"

Justin drew his breath in slowly, counting as he did so. "Truth is, Riley, they need your bed here. There are 20,000 patients coming and going, with lots of people needing orthopedic help. You're in between procedures and can travel. They'll have a spot when we come back."

"If they need my bed, you can take me into San Francisco and dump me on a street corner—I'll join all the others holding out a tin cup for money."

Justin shook his head. His cousin had always been emotional—but he usually dealt with it by being funny or sarcastic. This was different. Still, maybe it was best to deal with him in the usual way.

"That would probably work—you *do* look more pathetic than usual, so you'd probably get a lot of cash." He felt bad as soon as he said this, not for Riley's sake, but for insulting anyone who did panhandle because of a disability. "Sorry, I shouldn't have said that."

Riley had glanced up angrily, but it faded. "You just don't get it, Justin. I don't want people back home to see me like this. The last thing I want is for people to fawn over me and treat me like a piece of china that'll break if they touch me. Plus, they'll all want to know what I'm going to do now that I'm out of the war. And I have no idea." The anger returned to his eyes. "The fact is, I'm not good for anything. A pilot who can't fly, who can't even write his own name. I can't be a clerk, I can't do . . . anything."

Justin sat down on the side of his bed. "Listen, Riley, I think I'm supposed to be all encouraging at a point like this and say there are lots of things you can do. And I believe that, by the way. You could be a flight instructor in San Diego, an aeronautical engineer in Los Angeles—there's a lot you could do with what you know about planes. But all of that's in the future. Right now, you have to deal with pain and asking people for help, and there's just nothing positive about that. I don't know what else to say other than I'm here for you. I always will be. And so will your family—and mine."

Riley shook his head. "I look ridiculous, you know. My right shoulder droops. I can't walk—why would I want anyone else to see this?"

For the first time, Justin laughed. "Are you kidding? You're still as handsome as ever, with that Hollywood face of yours, so you'll just dazzle them with your movie-star smile, like you've always done."

Riley punched him with his left hand. "It's true that I'm better looking than—well, almost everybody." That encouraged Justin. But then Riley said, "How would we even get there? I can't walk; I can't hobble. I have trouble going to the bathroom!" He started smoldering again.

"Two ways—we could take the train, book a cabin on a sleeper car. They serve food in the room if you like, and I can help with the bathroom. The other is to book a flight on a military transport. That would be a rougher ride, but we could make it home in two days instead of five. Your choice."

"I didn't say I'd go."

"But if you *did* go, which would you choose?"

Riley Bracken shook his head. "Just what do you *think* I'd choose? I'm a pilot, for cripes sakes."

"Military aircraft it is. I'll get to work on it."

"Still haven't said I'm going."

"I know."

April 1943
Downtown San Francisco

"Thank you! We appreciate the ride!" Al Jowdy tended to act as spokesman for the group.

"Always glad to help boys in uniform. Enjoy your time in the city!"

The three seamen watched as the driver of the '39 Chevy pulled away from the curb and disappeared up Geary Street in San Francisco. Not wanting to spend their hard-earned money on bus fare, they'd hitched a ride with a friendly driver. Now they were standing on the corner of Union Square across from the world-famous St. Francis Hotel. Al Jowdy turned to Alex Mihalka and Elmer Breeze and lifted his shoulders in a "What now?" shrug. Alex responded with, "Let's get some food—how about we try something in Chinatown? We can ride the cable car up Powell Street and then find a restaurant."

"Chinatown?"

Alex smiled. "Have you ever had Chinese food?"

"I don't think so—I've just had food."

"I think you'll like it," said Elmer. "I had a few days in San Francisco before shipping out to Pearl Harbor and I fell in love with the place, including Chinatown. It's *so* different than any-thing I'd ever experienced. Let's go."

Go they did, hanging onto the side of a cable car to take the work out of climbing the steep hill. Al watched in fascination as the cable car operator squeezed the long lever that grabbed hold of the cable running under the street to move the car at a steady nine and a half miles per hour whether going up- or downhill. That's why the operator was called a "grip." When they got close to a stop, Al watched as he released the claws from the cable and then pulled a separate lever to force wood blocks against the steel rim on each side of the cable to bring the trolley to a stop. When Alex and Elmer jumped off, he followed but glanced under the car to see a whiff of smoke rising from the wood blocks—made from the friction of slowing the 15,000-pound cable car.

"That's so amazing! How many of these routes are there?"

"Dunno. Something like twenty?" Elmer said. "They have millions of riders each year. Not bad for a system built more than seventy years ago. Can you imagine all those steel cables con-stantly turning under the major streets?" Alex and Al nodded, amazed as always by Elmer's knowledge of arcane things. "But now it's time to prepare yourself for a new adventure, Al. The shops and restaurants in Chinatown are *crowded*—and the fresh vegetables are different than almost anything we had to eat back home. There are a million things for sale, so don't buy the first thing you see."

As they turned the corner onto Grant Street, Al Jowdy's eyes grew wide and he let out an involuntary "Wow!" Grant was one of the oldest streets in San Francisco and the main thorough-fare of Chinatown. "I can't believe this!" It was a sight indeed: hundreds of colorful lanterns strung across the street, intricate signs on each of the buildings written in gold Chinese characters against a brilliant red background, and more people than Al thought possible—many wearing clothing that he thought existed only in movies. Pungent odors filled the air from street vendors cooking unfamiliar vegetables and meats, their kettles filled with rich broth and thick noodles. "This is *nothing* like San Antonio!" he laughed, and together Al and his friends set off on their new adventure.

April 1943

Penn Station, New York

"Do you smell that?" Riley Bracken asked this with more enthusiasm than anything he'd said since an enemy shell had blown up his Kingfisher and ended his career as a pilot. "Smells like New York!"

Justin Collier smiled. The trip across the country in military aircraft had proved more problematic than he'd hoped; they were bumped to a later flight in San Francisco, had a rough landing in Salt Lake City, ran low on fuel as they approached Omaha, and ended up stuck in Cleveland for a day because of bad weather. Then they were diverted to a military airfield in Newark rather than New York, so they'd had to transfer by train into Manhattan. All of this with Riley in a wheelchair as Justin worked to manage their seabags. But Justin was patient, despite Riley's bad attitude. The only bright moments were when Riley talked with pilots who were interested in his story. Even then he seldom smiled and brooded whenever the subject of seeing his family arose. But now they were in Manhattan, where they'd spent many afternoons and evenings prior to the war, and Riley's spirits brightened.

"I think we should take a cab to Queens rather than fight the subways," said Justin. The truth was that he was exhausted and wanted to get home as quickly as possible.

133

Riley nodded. He preferred the subway but knew just how troublesome it was for Justin to manage his wheelchair and their luggage. "Sure, but what do you say we stop at Delmonico's for dinner first, for old time's sake? Do you think we could manage that?"

Justin bit his lip. That wasn't what he wanted. But he nodded. "I think that's one of the best ideas you've ever had. In the old days we'd have gone to the Rainbow Room for a drink and to hear the orchestra." He said this without thinking, since the Rainbow Room on the sixty-fifth floor of the RCA building in Rockefeller Center was famous for the world's most spectacular view of the Empire State Building and downtown Manhattan, as well as for its dancing—and that was something Riley wasn't going to do. But it had closed in 1942 because of the war. "Sorry, that would *not* have been a good idea, even if it was open."

Riley raised his hand. "Stop. I think that's a great idea." He thought for a moment. "But I'm pretty sure the Copacabana is open if you're up to it. I know I'll stand out like a sore thumb, but it would be great to hear some live music and watch the dancers. My parents don't know what day we're arriving, so what say we get a hotel for tonight so we can stay out late and not have to find a ride home?" Then he seemed to catch himself. "But now it's my turn for a bad idea—the last thing you need is to push me all over New York City. They don't make it easy for wheelchairs, after all."

"We can manage. The Copa's on 60th Street, so let's see if they have a room at the Plaza. It's half a block from the Copa, so we could walk there and back."

"You sure? I'm kind of a pain . . ."

"It's been a long time for me, too. Good food and good music will do us both good. Plus, by staying in the city, there's time for a nap and a shower first." Justin motioned for a cab driver to come help him with the bags. "Take us to the Plaza Hotel." He hoped they could find a room for two serving naval officers. He also recognized that having elevators to help them to and from the room would make it all possible, to say nothing of bellmen to help with the luggage.

"Yes, sir. Right away, sir."

April 1943
San Francisco

"Where are we going to sleep? I don't have a lot of money—I send most of it home to my mother." Al Jowdy had been enjoying such a great adventure in San Francisco that he'd lost track of the time, but it was too late now to hitchhike back to the base before curfew.

Alex smiled. "Turns out I know how to manage this—one of our shipmates told me how to pull it off. Stick with me, and we'll be fine."

Al and Elmer looked at each other with raised eyebrows but decided they didn't have any ideas about what to do, so they fell in with Alex.

"Where're we going?"

"You'll see."

Al imagined Alex would take them to a city park so they could sleep on benches, and he was surprised when Alex stopped in front of a movie theater. "A movie? I can't afford a movie *and* a hotel."

"This is a twenty-four-hour movie theater. You pay admission and then stay as long as you want—they run movies all night long!"

"Twenty-four-hour movies?" Once again Al was amazed.

Once inside they settled in to watch the first feature film, followed by some cartoons and a newsreel. Then, before the feature started up again, Alex motioned an usher over. Al strained to hear what he was saying but couldn't make it out. But he did see Alex hand him a dollar bill—a large sum during the war. The usher nodded and pointed to some empty rows.

"What's going on?" Elmer asked.

"I gave him a tip to make sure he wakes us up just before sunrise so we can hitch a ride back to base before our leave is up. He said it's fine for us to put down enough seats in a row so that we can lay out and sleep. So we get movies and a bed for one low price." He grinned.

"Wow!" Al said. "You can figure out anything."

"I'm a bosun's mate, for crying out loud—I'm *supposed* to know everything! Now, let's stake out our seats before anyone takes them."

April 1943
Mare Island Shipyard

"No, no, no—that won't do, and you know it!" Stuart Appelle hovered over the civilian crew working to patch the holes that had fouled the fuel tanks with sea water. "Either fix them right or replace the whole tank—we don't want oil leaking because you're in a hurry to get out of here."

"Maybe we should call our union rep," the foreman said. "We're not in the Navy, and we don't answer to you."

"Maybe not, but your work does. You won't get paid until I sign off on this." He stepped forward to the man he'd been clashing with the past ten days and was energized when the other fellow stepped toward him aggressively.

"Everything okay down here?" the chief engineer asked.

Stuart leaned in one last time, the men watching him and expecting the two to come to blows, but then stepped back. "Just a little disagreement over some welds—nothing we can't work out." He turned to the foreman. "That's right, isn't it?"

The foreman glowered, but replied, "Yes, that's right. We have a bit more to do."

The chief nodded. "That's good. I'll leave you to it, then."

Stuart knew it wouldn't go down well if he got in a fight with a contractor—even if it was deserved. So he decided to take some of the heat out of the discussion. Turning to the contractor he said quietly, "It's just that we work below the waterline, so we take these repairs personally."

He watched as the foreman's face flushed, wondering if he'd made him even angrier rather than calming him down. But then the man stood down. "We understand—you deserve the best. We'll check it all again, just to be sure."

Stuart nodded, then went over to his worktable to give the welders some space.

April 1943
The Copacabana, Manhattan

"I can't believe this!" Justin cupped his hand over Riley's ear to say this, since the music made it difficult to hear. "They serve Chinese food at a Brazilian-themed nightclub!" He laughed. "How international can you get?"

Riley smiled but now regretted suggesting they come. Being wheeled into the club in his military wheelchair made something of a scene. He hated having so many eyes on him. The maître d' seemed put out at having to find a table that Riley could get to easily, and the staff had balked at moving chairs to make space for them. If he could do it over, he wouldn't have come, but they were finally settled and to leave now would look peevish and draw even more attention.

"The food is really good, if you like Chinese food, which I do—at least it was before the war. I don't know now," Riley said. "You didn't come here with me before the war, did you?"

Justin shook his head. He and Riley had been close growing up, but after high school they'd gone their separate ways. Even though they were just a couple of subway stops from Manhattan, Justin hadn't come into the city that often—the occasional school visit to a museum, a concert at Central Park—but Riley had loved the place. Justin could see that it was tormenting him to come back here in his changed circumstances.

"Not that I can remember—and I'd probably remember the Chinese food, since it's my favorite. These people can do noodles! Chow fun, chow mein, or noodles with brown gravy—I love it all."

Riley laughed. "I like Little Italy for noodles—it's deep-fried lemon chicken for me when I'm at the Copa."

"Why don't we order a couple of dishes each and share? You know, try lots of things?"

"Sure. That sounds okay." Justin wasn't going to worry about the cost of anything tonight. They'd sailed halfway across the Pacific Ocean, then flown across the whole of the United States to get here, and the last thing he was going to do was scrimp on one evening.

A new song started, and Riley turned to watch the famous chorus line come out, the women dressed in extravagant Brazilian costumes bursting with color. They danced with abandon to the strong Latin beat of the music. "I love the bongo drums," Riley shouted into Justin's ear. "I'd get up and dance if I could."

"Maybe someday you can—who knows?"

Riley pursed his lips. His bad mood had started to lift. "Maybe. For now, I can clap!" And clap he did—for the next hour—in between different courses of food, and conversation during the lulls. Sometimes he was bright and cheerful, other times withdrawn and quiet. But then an old friend of Riley's recognized him and came over to join him and Justin for a time. They had a lengthy conversation about all that had happened since they last met, including Riley's accident. His friend worked in Army intelligence and was back in New York from Europe to attend a conference where operatives were trying to catch up on all the latest techniques in spying on the Germans and Italians.

Riley thought nothing of their discussion, of course, but apparently his friend did because a few minutes after his friend left, the emcee raised his hand to quiet the crowd before announcing the next performer. "Ladies and gentlemen, before we do our next number—the one I know you've all been waiting for, I want to take a moment to recognize an old friend of the Copa—a Navy pilot serving in the South Pacific who's home on leave. Many of us remember him as a great dancer . . . now that's changed. Would you join me in welcoming a true American hero, Lieutenant Riley Bracken, recently in battle on the USS *Salt Lake City*, a heavy cruiser up in the Aleutian Islands—wherever that is." That brought a laugh. "We need to let him know that he's always welcome at our club!" The spotlight swung to their table and suddenly everyone in the room was standing and clapping as Justin pushed a thoroughly abashed Riley Bracken forward onto the dance floor. His dark navy blue slacks were still crisp, with the fold over the spot where his leg ended neatly pinned. Riley was clearly shaken but managed to raise his hand and wave to the crowd, hoping that it was over.

But the emcee had other plans. He walked over to Riley with

the microphone and asked if he would mind telling the crowd what happened. To Riley's surprise, words failed him—he choked up to the point that he couldn't get anything out. Normally loquacious, this was just too much. So Justin took the mic and briefly explained the Battle of the Komandorski Islands, including the moment when the shell had blasted Riley into the catapult launcher while blowing his scout plane into a thousand pieces of shrapnel before the plane itself was tipped over the side. In a room that was usually filled with noise, there was intense silence as everyone listened to the story. When Justin finished by explaining that it had ended in a victory for the American task force by keeping the Japanese well away from the Pacific Coast, the crowd cheered.

Then two things happened that would forever change Riley Bracken's life. The emcee came forward and handed him a piece of paper and explained to the crowd that it was a pass that gave Riley free entrance to the Copa without a cover charge for the rest of his life, which led to another round of applause from the audience and shouts of "Here, here!" And then the surprise of a lifetime: The lights went down, and the band struck up a Gershwin tune as the star of the evening stepped out into the spotlight, none other than Marlene Dietrich, the world-famous Hollywood star with a sultry singing voice. She came over to Riley as she sang the haunting words to Gershwin's "Embraceable You." A natural-born flirt, she ran her fingers through his hair and up and down his face, delighting everyone in the room when he blushed and then laughed. And then she surprised him by taking control of the wheelchair and moving it in tune with the music, in essence dancing with him despite his injury.

For Dietrich, this was part of her wartime life—she was a devoted performer on USO tours, bringing encouragement to

American troops in Europe as well as visiting the injured in military hospitals. Her wartime service was even more remarkable for the fact that she had been born and raised in Germany, but hated Adolf Hitler and the Nazis and so put her life at risk by going right up to the front lines where she could be captured by the Germans. Hitler had put a bounty on her head, but that didn't stop her from the USO tours. She loved America and appreciated the soldiers who were dying to defeat the people who had overtaken her country's government.

Even though she had entertained millions of people on screen and stage, on this evening, at this moment, she was devoted to Lieutenant Riley Bracken, who despite the embarrassment of being in the spotlight accepted her gift openly and gratefully. At the end of the song, she leaned down and kissed him, then asked a question while holding the mic away. She ended the act by saying into the microphone, "Ladies, he's single—and very, very, handsome—so you better hurry to get his number before I come back to New York and take him with me to Hollywood!" Well, the crowd loved that, and hooted as she pushed Riley back over to his table.

With the spotlight no longer on them, Justin said quietly, "Well, *that* was exciting," as Dietrich started a new song.

"A little humiliating—but you're right, it was exciting." In view of their earlier treatment, receiving a lifetime pass meant a lot. "I'm glad you brought me home. I feel like I'm at home." He looked at Justin, then put his hand on top of his cousin's. "Maybe I *can* do this."

As they prepared to leave, a man in a tuxedo came over to their table. Riley looked up as the fellow introduced himself. "Forgive me for butting in, but I'm a surgeon, John Ferguson, and I want you to know that if I can do anything to help with your shoulder and arm, I'll be glad to do it. It's my specialty. And I have a friend from medical school who specializes in prosthetics who works wonders for people. I'm sure the Navy takes care of its people, but I think we can do some things they can't." He handed Riley a business card. "Not to brag, but I'm considered the best in the business. I wanted to serve in the military, but they wouldn't take me because of an injury I had in high school." He looked down at his leg. "I too lost a leg, so I have a sense of what you're feeling. At any rate, I appreciate your service to our country, and I'd like to help if you'd let me."

"I . . . I don't know what to say."

Justin put his hands on Riley's shoulders. "Say yes. Just say yes. This is a great offer."

"But what about the Navy? They do own me, after all."

"I'll take care of the Navy," Dr. Ferguson said. "It's all about paperwork with them. I'll see that you get transferred to a base here in Brooklyn, and then we'll meet with you. Let us do this for you."

Once again Riley found it hard to speak. "Sure—that sounds swell. Thank you!"

The doctor shook Riley's hand, and Justin forced himself to take some deep breaths. For the first time since the Battle of the Komandorski Islands, he felt as if he finally had his cousin back.

Chapter 10

THE BATTLE OF ATTU IN THE ALEUTIAN ISLANDS

May 1943
Near Attu Island

"Now hear this! Now hear this! Jowdy, AA, report to the bridge. Repeat, Jowdy, AA, report to the to the bridge!"

On the fantail, scrubbing salt deposits from his forty-mm gun, Al Jowdy felt like someone had just slapped him across the face.

"Jowdy! What have you done this time? The bridge!"

Al turned to Elmer Breeze with an ashen face. "I haven't done anything, Chief—I mean anything more than I usually do. Why would I get called to the bridge?" It was unheard of that an individual sailor out of a crew of 650 would be summoned to the bridge—at least for anything less than a serious offense. "What do I do?"

"What do you do? You go to the bridge before the master at arms comes looking for you. Get out of here!"

"Yes, Chief!" Jowdy ran his hand through his hair and then pulled his cap down tight on his head and started forward to the series of ladders that would take him up to the bridge. This was a journey he'd never expected to take. When he made it to the top he nervously stepped through the door onto the bridge, where an ensign saluted and asked his name and purpose.

"Jowdy, sir! Albert. Reporting as requested."

"Jowdy!" Al jumped at the sound of the captain's voice; the color now fully drained from his face.

"Yes, sir! Captain, sir! Captain Rodgers, sir!"

"At ease, Jowdy. I have a question for you."

"Sir?"

"When was the last time you wrote home to your mother?"

"My mother?" Al shook his head to clear it. Had the captain just asked him about a letter to his mother?

"Yes, Jowdy. When was the last time you wrote to your mother? I have reason to believe she hasn't heard from you in months."

"Uh, I'm not sure, sir. It has been a while since I wrote to her. She has nine kids, and I didn't think anyone would miss me."

"Jowdy, the correct answer is that it's been *six* months since she's heard from you. And that's just terrible—your poor mother has no idea if you're alive or dead. She wrote a frantic letter to the Navy Department in Washington, who sent a dispatch to the Pacific fleet, who forwarded the request on to me to find out why you would neglect a woman like that! Well?"

Jowdy swallowed hard. "I . . . I . . . should have written to her, sir. I'll see to it right away."

"Not good enough. I need to make sure you write to her. You're to report to the chaplain forthwith. He'll help you get a letter written and make sure it gets posted. Do you understand?"

"Yes, sir. Report to the chaplain, sir." Al's heart was racing— he was a religious person, but not one to visit the chaplain.

"And Jowdy, I don't expect to *ever* receive a message like this again—you will write to your mother weekly for as long as you're assigned to the *Salt Lake City*. Is that clear?"

"Yes, sir—it will never happen again. I promise! I mean, it will happen, my writing letters . . . to my mother . . ."

"Then off you go." Jowdy saluted, and the captain returned his salute.

"Well?"

"Uh, yes, sir." Jowdy spun around, taking his one and only look at the bridge of a heavy cruiser, in the process catching sight of men doing their very best not to grin. Another reason to be wary of officers. He turned on his heel and made his way to the door.

As he did, he heard the captain call out, "Straight to the chaplain—he's going to report back to me." Al nodded but didn't reply. He simply couldn't get off the bridge fast enough.

When he arrived at the chaplain's cabin, he found that he'd already been briefed. "Pretty terrible to leave your mother fretting like that, Jowdy."

"Yes, sir. I didn't mean to worry her—it's just that there are nine of us and I didn't think she'd have time to think about me. And I'm just not very good at writing."

"Well, she does think about you, so we're going to write a letter to catch her up on the last six months. I think five pages should be about right."

"Five pages!" Al had never written five pages of anything, let alone a letter to his mother. "But I thought the most you could send was one page!"

"That's true unless it's an exceptional circumstance—and this qualifies. We'll send it on my authority." The chaplain twisted up his mouth in a curious way. "Do you think the captain of a battle cruiser has time to spend with each of 650 men telling them to write a letter home?"

Al muttered, "I didn't think he had time to tell one enlisted man—until today."

The chaplain laughed. "Well—he doesn't. So we're going to make sure that your mother is happy to hear from you and she knows everything she needs to know to feel you're okay. When we're done, you'll know how to write a letter so you can do it every single week from now on—do you understand that?"

Al nodded. It would have been easier if the chaplain had asked him to chip paint.

"I'll help, so let's get started."

As it turned out, Al Jowdy had a lot to learn. It took five hours in the chaplain's office to finish the task.

May 1943
On the bridge near Attu Island

"I'd forgotten how boring it is to be in the peacetime Navy."

Justin Collier laughed at this from Commander Bitler. "We're keeping Alaska safe from the Japanese, sir!"

"Oh, right! Because they have so many capital ships that they can fight the United States in both the South Pacific and the wastelands of the Arctic." They were standing on the outside bridge. Commander Bitler stretched. "It feels like the war's passing us by."

Everyone on board felt that way. After the Battle of the Komandorski Islands, followed by the long refit in San Francisco, nearly everyone yearned for excitement. Of course, some were happy to be out of harm's way, but most ached to get back into action. It was the great irony of war: when you were under attack, you offered up desperate prayers pleading never to have to go into battle again. Then when the action passed, you were desperate for something meaningful to do. Justin added, "Well, whatever we're doing must be working; we haven't seen a trace of the enemy for months."

Bitler smiled. "It's inevitable that the United States will win this war against Japan—they can't keep up with our production or our manpower. The US has nearly double the population. We have abundant natural resources while they have to import nearly everything. They'll simply run out of people and steel a long time before we do. So, the only question is, how many people on both sides have to die before they surrender?"

"It does seem like we have the upper hand. Ever since Midway we've been pushing them back an island at a time. Although it gets tougher with every island."

Commander Bitler sighed. "Well, we still have a ship to run." He motioned for Justin to follow him to the inside bridge. "Mr. Collier has the conn!" The men on the bridge crew acknowledged the change in leadership. "I'm going down to the fire control center to meet with Ross Allen. I want to make sure we don't get out of balance on our munitions in future battles—having men lug shells from the forward magazine to the aft magazine is unacceptable. We need a better plan."

"Yes, sir."

"Call me if anything comes up." He smiled. "Like if the Japanese decide to abandon their home islands and move to Alaska!"

Justin Collier laughed. "Aye, sir. I'll watch for the moving vans."

May 11, 1943
On the bridge

"Now hear this! Now hear this! General Quarters, General Quarters; all hands man your battle stations. The route of travel is in support of beach landings. Set material condition Zebra throughout the ship. Reason for General Quarters: preinvasion shelling. All hands man your battle stations!"

Justin flipped off the switches to the shipwide loudspeaker system. "It seems our boredom was a little premature," Executive Officer Bitler said. "We get to fire our guns after all."

Justin smiled. "Yes, sir. Given what the Army faces in invading this island in snowy conditions, I'm glad we're here to help them, but not actually out there with them. I always thought May was supposed to be warm!"

"This is about as close to war in Europe as we're likely to experience. But from what we've learned so far, it's going to be a lot tougher than anything we've faced before. The Japanese infantry has been tenacious in trying to keep the islands they've won."

Justin nodded. It was true what Bitler said—war was hard to understand as it was, and this was going to be an even more difficult and unpredictable situation. "Lives wasted for no rational reason." Justin shook his head.

"Captain on the bridge!" Like all the others, Justin snapped to attention until Captain Rodgers gave the "at ease" command. He motioned for Justin and Worthy to come over to the plot table. "We're the biggest ship in the area, so we'll take the lead in softening up the beaches. I want the ship to steam slow and steady up and down the front so we can pound them. The more we kill, the fewer there are to kill our boys. And while beach operations often leave a lot of enemy survivors, we can muddle their brains so they're not as effective in the fighting."

"Aye, sir," Commander Bitler said.

"I'm going to the fire control center to monitor the firing pattern. I'll leave the bridge to you." With that the captain, whom Justin thought of as a whirlwind who blew in and out of places with incredible energy, disappeared from the bridge.

Bitler said, "Other than firing the guns, there's not a lot for us to do. We have no reports of enemy ships in the area. Why don't you go to your duty assignment at Signals? My guess is we'll get a lot of chatter in the next week or so as we pry them loose from the island. We're at General Quarters just in case there are enemy ships steaming this way, but I think the risk is low. And there's no report of heavy artillery on the island that can hurt us."

Justin saluted. "Aye, sir. I'm off to Signals, then." But before he could leave, a messenger came through the door.

"With respects from the captain, Mr. Collier, he'd like to see you in the fire control center as soon as possible." The young man saluted, and Justin returned it.

"Wonder what that's about," Worthy Bitler said. "That's not your normal duty station. Something's afoot, I think."

Justin smiled, then left for fire control, wondering what was in store.

May 12, 1943
Beach Red, northern Attu Island

"You do realize we're capable of calling in coordinates ourselves, Mr. Collier? We don't need a Navy officer to supervise us."

Justin bit his lip, then shivered. In an unusual move the day before, Captain Rodgers had asked Justin to join the Provisional Scout Battalion under the command of Army Captain William Willoughby to be among the first Americans to land on the island in advance of the main recapture effort. The idea was that the

Navy could provide better support for ground troops in future landings if they had firsthand knowledge of what it was like on the beaches during an invasion. Major General Albert Brown had agreed to the temporary assignment. Justin was excited by the opportunity, but also apprehensive—beach landings had the highest casualty rate of any action in the Pacific War.

Responding to Willoughby's challenge, Justin replied, "I'm here as an observer—nothing more. I'll help any way that I can, but that's entirely up to you, Captain Willoughby."

"We're each trained for different things—you have your job to do, and I have mine."

"Yes, sir. Of course." Justin referred to Willoughby as "sir" as a courtesy. Since Justin's rank was equivalent to that of an Army major, Justin outranked Captain Willoughby.

Willoughby paused and took a long drink of water from his canteen. Shells from the Navy task force were still passing overhead, smashing into the tree line some fifty feet from the beach. The scouts had made their way to the beach under the cover of early-morning darkness and were now digging in so they could do reconnaissance sorties in advance of the main landings. "Sorry, Commander. We need your support and are glad to have a heavy cruiser backing us up. And chances are good that if we do need something special, they'll pay more attention to you than to me."

Justin wanted to say that the Navy would support the Army no matter who called it in, but recognized this as a peace offering, so he just nodded. "I'm used to hearing the guns as they fire on the ship, which is hard on the ears. But being here and hearing the whine of the shells as they pass overhead and explode behind the trees is really kind of awesome."

"And you just pray that your Navy gunners don't get sent the wrong coordinates. I was on Guadalcanal when some nitwit sent in the wrong coordinates and suddenly our navy was bombing us instead of the Japanese! You talk about chaos—you think you'll lose your mind when those big shells come raining down."

"I was knocked silly during the Battle of the Komandorski Islands when a twelve-inch shell smashed into the superstructure of the *Salt Lake City* behind the bridge. I had to pick myself up off the floor. The blast leaves your brain scrambled as you try to figure out what just happened."

Willoughby was quiet for a few moments as he pondered this. It was easy to think of the Navy as less valiant than the infantry since they seldom came face-to-face with the enemy, but now that he thought about it, they were sitting targets out there in the ocean. "I guess we each have our own problems. I can't imagine getting sunk in the middle of the ocean to drown, freeze to death, or deal with sharks. At least here I can dig a deeper foxhole when the enemy fire gets too hot; you guys have no place to go." Justin just listened. Finally, Willoughby stuck out his hand. "Welcome to the Army, Mr. Collier. You're now an honorary member of the 7th Scout Company, 7th Reconnaissance Troop, 7th Infantry Division—the 'Lucky 7s'!"

"Thank you. Seven's my lucky number as well. And Justin's the name." He smiled. "I'm honored to serve."

"Right then. You can call me Will. Here's your situation report: We're here on the beach, and we need to be over there near the base of those mountains," he said, gesturing at the map. "With the tons of high explosives that the *Salt Lake City*'s been dropping on this area you'd think there wouldn't be a Japanese soldier left within a mile of the place, but just as soon as we start running across that open space you'll be surprised at how many are still alive and ready to fight. Just remember to stay as low as possible and run as fast as your legs will take you."

Justin felt a wave of fear wash over him, and he worked to steady his breathing. There were people out there—not very far away at all—who wanted to kill him. "Okay," he said, "just a moment ago I thought I was going to freeze to death in this weather, but now not so much." He took a deep breath and then said, "I'm ready."

Willoughby motioned to the others in his group and then said. "All right, then—let's go!"

May 29, 1943
Chichagof Harbor, northeastern Attu Island

Captain Will Willoughby shook his head. "My guess is that today's the day. The remaining Japanese that we haven't already killed will either surrender or die in a final suicide attack. I don't see how they can hold out any longer."

Justin nodded. He had never been so cold in his life. At this point more than 1,000 Americans had been either incapacitated or had died from exposure to the harsh Arctic weather. The temperature was imposing a higher casualty rate than the Japanese. Fighting in the heavy scrub brush of the island was ferocious, with treks across mountain passes in the snow, the enemy infantry fighting for every inch of ground as the Americans drove them back onto the Chichagof Peninsula. After two weeks of fighting there was no place left to retreat to. They had the ocean against their backs and no fleet to rescue them.

But Justin had learned enough in the hand-to-hand combat of the past two weeks to know that the normal rules of war didn't apply here. The Japanese commander, Colonel Yasuyo Yamasaki, should have surrendered a week ago to save as many Japanese lives as possible. Instead, the confirmed number of Japanese dead was approaching 2,000 men. The odds were terrible for the Japanese forces—15,000 American ground troops to 3,000 Japanese. Yet they continued to fight. Justin now knew what it was like to be in the infantry—the physical suffering was intense, the constant bombardment disorienting.

"By all rights, they should surrender," Justin replied. "One white flag and we'll feed them, get them to safety from the weather, and take them to a secure prisoner-of-war camp to wait out the war. This suffering is entirely their choice."

Captain Willoughby looked at Justin and said quietly, "Your suffering is by choice, as well. You could have gone back to your toasty warm ship anytime you wanted. But instead, you've gone through the worst of it right here with us." Justin couldn't tell if he was being complimented or criticized.

"You made me a member of the Lucky 7s—how could I leave my men until the battle is won?"

Willoughby continued, "And that's just it, isn't it? You're living up to your code. And your code—and mine—is that our squad comes first. Our men are who we fight for and with. I don't understand the enemy's code beyond that they're willing to fight and die for one man. A man they consider a god, but a man nonetheless. But they're living up to their code, too. It's frustrating that they could save themselves—and our men's lives as well, but they can't break their code."

Justin thought about that. He wanted to argue, but he knew Willoughby had a point. "I know. And I know this shouldn't matter, but I've been a little out of sorts since mail call yesterday."

"What's the matter? Bad news from back home?"

"It shouldn't be. And it's my fault. So a little while back, after our ship was damaged, I got homesick, and so I started reading through my letters from Heidi, my wife. And I don't know what it was, but I hadn't seen this in them before—she was talking a *lot* about this doctor she works with, Kani . . . she calls him Kani, not 'Dr. Caro.' And I got jealous. And I got worried. So I wrote an angry letter demanding she never speak to this guy again. And then I hadn't heard from her for a bit. Which is really out of character for her. Her dad was a lifer in the Army, so she knows what not sending letters means. And then yesterday I got a reply. And I'm an idiot. 'Kani' is her boss, and *everyone* calls him that. And he's married and has a ton of kids and Heidi's good friends with his wife, and they go to parties together." He pursed his lips. "I have an unbelievably great relationship, and I nearly killed it because . . ."

"Because you were afraid you were going to lose it. That you were going to die out here and let her and your family down." Willoughby was silent for a moment. "I underestimated you . . . and maybe the whole Navy. You've held up while others have succumbed. I'm glad you're here. You've saved a number of my men on more than one occasion, and nothing matters more than that."

"I've just tried to do my part."

"No, you've done a lot more than that," Willoughby said. "Like the second night you were here, and Lance Corporal Ryan dropped his canteen—then you shot the Japanese guy who'd heard it before he could shoot Ryan."

"So you know about that, huh?" Justin had tried to forget it, because it was the first time he'd killed a man with his own rifle, and it had made him want to throw up. He hardly felt heroic. Even though he'd given orders for the *Salt Lake City*'s massive armament to open fire on enemy ships and beaches, which undoubtedly led to many enemy deaths . . . killing a man one-on-one was different—it was his finger on the trigger and then a man he'd never met was dead just a few feet away. But the lance corporal was uninjured and grateful, so it had been worth it.

"I know everything that happens in this outfit," Willoughby said lightly, but didn't smile. "That was the moment when you were fully accepted into the group."

Justin nodded. "Thank you. I'm glad I've been here with you. I've seen a different side of the war here. I'll never talk bad about the Army again, no matter what." He smiled. "And I'm glad I've helped your men survive—they've returned the favor more than once."

There was nothing more to say, so the two men rested with their binoculars trained toward where they knew the Japanese were camped. Suddenly a strange and disconcerting noise arose from the forest—"Tennōheika banzai!" ("Long live His Majesty the Emperor!"), then "banzai, banzai!"

"We have our answer!" Willoughby shouted, the tone of his voice making it clear how disgusted he was. "They choose suicide!"

Justin felt the hair on the back of his neck stand up as he watched dozens of enemy soldiers burst through the underbrush, and he raised his rifle, sighted in on one of the men leading the charge, and pulled the trigger. The man fell but was quickly followed by another who ran right over the first man's corpse. Justin used rapid fire to continue shooting, killing at least a dozen of the enemy, as did all those around him, but it didn't seem to make a difference.

"Prepare to fall back!" Willoughby shouted. At this point a tactical retreat wasn't a failure, but simply laying a better trap. The enemy was bounded by water on three sides—where could they go?

Justin pulled himself up to a crouching position, ready to run. "Go!" Willoughby shouted. Justin stood up and turned his back to the advancing enemy, racing as fast as he could go. The fellow next to him was faster and Justin watched out of the corner of his eye as the young private pulled ahead of him, then watched in horror as the man took a bullet in the back. The force of his forward run plus the impact of a bullet traveling 3,000 feet per second sent the boy stumbling forward and then face-first into the ground. Even though he could hear the Japanese coming up from behind, Justin paused long enough to kneel down to help him, planning to lift and drag him forward. But as he rolled the body over, he could see that he was dead. "Come on, Collier— we'll come back for him!"

Justin accepted this as he raced for cover behind a rock. Then he turned and started firing into the enemy mob once more, watching as man after man fell to the ground. He felt that his face was flushed but didn't stop to think about it. Despite all their casualties, they kept coming. The image of the dead American intruded into his thoughts, even in the heat of battle. Somewhere in America a family was about to get a message that their son or husband or father had been killed. Would the same thing happen with Heidi and Verla and Emery? He wanted to run and hide— but could see that they were going to have to go into hand-to-hand combat, so he reached out to make sure his bayonet was still attached to his rifle. Almost out of ammunition, he carefully placed three more shots and then braced for the assault to reach him. But just as he was about to lunge forward, he was startled to hear the rapid fire of a machine gun from behind him, and he watched in fascinated horror as row after row of the enemy started falling to the ground. He whirled around to see that reinforcements were coming up from behind. The assault hesitated for a moment, and it was at that point that he heard Willoughby shout "Attack!" and along with the others, Justin raced ahead to engage the enemy directly. He used his bayonet to stab at men as they came near, injuring or killing several. But then a man charged at him with such ferocity that he knocked Justin's gun from his grip. Tackled to the ground and with the Japanese soldier on top of him, Justin wrestled for his life, doing his best to avoid the blows against his face and head. But he was no match for the other man's strength. The fury in his face was terrifying. Close to losing consciousness, Justin struggled to reach the knife in his boot, feeling a flood of relief when he caught hold of it. He pulled it out and stabbed the blade into the side of the man who had attacked him. Once, twice, and a third time before the man stopped struggling. With adrenaline flowing through his body, he pushed the corpse aside and shook his head to clear it.

By now the fighting had moved away from him, so he struggled to stand up, but found that his legs buckled. It was then that a medic came up from behind and said, "You better sit down, sir. Your face is badly beaten, and I don't think it's wise for you to go forward."

"What?" Justin put his hand to his face, and when he pulled it away, there was blood on the palm of his hand. "I'm not sure what happened." There was a powerful ringing in his ears that made it difficult for him to hear or think.

"Yes, sir. Stay still for just a minute." The medic dug a bottle out of his bag, poured some liquid on a strip of gauze, and said, "This is going to hurt—brace yourself."

"I'm okay . . ." and Justin screamed as the mercurochrome touched the wound on his face. A mercury-based antiseptic, it killed any germs it touched.

Justin tried to pull away, but the medic was insistent, putting his hand behind Justin's head to hold it in place. "There's a lot of germs out here and you need to sterilize that wound." Justin steadied himself and allowed the man to work.

When the medic finished, Justin forced himself to stand. "I should go forward and help them."

"No, sir. The Japanese are done for. You need to go back to camp and get some rest. You did your part—I watched you fight that man. You did your duty for sure."

"Thank you." Justin shook his head and blinked. It *was* hard to focus, and he wondered if he had a concussion.

"You just sit here quiet for a bit. You'll be safe—the enemy have been forced back. You can rejoin your group in a bit."

Justin sat down heavily. "Thank you."

"Yes, sir. Now I should move forward to help others. You'll be okay?"

Justin nodded. He knew he'd be physically okay, but how would he ever mentally get past what had just happened? He bit his lip as hard as he could to steady his nerves, and then listened to the fading sounds of battle in the distance as he watched his hands shake from adrenaline and fear.

May 31, 1943
Captain's quarters, USS *Salt Lake City*

"You're a mess, Mr. Collier."

Instinctively Justin raised his hand to smooth his hair. "Yes, sir. Sorry, sir, but they told me to report directly to you as soon as I was on board the ship. I haven't had a shower in two weeks, I'm afraid."

"At ease, Collier. I understand." Captain Rodgers motioned for his third officer to take a seat. Commander Bitler was also present. "You can go get cleaned up if you like and even get some rest before making your report—I confess that I've been anxious about you and the operation, particularly when I heard that you'd been hurt, so I asked you to come directly."

Justin accepted the offer to sit down. "I'm fine—they kept me in the battalion aid station for a day, even though my wounds are superficial."

Captain Rodgers held his tongue—his operations officer had a black eye, a swollen cheek with an ugly gash that should have had stitches applied, but instead was covered in the sickly yellow-green color of mercurochrome, and he walked with a limp when he came in.

"Tell me what happened."

"We had 549 men killed and 1,200 injured. The foul weather played a big part in that. It was war at its most violent. The Japanese had 2,872 men killed or who committed suicide—virtually all of the men on the island, including Colonel Yamasaki. I watched men slash open their own bellies to avoid being taken prisoner. So far there are just twenty-eight surviving prisoners out of the 2,900 who garrisoned the island, although we believe there are still some hiding out in caves or in the forest. I don't see how they can survive long in this weather." He realized he was rambling, so he shook his head. The images of battle, of watching the enemy attack against all odds—it should have been inspiring that men would fight so hard for their country, but to him it was just a waste.

"What about you? It looks like you had some tough fighting."

"Yes, sir. Most of the time it was firing from a foxhole or from behind a secure position. But on the last day of battle, they came forward in a banzai attack, and it degenerated quickly into hand-to-hand fighting—that's how I got all this."

"I shouldn't have sent you over there. The reports you radioed to us throughout the event were very instructive, but it wasn't worth it to put you in harm's way like that."

"That's not how I see it, sir. I'm an American at war with

Japan—and now I've experienced it from a new point of view. There's no reason I shouldn't face the same danger that the men in the Army do. I'll never look at them the same way again. Being face-to-face with the enemy takes a different kind of courage." He inhaled slowly. "It's as close as I'll ever come to what used to happen in the days of sailing ships—coming close enough to board another ship and fight hand-to-hand until one or the other side prevailed." He paused. "I admit that I like our kind of war better."

"Well, I've put you in for a Purple Heart. I think General Brown might have put you in for something else. I'm proud of you for standing firm. You've done right by the Navy." Captain Rodgers stood, as did Commander Bitler. "Now, I really can't have a senior officer looking that tattered, so go get yourself cleaned up and then sleep for as long as you like. We'll keep you off the duty roster for a day or two."

Justin stood and returned his captain's salute. "Thank you, sir." Worthy Bitler grabbed his bicep and said he'd like to walk Justin to his berth.

Chapter 11

HAWAII

October 1943
Aiea Naval Hospital, Oahu

"Let's take a look." Justin was just a bit peeved he was meeting with a plastic surgeon at his wife's insistence. He'd have brushed it off if she wasn't in the room with him.

"Significant scar tissue, to be sure. Gives you a rugged appearance, Commander."

"Rugged is one way of looking at it. Heidi thinks I'm disfigured."

"I do not, and you know it." Heidi frowned. "This isn't about how you look—it's about your health." Justin shrugged his shoulders—he didn't want to fight with her, but he was embarrassed to be here.

"Tell me how this happened?"

"In a fight with a Japanese soldier in a banzai attack. I think he hit me so hard it tore the skin. If he'd had a knife, he would have killed me, so I think it's just tearing from our fistfight."

"That *is* why it's so jagged." The doctor motioned for Heidi to step closer. They knew each other from her work at the hospital.

"They must not have stitched it, which allowed it to pull apart while healing. That's what created all this scar tissue."

Justin wanted to explain that the aid station on Attu had been overwhelmed by the number of casualties, and a gash on the cheek hadn't been important enough for attention. And by the time he made it back to the ship, the surgeon had said that the wound was too old to stitch. But he knew they could see all that for themselves.

The doctor straightened up, and Heidi returned to the chair at the side of the examination table. "I think you'll be okay if you decide to leave this as is," he said. "Your biggest risk is that with that much scar tissue, as you grow older and the skin ages, you'll have near-constant pain. Or we can cut out the excess scar tissue and create an almost invisible line. It would look better—and be better for your health in the long run." The doctor was sensitive to the tension between Justin and Heidi.

Justin turned to Heidi, who returned his shrug. He'd offended her.

"How long would it take to heal? We're here for a month, but then I need to be cleared for action."

The doctor nodded. "If we get right on it, we can have you ready. It really will be better all around."

Justin turned to Heidi and motioned for her to come close so he could put his arm around her. "I appreciate that you are both watching out for my best interest. And the truth is I'm startled by my face each time I look in a mirror. So I think it's good if we proceed." He turned to Heidi and said, "Thank you."

A tear started down her cheek, which she quickly brushed away. "You're welcome. He's the best surgeon in the islands, you know." Justin nodded.

As they left the hospital, Justin wordlessly extended his hand to Heidi. She hesitated, then took it in hers. "You seem so distant," she said with as little emotion as possible, leaving it as a statement or a question—it was up to Justin to decide.

They walked for a time before Justin said quietly, "A lot's happened. For the first time I feel separated from the crew." He walked on. "Everybody is so nice to me, and they keep treating me like a hero. And for a while there, I thought I'd lost you. That I'd said the wrong thing in my letter. I learned a lot from your reply."

"It took me a little while to figure out how to respond. I'm glad that it got through. From what you've told me, it was an extraordinary two weeks."

"That's just it—it *was* extraordinary for me—hand-to-hand combat, living in a foxhole. It was awful and thrilling. And I have nightmares. But it was just business as usual for the men I served with. They'll get a battle star, which they certainly deserve, but . . ." His voice caught, and he shook his head.

"But—what else happened?"

"But the captain has nominated me for a Purple Heart, and General Brown nominated me for the Silver Star." He stopped in his tracks. "It's so embarrassing. I don't deserve it." He took a deep breath. "I mean, think about it, Riley lost his leg, and all I have is a cut on my face—they're hardly comparable."

Heidi caught herself, deciding to pass on saying that medals are awarded based on what a senior officer thinks about a person's action in a combat situation, not what the person thinks about it. "So my suggestion that you have corrective surgery means?"

"It's a plus *and* a minus. The plus is that getting rid of the scar will stop any new crew from wondering about how I got it. But getting surgery to correct a scar that my crew already knows about feels like vanity."

Heidi sighed. For the first time she understood his frustrating responses since the *Salt Lake City* had docked in Pearl Harbor a week earlier. He'd been oblique in his replies to her and the children's questions, had refused to go out to meals with other officers and their wives, and had pouted when she said she wanted to have his face checked out.

Justin wasn't done. "It's not just the medals or my face. In World War I they called it shell shock. I don't know what they call it now, but I think I'm experiencing it."

"Combat stress syndrome." When Justin hesitated, she added, "That's what they call it now—'combat stress syndrome.' It's a cluster of emotional and physical symptoms that men experience after a particularly gruesome battle. We see it far more often in the Army than the Navy."

Justin nodded. "'Combat stress'—a perfect description of a banzai attack."

She felt his grip tighten, and at the same time his hand trembled slightly. Normally she'd pull away because it hurt, but she just tightened her grip. Justin didn't notice.

"How about a milkshake at the Iceberg?" she said quietly. It was one of their favorite diners before the war, and now that the fighting had moved to the western Pacific it was once again doing a booming business. "Maybe we can talk about it."

"I'm an officer of the line—we don't get 'combat stress syndrome.' I'm responsible for more than 650 men."

"I have a better idea," Heidi said. "Let's go sit down on that bench over there. We'll get the milkshake later." There was a great deal to unpack in her husband's life—she'd been awakened by his nightmares, and had to explain to Verla and Emery when they told her they'd been awakened as well. She had her own kind of stress, as did all the spouses of active-duty servicemen who saw combat. But right now, she had to try to help her husband—there was no one else he could turn to without compromising the confidence of his crew and captain.

Justin inhaled sharply, held it, and then let Heidi guide him to the bench.

October 1943
High school aboard the *Salt Lake City* in Hawaii

"Please, Lieutenant Dimmeck, I think my head may explode."

Lieutenant Paul G. Dimmeck, who'd been a college professor in his pre-Navy life, chomped into an apple before replying. "Al, we've been through this before—if I'm going to help you graduate high school, you've got to do the work. I've taken the trouble to write to Texas, found the process for certifying you, received permission based on my credentials, and found the books you need to study. So, Mr. Jowdy, you are *all* the way in on this project. With three days on board and a day off for shore leave, this is the perfect day for you to buckle down. You can relax in town tomorrow." Al Jowdy shook his head. For one thing, shore leave was never relaxing. He appreciated the lieutenant helping him—he really did. But he thought he'd been done with high school when he joined the Navy. Now he was back at it, and he was pretty sure that Lieutenant Dimmeck was working him a lot harder than his teachers back in San Antonio ever had.

"Here's the deal, Al," Dimmeck said. "When you get home, you'll have to show your local school board the certificates I've signed, and then they'll require you to take one semester in person before awarding the diploma. In that semester they'll test you like crazy to make sure you've learned everything you need—and that will reflect on me. So we're going to turn you into a scholar. You'll be the best educated man in San Antonio."

Al sighed. Homework was not his favorite thing. But how could you turn down an offer like this? Plus Lieutenant Dimmeck was just a really good guy who had faith in Al for some reason, and he didn't want to disappoint him. He nodded and asked for help with the frustrating math problem in front of him.

October 1943
Oahu

"Dad—it's a letter from Uncle Riley!" Emery Collier, about six inches taller than when Justin had left for the Aleutian Islands the first time, came bounding up the steps of their porch waving a letter in his hand. Justin was always grateful that Riley kept in mind that Verla and Emery would be reading his letters and so kept his stories family friendly.

"Well, why don't you read it to me?" They were quickly joined on the porch by Verla and one of her friends, Mrs. Matsui's niece, Kiko. Heidi was working at the hospital, and Justin was home with a new bandage on his face that, for support reasons, covered his right eye. He couldn't solve all his issues on one trip home, but at least his face was likely to be in better shape after the surgery. At Heidi's suggestion, he'd confided his concerns about receiving the Silver Star, the third-highest medal for valor in the Navy, to the ship's chaplain, who'd urged him to accept, saying, "Medals aren't just for the person receiving them—they're to inspire others to their best effort. Your medal is an award for the ship as well as for you, and the men are proud of you." Justin was still self-conscious about it but decided to act with grace at a ceremony that was scheduled to take place just before the ship was to leave on its next sea assignment. More important was that he was also to be promoted to commander—a great honor and an increase in pay.

"Okay," Emery said cheerfully, "here goes." He opened the flap of the letter with his thumb, then took the onion-skin paper out of the envelope and unfolded it carefully. He set the envelope aside so he could save the stamps to add to his collection. Emery cleared his throat and started reading:

"Dear cousin, cousin-in-law, and favorite niece and nephew,

"I'm okay. Dr. Ferguson is as good as he said he was—he did surgery on my shoulder, and I already have a lot greater range of motion. I'm hopeful about that. And my new prosthetic leg hurts like crazy, but I'm slowly getting used to it. I walk like I'm eighty years old. The good news about that is it just might give my awkward nephew a chance to equal me on the surfboard—one and a half legs against two seems like a fair fight."

Verla laughed as Emery protested that he was not "awkward," but Justin was pleased to see that Emery was flattered to be remembered. "I was better than him when he had two legs, and he knows it," Emery said, laughing.

"The Navy's given me the option of an honorable discharge with disability, or of staying on and becoming an instructor at a flight academy. Haven't decided, although I'm pretty sure my favorite cousin (also my least favorite, since he's my only cousin) would say I should stay in the Navy. We'll see—I'm still a couple of months away from being released from physical therapy. I did have another dance with the darkness lately, but it's okay now."

"What does that mean?" Emery asked.

Justin felt sick to his stomach, but the last thing he wanted to do was alarm Emery. So, he settled for, "I'm not sure—you know how he likes to go to dance clubs in Manhattan. I think that's the name of one of them." He could see that Emery was willing to accept that, but Verla looked uncomfortable. Clearly his cousin wasn't out of the emotional woods yet.

"Your parents miss their grandkids—they tell me about it every time I see them. So does their uncle, for that matter. It would make the decision a lot easier if they had an aviation school in Oahu. Why everyone doesn't move there is beyond me—New York's already cold and dreary, and there's not a single palm tree anywhere. Well—that's all I can fit on the page, so better go for now. Tell Heidi thanks for sending the macadamia nut cookies—I know you didn't make them, Justin. No one here even *knows* what a macadamia nut is, so it was a treat. Yours truly, the best uncle in the world."

Emery smiled. "He seems happy—I miss him."

"He's funny," Verla's friend said. "But what exactly happened to him?"

Emery was only too glad to tell the story, and Justin was fine to let him, since it was clear the story wasn't fully written.

Chapter 12

TAKING THE BATTLE TO THE ENEMY

September 12, 1943
A new captain welcomed by the ship's
newspaper, the *Saltshaker*

"Captain Leroy W. Busbey came aboard the SALT LAKE CITY and took over his command on Sat., Sept. 4th. The officers and men welcomed him with the confident feeling that the high quality of our leadership has been sustained. The Swayback can sense a Master and knows that her famed fighting qualities are again under skillful direction.

"Captain Busbey comes to us with a long and notable record of service in this man's Navy. He graduated from the Academy in 1917 with the class of 1918.

"He has served on submarines, destroyers, cruisers, and battleships. He was engineering officer of the NORTHAMPTON and later was executive officer of the ARKANSAS. He has come to us directly from the staff of Vice Admiral Sharp, where he was operations officer of the Atlantic Service Force. We feel that Captain Busbey is happy to be with us and we assure him in turn of our pride in being under his leadership. For we know that under him the SALT LAKE CITY will continue to be a decisive factor in the successful prosecution of this war."

November 20, 1943
Off the coast of Betio Island in the Tarawa Atoll

"This is quite the armada—the Japanese don't stand a chance!"

When newly promoted Commander Justin Collier didn't reply, Commander Bitler turned and looked at him quizzically. "Do you disagree?"

Justin drew a deep breath and glanced down at the brief he'd been studying that summarized the strength of the task force. "No, sir. I *do* agree with you. It's an amazing sight—five aircraft carriers, three battleships, two heavy cruisers, two light cruisers, sixty-six destroyers, twenty-two minesweepers, and eighteen transports and landing craft. Then 18,000 marines and 17,000 Army infantry—35,000 invaders against 4,000 Japanese defenders. I doubt there's ever been anything quite like it."

"And yet you don't seem enthusiastic."

Justin turned and smiled—something he didn't do often anymore. "There's no question we're going to win. My guess is the next three or four days are going to be noisy. But since this is the first major opposed beach landing in the South Pacific, I'm not sure anyone's prepared for just how ferociously the enemy on that little spit of an island are going to fight. I think we'll lose far more men than expected." Betio was just 300 acres, shaped like a swordfish, two miles long and a mile at its widest point. But it featured a Japanese aircraft landing strip and a fierce array of defensive armament: fourteen naval guns captured from the British in Singapore, including eight-inch guns that matched the *Salt Lake City*'s, protected in heavy concrete bunkers.

Commander Bitler was quiet for a moment. "Your experience in Attu informs your opinion?"

Justin nodded. "Yes, sir," he said, remembering conversations he'd had with Captain Willoughby in the spaces between enemy encounters. "We're fighting for freedom, for our way of life, for our families. At heart, we're fighting for our brothers, whether they're an infantry squad or our shipmates. The Japanese are fighting for their way of life, too, but from my point of view, it's mostly about fighting for their emperor, and their honor requires that they kill as many of us as they can. And it doesn't matter if they die, or their squad dies. As long as they're honoring the emperor, nothing else matters." He shook his head. "But even knowing that, I'm not sure what we can do differently here. They are who they are, we are who we are, and if we want this as a forward staging ground to close in on their home islands, we need to root out every single Japanese soldier on that island, in every single one of their couple of hundred pillboxes. I just hope our preinvasion bombardment softens the place up for the marines who will be going in tomorrow."

"Well, we're certainly going to do our part." Bitler stretched his arms and torso and then said in a loud voice, "Mr. Collier has the conn!" The bridge crew acknowledged the change in leadership. "I'm going to the fire control center. We're moments away from waking up Betio with a rather big surprise." Bitler laughed. "Can you imagine the shock they're feeling right now, seeing what we've got out here!"

It was a fearsome sight indeed—the largest US armada so far. For his part, Justin found himself aching inside, wishing that he could be with the marines who were even now transferring from their transport ships into the lightweight wheeled landing craft that would have to float their way over the jagged coral reef that surrounded the island and then make their way across the lagoon under heavy enemy fire. It wasn't that he was anxious to be killed, but the thought of standing passively by while they risked their lives was a different kind of torture.

Fresh water

"Sir, I think we have a problem."

Since his promotion to Chief Machinist's Mate, Stuart Appelle had assumed additional responsibilities, including the evaporator-condensers that converted sea water into fresh water for drinking and to feed the boilers for propulsion and to power the electric generators. Fresh water was as essential as air for the operation of the ship and the welfare of the crew.

Appelle put down the clipboard he'd been studying and moved closer to Walter Freysinger, a water tender and one of the many seamen responsible for monitoring, maintaining, and cleaning the large evaporator-condenser units. "What's the problem?"

"We're having trouble holding the vacuum on Unit Two. It's running hotter than necessary and using a lot more fuel. Plus, it strains the evaporator. I recommend we shut down the whole unit to check the seals in the cooling system."

Appelle nodded apprehensively. "How quick can you get it done?"

Freysinger shook his head. "Hard to tell, Chief—at least four hours, but could be longer."

"Sounds like we should be fine operating at low speeds—our other units can provide plenty of fresh water to the active boilers. I'll have the bridge instruct the crew to go to 'essential use' only while it's down, but I see no problem unless we go to flank speed for an extended period," Appelle thought aloud.

"Aye, Chief."

Appelle nodded. "Very well. I'll pass the word along. The quicker the better, Mr. Freysinger."

"Aye, Chief. Fresh water is one of those things people take for granted until there's a problem. We'll get this done in quick order."

Appelle picked up the interphone and heard, "Bridge here!"

"This is Chief Appelle. We're taking one of our fresh-water units offline for repair. Advise that we go to 'essential use' only for the crew."

"Understood. Advise when the unit comes back online."

Appelle made his way back to the boiler room to see if they could economize on using boiler water so they wouldn't draw down the reserves. After explaining the situation to his boiler crew, they felt they could take one boiler offline and still meet the needs of the ship, since they were moving at slow speed while positioning to fire on the beaches.

"It's always something," Appelle said to himself. "Always something."

In the crow's nest off Betio Island

"Coming up early to relieve me?" Seaman Sandy Oppenheimer said cheekily without turning to look at who had ascended the perilous ladder to the crow's nest at the top of the signal tower. It was possible to spot an enemy ship approximately sixteen miles away when standing on the deck of the *Salt Lake City,* but twenty-five miles away from the crow's nest. While radar gave the earliest warning, it could be fooled by unusual weather conditions, so it made sense to have human observers in battle.

"Sorry, no," Commander Justin Collier responded quietly.

"Just coming up to survey the landings from a new vantage point."

Oppenheimer swung around at the sound of an unfamiliar voice, and the shock of seeing the operations officer stepping onto the small platform caused him to snap to attention with a "Sorry, sir, I had no idea . . ."

"At ease. I know it's unexpected." Justin shook his head slightly to clear it. It had been many years since he'd been an ensign assigned to watch duty in the nest, and he'd forgotten just how many rungs of the ladder you had to climb to reach the observation post. He didn't get vertigo, exactly, but the motion of the ship was exaggerated at this height, and it took some getting used to in order to keep your balance and not get a headache. "Mind if I join you for a minute?"

"Of course not, sir. Glad to have some company."

Justin knew that he wouldn't make good company but was sensitive to the feelings of the young man, so he chatted awhile about his days on the signals watch. "Haven't I seen you somewhere else on the ship?"

"Stores department, sir. I run the Pogey Bait. But the crow's nest is my combat assignment when we're at General Quarters. I don't get called up here often, but my name came up in the rotation today, so here I am."

"The Pogey Bait. Wish I was there—a bottle of cola settles my stomach, and I could use that right now." He smiled, and Oppenheimer nodded.

"The swaying gives me a bigger headache when we're moving slow than when we're under power—more of a rocking motion than I like. I think it's natural if it's getting to you a bit, sir. No offense intended."

"None taken. I'm glad you're up to it. The eyes of the ship, so to speak."

Justin moved to a corner of the platform where he could look down on the lagoon and beaches of Betio Island. The preinvasion bombardment of the island had finished a few hours earlier, and now the ship was firing at specific sites called in by men in the landing craft. From this vantage point, Justin could see the troubles the landing craft were encountering—many had their hulls damaged trying to float over the jagged coral.

"The Water Buffaloes are doing better than the Higgins boats, looks like," Justin said quietly. The LVT-2 "Water Buffaloes" were armored amphibious transports propelled through the water, over the reef, and over land by tracks on either side. Higgins boats were light, unarmored shallow-draft transports with greater capacity and more maneuverability. But they were getting caught on the coral reefs and having to be abandoned, leaving their marines exposed as they waded across the lagoon toward the shore.

"Yes, sir. Can't be easy to have to wade that far under fire."

Justin watched in fascinated horror as he saw the marines crouching to keep their heads barely above the surface of the lagoon to reduce their profile to snipers on the shore. With his field glasses he could see every time a bullet hit the water by the tiny splash it made, and the surface of the lagoon looked like it was experiencing a deadly downpour. Worse, dead American marines floated in the water with no way to retrieve them until a beachhead was established.

"If I may ask a question, sir?"

"Of course."

"I thought the tide was supposed to be high enough that the Higgins boats would clear the reef."

"It was. In normal conditions the tide would have provided

five feet of water above the reef—that's what we were counting on. But today, when we need a good high tide the most, there was an unexpected neap tide. It keeps the tide far lower than usual."

Sandy Oppenheimer was about to express how bad he felt for the troops, but he saw Commander Collier stiffen. "Did you see that?" Justin asked.

"See what, sir?"

He motioned to a spot, and gave its coordinates so Oppenheimer could look at it through his high-powered binoculars.

"I see a bunch of scrub brush, if I'm looking at the right spot."

"Yes, but do you see smoke every now and then from what I assume is a machine gun?"

Sandy Oppenheimer strained to find what the commander was asking him to see. But there was nothing. Then, just as he was about to turn away, he saw some bushes flatten and a whiff of smoke drift away.

"I see it, sir—it's a pillbox, isn't it?"

"Oh, I'm glad you see it too. Yes, it's a very well camouflaged pillbox—one whose defenders are smart enough to fire infrequently and in very short bursts. That gives them the chance to sight in on a specific marine, or group of marines, and shoot them without drawing shore fire."

He turned to Oppenheimer with fire in his eyes—"But we can do something about it." Justin fumbled for the interphone.

"Hit the deck, sir! Incoming!"

Justin's military training asserted itself and he flattened himself to the steel plating of the platform. He listened as a large shell whistled overhead. One of the eight-inch guns on the island had decided to take a pot shot at the *Salt Lake City*. There were so many ships supporting the landing that they had been singled out only a few times.

"Glad they're not very good shots!" Justin laughed. They felt the *Salt Lake City*'s big guns return fire on the shore battery that had fired at them.

"Still gotta get that pillbox!" Justin picked up the interphone, identified himself, and gave the coordinates of the enemy snipers. "Pass this on to fire control immediately."

He and Oppenheimer stood back up. "Now watch what happens." They knew the guns wouldn't fire until the exact moment that the ship rolled to the right position for the firing solution. "Should be right . . . now!"

They saw two of the *Salt Lake City*'s guns flash. "They fired, sir! They fired!" Collier and Oppenheimer watched as two explosions churned up the sand at exactly the spot that they had called in. But more than sand went up into the air—there were huge chunks of concrete, as well. While it was unlikely that the blast had completely destroyed the pillbox, the direct hits would have knocked the people inside senseless and hopefully destroyed their gun from the blast gases going through the gun opening.

"I think we got them, sir."

Justin turned to the young man. "I think so too. You can return to your normal scanning for enemy aircraft or ships—I'll keep an eye on that spot to see if we got them or not."

Justin watched anxiously until he was convinced that they had taken out the pillbox. There were no further wafts of smoke coming from that spot. In the grand scheme of a massive battle, one pillbox was of little consequence. But to the marines in the lagoon—who knew how many would live who would have died without that action?

Justin stood up and pulled the binoculars from his eyes, allowing them to rest against his chest. "Well, Mr. Oppenheimer,

I'm afraid that other duties call. I'll leave all this in your very capable hands."

"I'm glad you came up, sir! It was nice to talk with you."

"I'm glad too. I think we saved some lives today." With that Justin started the long descent down the ladder.

On the fantail

"Watch out, Jowdy!"

Al Jowdy wasn't sure what he was supposed to watch out for, but then nearly tripped as a stray casing from the forty-mm gun rolled under his feet. Stooping to pick it up, he issued a mild curse—not even feeling guilty for it, although an image of his mother telling him not to talk like that did come to mind. "How many of these things can our stupid guns shoot—I think we've lifted a thousand pounds of casings!"

"Oh, we're just getting started," Elmer Breeze said. "Watch your step."

One of the *Salt Lake City*'s primary responsibilities was to protect the five aircraft carriers in the task force from attacks by Japanese aircraft, and this morning there had been repeated torpedo plane attacks from nearby islands. It was hazardous in the extreme for the attacking Japanese, since the Americans could throw up high-explosive Bofors shells as well as send out fighter aircraft to engage them in aerial combat, but it was also extremely dangerous to the carriers. It was infuriating that an 800-pound torpedo could severely damage—or even sink—a 35,000-ton aircraft carrier. But that was the state of modern warfare. It was a single torpedo that had damaged the mighty German battleship KMS *Bismarck*'s rudder at the beginning of the war that led to the ship's destruction. And it was just two torpedoes that put the final nails in the coffin of the USS *Yorktown* at the Battle of Midway.

Enemy torpedo plane attacks were very high risk to both sides—and it was up to the gun crews of the *Salt Lake City* to stop them.

As gunner's mates, Jowdy and Breeze and the others on the crew assisted the gunners in any way they needed, including helping to clear jams in the feeder mechanism that sent the shells up to the guns, as well as corralling spent shell casings after they'd been fired and ejected to store until they could be returned to be reloaded for future battles. It was hard work, particularly in September in the tropical summer of the South Pacific. While his childhood in Texas had accustomed Al to high humidity, this was different, with all the smoke from the guns fouling the air and the constant *pom pom pom* sound of the antiaircraft forty-mm guns throwing up as much high-explosive fire as possible. Still, it felt good to be in the fight again, instead of just preparing to fight.

"There's one coming in now!" Al shouted, pointing at the closest aircraft carrier. A Japanese torpedo plane—their equivalent of the American Dauntless—had come screaming across the sky in a very steep dive from high altitude and was leveling out just feet above the ocean as it lined up to release its torpedo on a direct path to the carrier. Fortunately, the gun's spotters had seen it too, because the double mounted guns swung on their platform in the direction of the newest threat and started their systematic *pom pom pom pom* firing sequence. Al watched in fascination as dark puffs of smoke appeared in the sky in front of the attacking enemy aircraft. "All you gotta do is fly into that cloud . . ." Al said anxiously. Although he didn't think about it at the time, he and everyone else working the guns were holding their breath as the flight path stabilized—the best chance for the gunners to sight in and get a hit. *Pom pom pom pom pom!* Just when they thought it was too late, the enemy aircraft exploded in a brilliant flash of light and a shower of debris.

"It's a hit! It's a hit!" Al shouted jubilantly. And of course, he wasn't the only one. All the men were cheering—certain that it was their gun that found the target. But what really mattered is that they had hit it *before* the torpedo was released, meaning the aircraft carrier was saved from an almost certain impact. Even the normally stoic Elmer Breeze was jumping up and down.

For the moment, there were no more aircraft visible, so the guns fell silent. "I don't think I've ever seen anything like that," Al said, taking a moment to catch his breath. "My mom told me to never look at the sun because it can burn your eyes, but this had to be nearly as bright as that."

"It was a triple explosion, you know," Elmer said. "First our shell exploded, and that ignited the aircraft fuel, and then the torpedo exploded from the heat and pressure. It's no wonder it was so spectacular!" He laughed as he said this, relieved of the tension that had been part of every engagement with an enemy aircraft that day.

"Well, it's something I'll never forget," Al said. The adrenaline they'd been running on ran out and a wave of weariness swept over them. "Speaking of the sun, it looks like it's going down fairly soon. Do you think there will be any more attacks?"

"Who knows?" Elmer said. Now that the guns had stopped firing, the gunners were busy starting the lengthy process of inspecting and cleaning them, leaving Al and Elmer to return to the task of packing the spent shell casings into storage containers. The entire country was doing everything it could to conserve metal to make sure the military received what it needed in the way of new airplanes, ships, trucks, jeeps, and—most of all—ammunition. Saving shell casings was an essential step in that process.

"Well, if *I* was them I'd head in for the night. They've been flying missions all day and haven't hit a single carrier. I think those boys need a good talking to about their shooting!"

Elmer Breeze laughed. Al always had a unique way of looking at things. "You're probably right—I think we're done shooting for today." And with that they put their backs into the task at hand, content that the lives of hundreds of men on the carrier had been protected because of their actions. It was a great feeling.

November 23, 1943
On the bridge

"I'm sorry to say that your fears were confirmed," Commander Worthy Bitler said.

"Yes, sir." Justin Collier shook his head. "Just seventeen prisoners out of more than 4,700—the rest dead because their honor code demands that they commit suicide rather than be captured."

The Americans had won the three-day battle after fierce hand-to-hand combat on the island as every single pillbox was attacked with flamethrowers, shore artillery, and men crawling up and forcing their way through. Despite the overwhelming naval and infantry advantage, the campaign still cost more than a thousand US lives and 2,000 wounded—all for an outcome that was never in doubt from the beginning.

"Apparently there are a hundred or so Korean slave laborers who managed to surrender. They were smart enough to fly the white flag."

Justin nodded. From what he had heard, the Japanese treated other Asian prisoners even worse than they did their American prisoners—and that was hard to comprehend, since they were so cruel to the Americans. They had particular vitriol for Koreans. He was glad that these Koreans had escaped from the Japanese to the American side.

"Well, we achieved our objective," Bitler said. "The Seabees have already started refurbishing Betio's airstrip and will work their magic building Quonset huts and everything else needed to turn this little island into a forward base for American bombers. We just cut the distance from our front line to Japan by more than two-thirds. It's a battle well fought and won."

"And we shot down a torpedo plane—that's tough to do. I've given the gun crew extra tokens to use at the Pogey Bait. They were excited."

Bitler nodded. He was pleased that it seemed that Collier's attitude had lightened, and he was almost back to his old confident self.

Chapter 13

SHORE LEAVE, NEW YORK CITY

April 1944

West of the Hawaiian Islands,
en route to Pearl Harbor

"We've had a very busy six months," Captain Busbey said to the officers dining with him in the officers' mess. The others at the table nodded. "In fact, I've got five dollars for anyone who can name all the islands we bombarded. But you lose two dollars if you try and fail."

Some of the hands that had first been raised dropped to the side. "Okay, Mr. Allen, as chief gunnery officer I think you've got a good shot at it. Go!"

Ross Allen started out confidently, "Wotje and Tarao, Majuro and Eniwetok, in the Marshalls." He hesitated. "Palau, Yap, and Ulithi in the Western Carolines." He bowed as everyone applauded.

"Oh, that's good—but I'm afraid you left out two of the minor islands. Who's willing to risk two dollars to fill in the missing pieces?"

After a moment's hesitation, Justin raised his hand. "Ah, Mr.

Collier, our resident historian." It was true—Justin kept track of everything. He had clipboards for every single department he supervised and kept detailed logs of all his interactions. A naval ship at sea is orderly, with deck logs and inventories aplenty, but Justin took it to a new dimension. "Well?"

"I believe Lieutenant Allen missed Kwajalein in the Marshalls and Woleai in the Carolines. But it could be argued that they really don't count since they weren't our primary targets."

"Kwajalein!" Ross Allen made an exaggerated slap of his right hand to his forehead. "How could I forget the tropical paradise of Kwajalein?"

The captain ignored this display and turned to Justin. "You have a great career ahead of you in politics, if you like," the captain said, "with your attempt to both win the bet and stay on Mr. Allen's good side. But a bet is a bet and you won, and Mr. Allen lost. You win my five dollars while I'll be glad to collect two dollars from you, Mr. Allen."

"Is ship's scrip all right?" Ross Allen asked. The *Salt Lake City* had its own coins and paper scrip which could be used as a substitute for dollars on board but was less likely to be stolen on shore since its usefulness was limited to the ship.

"Afraid not. I want the real thing—crisp dollar bills."

"Aye, sir. But next time we're assigned to blast the heck out of a beach, perhaps you'll let me observe from the bridge with a clipboard in hand, instead of down there where the guns are going off."

This created an awkward pause until Justin replied easily, "I'd be careful about that, Ross. It takes years of experience to get those clipboards just right—I don't think you've sharpened enough pencils yet to try it on your own. I wouldn't want you to hurt yourself!"

Ross Allen smiled. "Fair enough." Then he grew serious, glad that the insult he'd spoken in anger had been brushed aside. Everyone in leadership knew that Justin didn't deserve to be criticized. "But since you really do watch out for our best interests, Mr. Collier—and I say that sincerely—perhaps you could share some of that good fortune in one of the local establishments in Pearl when we land?"

"With pleasure." Justin raised his drink and said quickly, "To the *Salt Lake City*, the best-run ship in the Pacific Fleet."

"To the *Salt Lake City*," everyone replied as they raised their glasses to complete the toast.

Six months is a long time to be at sea, Justin thought to himself. It was astonishing, looking back, just how many thousands of shells they had fired in support of landings, to fend off aircraft attacks on their own ship as well as the aircraft carriers in the task force. It was no wonder Ross Allen was testy. *We need some shore time for the men to blow off some steam.*

April 1944
Honolulu

"What do you think?"

"I think . . ." Heidi Collier bit her lip. There were so many reasons to say no, but the fact is that it would put the family together for at least two months—and she realized they really needed that.

"I like the idea," said Emery.

"But what about school?" Verla asked. "We're in the middle of the semester."

Justin wanted to try to sell it, but realized it was better if he let them come to the answer on their own.

"I'm sure the school could give us assignments we could

supervise while traveling," Heidi said. "That might not work in usual times, but the last three years have been anything but usual."

"*Homework?*" Emery said.

"You thought you could just drop out of school for two months?" Verla asked.

"I guess I hoped . . ."

At that, everyone laughed. "Sure," Heidi said to Justin. "Why shouldn't we go home to New York? You've been out to sea all this time, but I guess that the three of us do have a little island fever, and a change would be good for us."

Emery shouted hurray and Justin stood and drew them into a hug. "This will be great," he said. "I'll go to work making it happen." As they pulled apart, he smiled. "I look forward to this—more than you know."

"And we get to go see Uncle Riley?" Emery asked in confirmation.

"I think we can make that happen."

"And your grandparents," said Heidi. "It's been so long since I've seen them." She wiped a tear and then turned to Justin. "Thank you." He nodded and drew her close again.

The wear and tear from their recent battles was great enough that the *Salt Lake City* was scheduled for a refit in the repair docks at Mare Island near San Francisco—a refit that would take at least two months. So Justin had casually mentioned to the captain that he had family in Queens, an easy train ride away from the Camden, New Jersey, shipyards where the *Salt Lake City* was built in 1929, and where some crucial equipment was being fabricated. He knew having firsthand conversations with the design engineers would help the crew transition to the new equipment. The captain had taken the bait, thinking aloud that if Justin were to take leave and travel to New York with his family, he could meet with the shipyard engineers to answer some questions they had about the equipment they were making. Justin had graciously agreed, making their family trip possible. Now he'd have priority finding room on a military aircraft that would take them to San Francisco and then a transfer to an express train to New York to visit their family.

"How will we get to San Francisco?" Emery asked.

"Well, we could find an empty troop transport," Justin said, "but that would use up most of our vacation. So I was thinking maybe we'd take a military aircraft home. I know a few people who could make that happen. Which would you choose?" he asked.

For one of the few times in his young life, Emery was speechless. He'd never been on an airplane, even though they were the most interesting things in the world to him. "You're serious? We can really go by plane?"

Justin smiled. "We really can, and it's up to me to make it happen. So after breakfast, your mother and I will take you to school, then we'll talk to your principal, and then I'll drop your mother off at the hospital, and I'll go down to the airfield to see what's available in the next few days."

"Oh, my goodness, we've got to hurry," Heidi said as she realized just how many millions of tasks had to be completed in a very short time—it was time for her to transition into combat mode.

And with that, the conversation buzzed as everyone hurried to finish their breakfast, acting like it wouldn't happen unless it all happened that very day. For the first time in months Justin was truly happy. He looked over at Heidi and smiled—something that she had longed for.

April 15, 1944
To New York via the *City of San Francisco*

"Oh, dad. This train is unbelievable!" Emery was enthralled as he gazed on the long sleek lines of the *City of San Francisco,* a streamlined diesel-electric train co-owned by the Southern Pacific, Union Pacific, and Chicago & Northwestern Railroads. While air travel from Hawaii to San Francisco was easy enough to arrange for a family, the same wasn't true from San Francisco to New York. The *City of San Francisco* was the fastest option from San Francisco to Chicago, where they'd connect to the New York Central's famous *20th-Century Limited* for a sixteen-hour trip from Chicago's LaSalle Street Station to Manhattan's Grand Central Terminal. There was simply no faster way for a family to cross the country—nor any alternative that offered greater style and comfort. The *City of San Francisco* reached speeds of up to 110 miles per hour on straight routes. It also provided spectacular views as it made its way through the Sierra Nevada mountains, including snow tunnels on the most treacherous parts of the journey, then beautiful vistas through the Wasatch and Uinta mountains of Utah as it made its way to Wyoming and then onto the Great Plains. Along the way they had dinner in the dining car served by white-gloved waiters, slept in their own Pullman sleeper each night, and enjoyed the views from the domed cars when they could. Service wasn't entirely up to prewar standards since many of the passenger trains were still being used primarily as troop transports, but Justin's status as an officer had enabled him to secure the best possible accommodations. It was expensive, but after two and a half years at sea with very little places to spend their earnings, Justin and Heidi had decided to trade money for time with their families in New York—plus enjoy the comfort of the best that the railroads had to offer.

Once transferred to the *20th-Century Limited*, they enjoyed following the famous "water route" along the shores of the Great Lakes. In 1943 the *Limited* was still pulled by a steam locomotive, but with remarkable art deco streamlining that gave it the sleek appearance for which it was famous. Even though it was not nearly as smooth as a diesel-electric, it too could reach speeds of over 100 miles per hour—the massive six-foot driving wheels turning at 500 revolutions per minute. Once they reached the New York state line, the steam engine was switched out at the Croton-Harmon Station to an electrified line into Manhattan to make it possible to breathe when the train descended into the tunnels beneath the city.

Despite the comfort, the family was still tired as the train approached the tunnel in Harlem that would drop them beneath the streets of Manhattan. Emery had fallen asleep, but Justin fulfilled his promise to wake him before their descent into darkness. There was just something remarkable about a train traveling under city streets, its electric motors drawing power from the city grid.

As the train came to a stop in the passenger tunnel, Justin stood and started collecting their carry-on bags. "All right, we'll find a porter to help us transfer our luggage to a taxicab—"

"I thought we were taking the subway!" Emery said anxiously.

"Not today," Heidi replied. "It's too many transfers to manage all our luggage. But I think your father's planning to bring us back into Manhattan to see the sights."

"I want to go to a show at Radio City Music Hall," Verla said.

"Movie or live show?" Justin asked.

"You can *choose*?" she said incredulously.

Justin nodded.

"Then a live show," Verla replied.

"I want to see the view from the Empire State Building," Emery said.

"Done! And what do you want to see?" Justin asked Heidi.

"I want to see a great big bathtub at my mother's house and no one interrupting me while I soak," she said, prompting a laugh.

The family was standing on the platform. Justin motioned to a uniformed porter to assist them. Justin gave him their luggage tags and the older man promised to meet them at the 42nd Street doors.

"He seems rather old to be lifting all that heavy luggage," Heidi said.

"Probably brought out of retirement since the young men are all at war. If I had access to the luggage carts, I'd do it myself, but there's a system in place."

As they walked toward the entrance to the massive Beaux-Arts main concourse, porters of the *20th-Century Limited* rolled out a stunning red carpet for the customers to walk on as they entered the 35,000 square feet of common space that brought commuters together with travelers from out of town.

Once inside, the family couldn't help but look up to the massive, sixty-foot-tall windows at each end of the barrel-vaulted ceiling, and then further up to the dark green ceiling where gold-leaf stars showed the constellations of the night sky. It was impossible not to marvel at the grand and glorious station built by Cornelius Vanderbilt at the height of his influence as the richest man in the world. "It's so beautiful," Verla said. "I'm not sure I've ever seen anything like it!"

Justin and Heidi looked at each other, knowing that Verla had been here before, but obviously when she was too young to remember. "It's good that you get to see it again—I still think of this as home, even though we've lived in Hawaii a long time now."

"I like Hawaii," Emery said firmly.

Justin laughed. "Me too! But we'll see what you think after you've had a chance to explore New York more thoroughly. For now, let's find our luggage and head out to Queens."

April 1944
Camden, New Jersey, shipyards

"I'm just slowing you down. I should never have come," Riley said.

"Nonsense. You know as much about this as I do, and part of the equipment that we're replacing affects the SOC catapult. Stop fretting—we arrived in plenty of time."

Riley Bracken had made it clear that he didn't want to be pushed around in a wheelchair, but he still walked slowly on his prosthetic leg. And while Justin acted calm, inside he was anxious about the timing of the various meetings, since they were scattered around different buildings in the large shipyard. Fortunately, the contractors had provided them a car and driver, who had met them at the train terminal and ferried them to their two previous meetings, where they'd discussed equipment in the engine room, then the forty-mm Bofors guns, and now they were about to have their final meeting. Riley was tired and grouchy.

"I'm sorry," a young female receptionist said, "but your meeting is in our upstairs conference room." She'd seen Riley's limp and was concerned for him.

"Not a problem." And this time Riley was right—he'd learned to manage the stairs at home and made quick work of these as he and Justin found their way to a second-story conference room, where piles of blueprints lay scattered about on tables and in chairs and on the floor. "Now *this* is how I like a room organized," Riley said.

"The mess tells me they're civilian contractors, not military," Justin said.

Just then, three men walked in and motioned for Justin and Riley to sit down at the table. The leader of the group quickly emerged as he said confidently, "It's not often we get to talk to people serving in the Pacific—so it's nice to have you. How can we help?"

Justin explained that the plans they'd received for how to replace the existing scout plane launcher would take a great deal of onsite fabrication, eating up valuable time in the last two weeks of the ship's refurbishment at Mare Island. "The problem we see is that the current design will change the traffic flow around the launcher, which would be a nuisance anytime, but could be very costly in battle. We're hoping to either understand the logic behind this design, or if you could consider modifications we could send by military air before they begin this project at Mare Island."

"We designed it for maximum launch efficiency," one of the men said defensively.

"I can see that," Riley said, "but it doesn't take into consideration the unique deck plan of the *Salt Lake City* and the *Pensacola*, the only two ships of this type in service." When the engineers looked at him skeptically, Justin explained that Riley was an experienced scout plane pilot who had launched from the *Salt Lake City* on numerous occasions, causing them to become more attentive to what he had to say.

"Could you wait just a minute? With a pilot in the room, we'd like to bring someone else into the discussion."

"Of course," Justin said, so they waited for a few minutes until the leader returned, followed by an attractive young woman dressed in the crisp Santiago blue uniform and beret of a WASP officer. The Women Airforce Service Pilots were civilians tasked to test military aircraft, to ferry airplanes around the country after manufacture, and even to train military pilots. Their service enabled more male pilots to serve in combat. The men in the room stood as the leader said, "Gentlemen, I'd like you to meet Miss Angela Millburn, a test pilot in the WASP program assigned to help us with the scout aircraft. She's a valued member of our team and may understand the discussion better than we do. Now, Lieutenant Bracken, could you show us what we're dealing with?"

"Sure." Riley pried his eyes off Miss Millburn and looked around the room until he spied a chalkboard. "Okay if I use that?"

"Of course." And with that, Riley launched a discussion that took more than an hour, with he and Angie Millburn going back and forth about various aspects of the launching platform and its placement on the deck. In the end, they came up with some simple but commonsense changes that would resolve many of Justin and Riley's concerns. The engineers promised to draft the changes over the next three days and then send them by air courier to San Francisco.

After the meeting, they made their way down the stairs—which was more difficult for Riley than going up had been—and then outside to their car. "See," Justin said, "I couldn't have done any of that. I'm glad you were here." Riley shrugged but seemed a little less sullen. Just as they were about to get in the car, they heard a "Lieutenant Bracken!" and turned to see Miss Millburn coming after them. Riley turned around immediately and started walking toward her.

"Lieutenant, I just wanted to say how helpful your comments were. I'd struggled with some of the same issues on my test flights but assumed there was nothing that could be done about it, since my job is to test the airplanes, not the launcher or the ship."

"Thanks. So maybe you can tell me about the WASP program. I've heard of it but thought you just ferried aircraft from the factory to the port."

"That is a primary job of the WASPs—so far, we've flown more than eighty percent of all those flights. It frees up men, you know. But a handful of us get to test aircraft."

Riley nodded, but then seemed to struggle with what to say next.

"I've got an idea," Justin said. "I was hoping to catch a bite to eat before we head back to New York on the late train. Is there any chance you could join us? Just something simple, and only if you don't have plans . . ." His voice trailed off as he realized that he had gone out on a limb with this—they'd just met this woman an hour earlier, and he had no idea if she was even single, or how interested Riley might be. Riley's glare told him that he was right to worry. "Of course, I know it's a spur of the moment thing, so if you can't . . ."

Angie Millburn looked at the two of them for a moment, particularly Riley, and then said, "I think I could handle a dinner, since it's military related. I know a good diner close to the 30th Street Station if you're on your way out of Philadelphia."

They hadn't planned to leave Philadelphia, just across the river from Camden, but it was easy enough to change their plans. "Yes—yes, that's what we were planning to do," Justin replied. "Let me check with our driver."

"I'll talk to him," Millburn said. "Maybe he could join us too? Is that against military protocol?"

"No, that's a good idea," Justin said, since it would make the driver more inclined to stretch his workday.

"I'll take care of it then." She spoke with the driver, who agreed, and Millburn agreed to meet them at the restaurant forty-five minutes from then.

Once inside the car, Justin said quietly to Riley, "A very interesting woman."

"Yes, yes, she is."

Chapter 14

SUMMER NEAR THE ARCTIC

July 1944
Near Adak Island

Executive Officer Worthy Bitler shivered and stamped his feet. "It's supposed to be *warm* in the summer—who forgot to tell the weather gods?"

"May I suggest we step inside and off the battle bridge, sir?" Justin said. They moved to the inside bridge. While not as cold as it had been during the Battle of the Komandorski Islands a year earlier, it was still just thirty-eight degrees Fahrenheit following the short sunset an hour earlier.

"It seems to me that there's a war going on somewhere—in Europe, in the Mediterranean, and even in the South Pacific—just not here," Worthy said.

Justin nodded. The threat of Japan launching an attack across the Northern Pacific had receded significantly after the fights a year earlier in which the *Salt Lake City* played such a prominent role. But Pacific command still felt it was worthwhile to keep capital ships in the area just to make sure the Japanese didn't see an opening to hit the North American mainland—an assignment

SUMMER NEAR THE ARCTIC

that was *not* a morale booster for the men of the *Salt Lake City* since it kept them isolated.

"The men gripe when we're out of the action, but they used to gripe when we were seeing continuous action," Justin said. "I suppose it's never quite right."

"Human nature. By the way, you never told me about your trip east. How did it go?"

"It was great. Heidi loved seeing her parents, and her parents loved seeing their grandkids, and we all had a fun time going to Coney Island and into Manhattan. My parents cried when we said goodbye, so I take that as a sign that they were happy we came. It was good for me to have that much time with them."

"What about your cousin, the scout pilot?" Bitler furrowed his brow. "I don't remember his name."

"Riley Bracken." Justin shook his head as he thought back on the experience. It was still complicated, and it was frustrating not having someone to talk to about it. He decided that he could trust Commander Bitler.

"May I speak candidly, sir?"

"Of course—I asked you."

"Thank you. Physically, he's doing quite well. He has a prosthetic leg that he's getting used to, and he's regained much of the use of his right shoulder. The leg still chafes when he does a lot of walking, but they're working to get a better fit to reduce that."

"Physically okay, but something's not going right?"

"Riley's always been an upbeat, cheerful, jokester type. He's the life of the party, and he was a quick-witted fighter pilot before he transferred to the scout planes. I could never figure out why he did that, but on this trip, he confided in me he'd started getting vertigo on the steep dives. He knew telling anyone about it would ground him permanently, so he talked his way into a scout plane so he could keep flying. And then . . . he lost his leg and can't fly for the Navy anymore. He's really struggled mentally with all that he's lost and not knowing where he belongs."

"Seems like he has a good reason to be down."

Justin nodded. "He does. But it's more than that. He gets . . . I'm not sure what the word is. They used to call it *melancholy*, but that implies sentimentality. Whatever he's going through is a lot darker than that—anger mixed with hopelessness. Despite all the people who care about him and encourage him, he still lapses into brooding."

"It's hard on a person to lose . . . not just physical ability, but a part of you that made you get up in the morning." Worthy Bitler hesitated, pondering whether he should say what he was thinking. He decided to go ahead. "For example, it seemed to me that you went to a dark place for a time after your injury—which looks good, by the way. The scar's hardly noticeable."

Justin nodded. "I did—maybe I went to the same place Riley is. I know this sounds foolish, but part of me wishes I still had the original scar." When he saw the surprised look on Bitler's face, he continued, "Don't get me wrong. I'm glad the plastic surgeon did such a great job. It's much better for the people around me—no one winces anymore. In fact, my impression is they hardly notice it. So it makes things easier for them, and I don't have to explain myself."

"And yet you wish you had the original scar? I don't understand."

"I don't know how to explain it—it's just that I watched so many men killed or wounded during those days on the island. Most of the wounded were disfigured far worse than I was, or suffered a catastrophic loss, like my cousin. Yet somehow I get out of it with nothing more than a scar—now an almost invisible one."

He was quiet again. "I'm over it—I'm glad to be back in action with all my assignments to keep me busy. But I was shocked at how deeply the experience affected me. There's more than just the invisible scar. I still have flashbacks to the face of the man who was trying to kill me."

Bitler was quiet, finally breaking the silence by saying, "My father had a friend who was paralyzed in the Great War. He had to learn to get around in a wheelchair and required help from others for even mundane tasks. Everyone in his family was helpful, but it was inconvenient, and he knew people were frustrated by it. At any rate, a couple of years after he got home, it was just too much, and he took his own life. The note he left said he just couldn't imagine continuing to live his life that way, so he ended it. I hope things get better for your cousin."

"Thank you for sharing that, sir—I've worried that Riley might do the same thing. It's clear to me that he can make a good life for himself if he's patient. But so far, all that he's seen are the limitations. I do understand his frustration—he's a guy who was right on the cutting edge of aviation who's lost that part of his life, and it's been hard."

"Wish I knew what to say, but I don't."

"There was one good thing that happened while I was there. I talked him into going with me to the Camden shipyards to discuss the SOC mounts, and while we were there, he met a WASP pilot who had experience with our type of scout plane. The two of them seemed to hit it off."

"A WASP pilot? I thought they transferred aircraft?"

"That's most of what they do, but she's also a test pilot. We went to dinner with her after the meetings, and she tried to convince Riley to come to work at the test yard where she's posted."

Justin nodded. "I think he's considering it—it would be good for him if he did."

Bitler nodded. "Well, all things taken together it sounds like it was a good trip then. The training classes you've held because of your work at the shipyard have been well received. So, I'd count it a success."

"Thank you, sir. I appreciate your support in helping me put it together."

July 1944

In the brig

"Jowdy!"

"Yes, Chief?"

"How is it that you've gained weight?"

"Chief?"

Al Jowdy knew full well why he was being asked this question. He was toward the end of his imprisonment in the *Salt Lake City*'s brig and was supposed to be living off nothing more than bread and water. Men almost always lost weight while "doing time," but Al was as well fed as ever. A prisoner, a galley steward from the enlisted mess, who was just about done with his time in the brig when Al arrived, had shown him that the brig shared a wall with the enlisted men's mess, and he showed him how to move some slats in the wall next to his bunk so that he could stick his hand through. The steward had made a deal with his shipmates that they'd sneak him food. Al, being Al, had talked the steward into cutting him in on the deal. He'd never been hungry this whole time in the brig.

"Well, Jowdy?" The guard was looking right at him.

"I guess when you're already skinny to start out, like me, it doesn't show as much. Plus, I came from a family of nine kids in

Texas, and there were a lot of times we didn't have much to eat." He hoped this would satisfy the guard, because Al fully intended to tell the next prisoner how to use the system and didn't want to spoil it.

The guard nodded. "I guess so. It really doesn't matter. Tell me again why you're here? I wasn't here when they checked you in." He looked down at his clipboard. "Insubordination and assaulting an officer? You don't seem the type."

"Uh, well, there are two sides to the story."

The guard pulled up a chair and said, "I got nothing better to do. Tell me about it."

Al loved telling stories, so he was happy to do so. "Well, I was coming back from shore leave one day and when I made it to the top of the gangplank I saluted the ensign at the back of the ship, just like we're supposed to do, and then I turned and saluted the officer of the deck. But he didn't like the way I saluted, so he gave me guff for it."

"Which an officer is entitled to do . . ."

"Yes, Chief. Well, I didn't like it, so I muttered something under my breath and that really set him off. In fact, he stepped forward and kind of punched me in the chest . . ."

"He hit you!" The guard's eyes widened at this, and the pitch of his voice rose.

"Yes, Chief, he did."

"So what did you do?"

"I did stupid, sir. I was so shocked by what he'd done that I just reached forward and grabbed him by his shoulders and picked him up and turned him around, and then let go of his shoulders."

"So—that's bad, but not toss you in the brig bad."

"Well, what I didn't know until it was too late is that I'd

turned far enough that when I let him go, he fell off the side of the ship into the water! And he *really* didn't like that!"

The guard busted up laughing. "Jowdy, are you telling me the truth? Did you really drop an officer off the side of the ship?"

"I did, Chief. I did."

The guard laughed so hard that he struggled to get his breath. "Well, that explains why you're here, I guess."

"The thing is, that when I was telling the XO, Mr. Bitler, about all this he was shocked that the officer had punched me. So, he put him on discipline too. I thought I might get off with only a warning, but he told me that I played a big part in—I think he called it a fiasco, whatever that is. And so that's why I've been on restricted rations."

"Well, that beats all—I've never heard a story like that in all my time as a master at arms." He shook his head. "I've just never heard anything like it."

"Me neither, Chief. I'll be sure not to do that again." But secretly Jowdy was all right with what had happened. During his weeks in the brig there were no decks to scrub, garbage to clean up, or guns to polish, and he'd eaten good food every day from the kindness of strangers on the other side of his bunk. He wouldn't do it again, because he was an honorable man who had just reacted to a confrontation, but being confined hadn't been that bad.

The guard stood up to complete his rounds. "Dropped him off the side of the ship. I bet he'll never tell that story to anyone!" That made Al laugh.

August 1944
New orders

"Captain on the bridge!"

"At ease, everyone." Captain Busbey walked to the ship's

public address system, where he motioned for Justin Collier to call the ship to attention.

"Now hear this, now hear this. All hands heave to—the captain will address the crew!"

Justin stepped aside, and the captain stepped forward to the microphone. "Men of the *Salt Lake City*, we have just received new orders." Captain Leroy Busbey paused to add drama to the moment, knowing that everyone would be anxious to know their new fate. He read from a printed dispatch he'd received just a few moments earlier from the signals department. "'From the admiral: The heavy cruiser USS *Salt Lake City* is hereby requested and commanded to return to Pearl Harbor for reassignment to the western Pacific. Make way immediately!'"

Cheers erupted in all corners of the ship, including the men on the bridge. They could say goodbye to the miserable cold and isolation of the Aleutian Islands, and say hello to the warmth of their Hawaiian homes before having to return to the war.

Chapter 15

A SEA CHANGE

September 22, 1944
Philadelphia, Pennsylvania

"Why don't you ever order a steak?" Riley Bracken asked.

"I'm just not that fond of meat," Angie Millburn replied.

Riley shook his head. "And you hardly ever drink milk or order cheese."

"I don't like the way I feel after eating it—I like potatoes and beans and rice and bread and peanut butter. And vegetables." Angie fixed her gaze at him. "That a problem for you?"

"Well, it could be." He struggled to figure out why it would be a problem for him—after all, she was an adult and could eat whatever she wanted.

"So while we're on the subject of what I like and don't like," Angie added, "I'm not at all sure why you think that everybody we talk to cares a fig about the New York Yankees—particularly when so many of the best players are off to war!"

"Oh, sure, but if it was the Phillies we were talking about . . ."

"Then everyone would be interested." She smiled.

Riley shook his head. "I just don't see how it can work out."

He shifted his gaze to take in the elegant setting—the Primrose Dinner Club in Philadelphia. He'd gone out of his way to make the reservation and to make sure that the waiters would bring the bouquet of flowers at just the right moment. He'd even tipped the bandleader to play their favorite song.

"How *what* can work out?" Angie asked.

"You and me—you don't like beef, I certainly don't like the Phillies, and you fly airplanes for the Army sometimes! I'm a Navy man."

Angie nodded. "I can see why that's a problem for you." She stirred her fork in her salad. "But we both do like airplanes . . . and you're *nearly* as good a pilot as I am, so that's something." He tipped his head, waiting to hear what else was coming. "And we both agree that you're quite handsome."

He nodded in agreement. "Well, that part's certainly true."

"And the way you look at me suggests . . ."

"That I think you're the most beautiful woman in the world?"

"Exactly. Do I have that right?"

"You do have it right—you are the most beautiful woman in the world."

"Well then, despite the differences, I'd like to suggest that right now is about the best time for you to try to win me over, since more than seven million soldiers and sailors will be coming home when the war ends, and that will significantly increase the competition for my affection." She batted her eyes.

"Well, that's about the least of my problems—not one of them is as clever or smart as I am, and how many of *them* want a pilot for a wife? It's kind of hard on a man's ego, you know. It takes someone with humility—like me—to admit and admire your talent!"

Angie burst out laughing. "Now you've gone too far—putting

humility in the same sentence with you!" Riley acted wounded, then smiled.

"Maybe we do have some things in common," Riley said, "but I can only take beans and rice so often, you know."

"There are lots of restaurants where a man can get whatever he wants for lunch—as long as he's home for dinner."

Now it was Riley who laughed. "Okay, I suppose it has a chance of working after all."

"You still haven't told me what 'it' is," Angie said—genuinely curious now.

"Oh, right—let's fix that!" He caught the attention of the maître d' and motioned for him to put the plan in action. A few more hand signals to people around the room, and the lights dimmed and the band started playing George Gershwin's "Embraceable You." Angie watched transfixed as Riley mouthed the words to the song.

Just as the song ended, one of the waiters came forward and handed Angie a large bouquet of red roses with a note and a small gift box attached. Riley was pleased to see her blush. "Well, open the note and then the box."

"Riley, what are you up to?"

"Just open the note."

So she did. It read:

"When a man finds the best friend he could ever hope to find, and loves her with all his heart, it's customary for him to get down on one knee to ask her to be his wife. For me that's a little awkward, so perhaps you'll accept my hand instead, as I ask you with all the love I can muster, 'Will you marry me?'"

She caught her breath and looked up as Riley extended his hand—"Will you? Will you marry me?"

"Oh, Riley! Of course I will. How could there ever be anyone but you?"

It was embarrassing, but Riley had to wipe a tear away from his eye before he could pull her close to him in the booth to kiss her and stroke her hair. "Thank you," he said. "Thank you from the bottom of my heart. There was darkness, and now there's light, and all because of you."

"I love you," Angie said. "I don't know if I would have believed how this whole thing came together, but I know I've had someone looking out for me. And for you. You're the one for me!"

He straightened up. "Well then, if we hope to make this official, you better open the box!" He untied the ribbon that attached the box to the flowers and handed it to her.

"I don't know what to expect!" After opening the small box and pushing back the tissue, she gasped. "Riley—it's so beautiful!" The ring was made of yellow gold and featured a brilliant red ruby surrounded by a wreath of small diamonds. "This is too much—you shouldn't have!"

"I wish it could have been a diamond instead of a ruby, but they're too rare for now."

"Oh, no—the ruby is so beautiful. It's my favorite color!" She started to slip the ring on her finger but stopped, insisting that Riley do it instead. Once it was on her finger, she held it up to the light and smiled. "I'm engaged! You're engaged! We're engaged!"

"To each other!" Riley laughed. "How about we get married tonight?" he asked.

That settled her down. "How about we get married next fall? It takes time to plan a wedding."

"How about June?" Riley asked hopefully. That seemed far too long to him, but he hoped to pull it back from next September.

"June?" She stopped and thought. "But why not? June it is."

"I'd like to ask you to dance, but I really don't feel ready—I'm still quite awkward."

"That's all right. Could I take you flying tomorrow, and we'll celebrate that way?"

Riley nodded. "That'd be great—perfect, in fact. Nothing too extreme in terms of aerobatics, though, okay? I'll be happy just to be up in the clouds with my sweetheart." And then he added, "I love you, Angie Millburn."

"Love you too, Riley Bracken."

October 5, 1944
Camden, New Jersey

"I can't believe it! They're decommissioning me and the rest of the WASPS! After everything we've done to help this lousy war effort, they're firing us."

Riley Bracken considered carefully how he should react to Angie's outburst. He was pretty sure that he shouldn't point out that since she'd never been commissioned—the WASPs were a civilian unit—it was impossible for her to be *de*commissioned.

"I think everybody's going to be out of a job soon. Most predictions are that the war in Europe will be over in a month. No need for as many military aircraft—"

"But the war in Japan is still going! They still need to get aircraft to the Pacific!"

He slipped the back edge of his lower lip between his teeth and pressed them together gently. "What are you going to do?" he asked.

Angie turned to him with fire in her eyes. It was one of the things he'd come to love about her—her cool professionalism on duty and her energy when off. Since they had become engaged two weeks earlier on what might have appeared to be a whim, but that absolutely was *not* a whim, life had changed dramatically for Riley Bracken. His concerns about his missing leg were swallowed up in the sheer joy of finding someone who loved him as much as he loved her.

"What am I going to *do*?" she asked. "I'll tell you what I'm going to do—I'll do what all the other pilots are going to do. I'll get a job flying for the post office. Or I'll go to work for one of the passenger airlines they keep telling us will soon fly more people than travel by rail. Or maybe I'll just extend my enlistment in the Army Air Corps and be part of the peacetime Army. That's what I'll do—one of those things. Oh, wait! Those jobs aren't available to women—only men! No women need apply. How could a woman even *think* about taking a job away from one of the boys?"

Riley inhaled slowly. His mother had given him just one piece of advice when he told her that he had proposed to Angie: "Listen more than you talk." That was it—and fortunately her words came back to him now. "What can I do?"

She turned and glowered at him. What she needed now was a good fight. But as she saw the sincere look of concern on her fiancé's face, she relented. She did need a fight, but not with Riley. She sat down heavily. "I don't know—I don't know what I should do, and I don't know how you can help."

Riley nodded. "It's a bum deal for sure. There's no telling how many lives you saved because of your test flights. That crash on takeoff that nearly killed you *would* have killed someone on the deck of an aircraft carrier. Instead, they found the defect, fixed it, and told you 'thanks.'"

She smiled. "That was exciting. It's probably the closest I'll ever come to knowing how you felt when you got blown up. I was scared out of my wits."

"I'm just glad you got out of there in time."

She got up and sat on the side of his chair. "We'll figure it out, won't we?"

Riley nodded. "My guess is that aviation is going to become one of the biggest things in the economy. There's going to be all kinds of jobs for great pilots. Maybe they'll let women be test pilots for those commercial albatrosses you talk about. That would be fun, wouldn't it, as you slowly lift off the runway, making sure you don't spill anyone's coffee in the back. They'll call you 'Slow and Steady Angie'!" She slugged him.

"This from a guy who flew a Kingfisher—talk about slow."

"Not on takeoff! You got blasted into the wind pretty darn fast."

"Well, there's also room for you in aviation. If you keep getting As on your math tests in the engineering class you're taking, you'll probably be designing those big fat passenger birds."

"Not me . . . but I may be able to sell them. I'm not bad at glad-handing and backslapping." He thought about it for a moment. "You know, that's not a bad idea. Maybe we could open a company together where we represent the manufacturers to the people buying the planes. You take them on test flights; I talk them through the details of the deal. That could actually work, you know."

She smiled. "Darn you, Riley. I want to be angry. And you're ruining it for me."

He reached over and drew her close for a kiss—which turned out to be a very passionate one. Through their relationship, Riley Bracken had found his way out of the blackness and back into the light.

Chapter 16

AN UNUSUAL REQUEST AT OKINAWA

April 1, 1945
Okinawa
With Task Force 54 Gunfire
and Covering Unit 5

Justin Collier shook his head to clear the eardrops that the doctor had placed in his ears. In six months of battle since leaving the Aleutian Islands, he'd been troubled by hearing loss. Voices on the bridge were muted and difficult to follow.

It had started with the beating he'd taken while serving with the Lucky 7s. The condition worsened during the firing of the big guns in support of beach landings at the Volcano Islands and Iwo Jima—a bloodbath for both sides. Iwo Jima had captured the imagination of the American public because of a remarkable photo of marines raising the flag atop Mt. Suribachi taken by the war photographer Joe Rosenthal.

That moment came near the end of an ordeal that had pitted 110,000 marines against 20,000 Japanese infantrymen. Conditions on the beach were miserable, with fine volcanic ash making it impossible for wheeled vehicles to make their way up the beach, leaving it to the men to struggle in the soft ash, and no ability to dig foxholes. It was the first time in the war that total US casualties (wounded and killed) exceeded that of the Japanese. The *Salt Lake City* had joined in preinvasion shelling, as well as providing defensive fire for attacks on US carriers. The guns fired relentlessly, and yet their barrage still left most of the Japanese alive to resist the US assault. At the end of the battle, more than 18,000 Japanese defenders were dead, while the remaining 2,000 died slowly of starvation or from being flushed out of their hiding places by marines with flamethrowers. On the US side, 6,000 marines were killed and 21,000 were wounded.

"I think I understand why I have trouble hearing after the guns fire, but I don't understand why I have this ringing in my ears all the time. It's enough to drive a person crazy!"

"You have a condition called 'tinnitus,'" the doctor replied.

"Tinnitus?"

"It's derived from the ancient word *tintinnabulation*, which means 'ringing, tinkling, or jingling of bells.' Many of our men are complaining of it. It's a sign of permanent ear damage at the frequency you hear the ringing."

"To me it's more of a steady whistle in both ears that's loudest when everything else is quiet. Most of the time I don't notice it, but I think it must impact my ability to hear, because it's difficult for me to follow conversations as easily as I once did." He paused. "And it's always present if I happen to think about it—like right now when I'm talking to you. Is there anything that can be done for it?"

The doctor shook his head. "I'm afraid there's no cure. Hopefully there will be research into it since so many people in all branches of the military are exposed to damaging levels of sound from the weapons we fire."

This was discouraging news. Justin had assumed it would clear up over time. "What causes it—the ringing?"

"There are some medical conditions that cause it, but in your case it's almost certainly because of the shelling. The extremely loud noise of the guns damages tiny hairs in your inner ear, the cochlea, so they no longer transmit sounds of a particular frequency to your brain. It's a paradox, but you're *not* hearing anything—there's no external noise. But since your brain expects to receive feedback from your ears at all frequencies, when it doesn't, it creates the perception of sound to fill in the missing information."

"You're kidding—that sounds just like my cousin who lost his leg in combat here on the *Salt Lake City*!" Justin responded. "He tells me that there are times when he wants to scratch his missing leg because it itches. Of course, there's nothing to scratch, so it drives him crazy."

"Similar—in his case the limb is gone. In your case the stereocilia cells are damaged and nonfunctioning, but the effect's the same—you're sensing something that isn't there." The doctor added, "The problem for speech is that the injured cells are at higher frequencies that help you hear sounds like *S* and *D* and *T*, so your brain isn't receiving the information it needs to tell the difference between words like 'sealed' and 'field.' That's why you struggle to make sense of conversations."

Justin nodded—he did have trouble with those sounds. "Well, I guess I'm lucky in that even when I do notice it, I'm able to function. I just wish I could hear better. I hate asking people to repeat themselves."

The doctor sighed. "Wish I could help—just do your best to

protect your ears when we're firing. I understand it's all about to start over again here at Okinawa."

Justin nodded. It was about to start over—this time with more than 800,000 American troops against 120,000 Japanese. And the *Salt Lake City* was just one of a stunning 1,600 US naval ships with a total complement of 350,000 sailors and officers. It was the largest naval armada in the history of the world, and the *Salt Lake City* would have its own unique role to play.

"All I can say, Doc, is that if ever there was a 'big one,' this is it!"

April 1, 1945
In the engine room

"Mr. Appelle, can I see you for a moment?"

"Of course." Stuart stepped away from the group he'd been meeting with about a boiler problem. When he reached a quiet spot, he saluted the chief engineer and said a crisp "Sir!"

"Can you imagine how much fuel oil it takes to get 1,600 ships to this spot this close to Japan and this far away from the United States? And we've been burning through ours while we're sitting here idle." The chief engineer shook his head. "It's like we're playing a chess game with 1,600 pieces, all of which need fuel."

"Yes, sir," was all that Stuart could think to say. He had no idea where the boss was going with this.

"Yes, well, you and I aren't responsible for the other 1,599 ships out there—just the *Salt Lake City*, and I've had a request in for weeks for refueling."

"Yes, sir. It's my understanding that's to take place tomorrow."

"And that's because *you* don't think like a land-based fool who's out to impress an admiral. We *were* scheduled for tomorrow, but now it seems that our allotment has to go to Rear

Admiral McCormick in Unit Three to feed his thirsty old bat-tleships *Idaho* and *Tennessee*. So we'll be put off for at least three days, maybe up to a week."

Stuart whistled. "That'd cut it pretty darn close." He was al-ready running the numbers in his head. It's not like they'd have to cover a lot of distance during the battle—there were US ships completely surrounding the island. But it took an incredible amount of steam just to make fresh water, generate electricity, keep enough power to the propellers to maintain steerage, and to power all the pneumatics and other machinery on the ship, including the gun platforms. He'd already noticed that the *Salt Lake City* was floating high in the water because their fuel tanks were so low.

"How can I help?"

"We need to implement extreme conservation measures. The captain's aware of the problem and has given us permission to shut down the boilers to the bare minimum. But it's crucial that your men be prepared to fire them up at a moment's notice if the battle demands it."

"Yes, sir. I understand. With your permission we'll keep a minimum fire so that we always have a small head of steam . . ."

The chief shook his head. "Afraid not, Stuart. We must let the idled boilers go cold—I know it's dangerous, but we simply can't run the risk of running out of fuel. So, drill your emergency restart procedures and cross your fingers."

"Aye, sir. No hot showers for now." He smiled and saluted. The chief nodded and returned the salute.

April 1, 1945
On the fantail

"And to think that I joined the Navy for adventure and new experiences—and it's like a broken record. It keeps playing the same note over and over again," Al Jowdy said.

"I know what you mean," Elmer Breeze replied. "These battles all play out the same way—we fire on the beaches, our guys get clobbered on the landing, we do our best to fight off air attacks on the aircraft carriers, and we always win the battle in the end. Lots of noise and lots of smoke."

"I think this one may be different!" Al and Elmer turned at the sound of Alex Mihalka's voice.

"Why?" Al asked.

"Because for the first time we're in range of enemy aircraft from the home islands, as well as the ones we usually see from closer islands. I think they'll send a lot more aircraft than we've seen in other battles. And with more than a thousand of our ships to attack, it's going to be really hard for us to protect them all. I'm afraid we'll lose a lot of ships and men. And if they can't sink us from the air, their kamikaze pilots will simply fly their planes right into us."

The three of them stood silently for a time. "Well, I don't like *that* prediction," Elmer said. "We're the good guys here."

Al nodded. "I just hope they don't come after us," he said, a response that hung heavy in the air.

April 6, 1945
On the bridge

"This is odd," Captain Edward Mitchell said. He had assumed command of the *Salt Lake City* from Captain Busbey after their October resupply in Hawaii.

"Sir?" Worthy Bitler said.

"Would you ask Commander Collier to meet me at my cabin?"

"Of course," Bitler said, curious about what was in the message the captain had just received. He stepped to the interphone and paged Commander Collier to the captain's cabin.

Justin Collier had been meeting with the chief engineer to discuss some required maintenance on the boilers and to give him the good news that the *Salt Lake City* would finally be refueled the next day. When he arrived at the captain's cabin, he knocked on the door and waited for the "enter" command, then stepped inside.

"You wanted to see me, sir?" Captain Mitchell motioned for Justin to sit down. Rather than address him, Captain Mitchell handed him the cable, which read:

From: Rear Admiral Bertram Rodgers, Unit 3,
USS *Tennessee*
To: Captain Edward Mitchell, USS *Salt Lake City*
Subject: Request short-term transfer of Commander Justin Collier to USS *Tennessee* for consultation and instruction of signals department re: island bombardment.

Previous experience indicates Cmd. Collier has unique knowledge that will benefit Unit 3 ships in communications with ground forces on Okinawa. If you can safely release him, please arrange transport to *Tennessee* for 1-week assignment. Your discretion whether to approve or deny.

RA Rodgers

When Justin looked up, Captain Mitchell asked, "Any idea what this is about?"

"I don't know, sir. I served with Admiral Rodgers when he commanded the *Salt Lake City*, but I don't know what he has in mind." He thought for a moment. "Unless it has something to do with an assignment that made me part of a landing party during the Battle of Attu Island in the Aleutians. I was embedded with the attacking forces and got to know their protocols pretty well. But I'm not sure that's it."

"Well, it's irregular, but it may be good to put some of the weight you carry on your shoulders on your subordinates for a week. I'll treat it as a training exercise. That is, if you want to accept the temporary assignment."

Justin nodded thoughtfully. "I'd like to accept. Admiral Rodgers is an expert in intelligence, so he must think this is important."

"Well, then—it looks like you're off on an adventure. I suggest you have one of our scout planes ferry you over there—there are too many ships out there to make it safe for one of our small boats."

"Yes, sir. I'll see to it immediately."

April 6, 1945
At the SOC launcher

"Whenever you're ready, Commander."

"Thank you, Mr. Rowan."

Justin Collier had stowed his seabag in the space behind his seat and was now preparing for the shock of takeoff he'd heard so much about from Riley. He was surprised to realize that in all his years in the Navy and on the *Salt Lake City*, this was his first flight in a scout plane. For the past few minutes, while their flight plan was being transmitted to ships in the area so that they wouldn't be shot down by friendly fire, Dan Rowan and Justin had been chatting about Riley and his engagement—which Dan hadn't heard about until Justin had responded to his question about how Riley was getting along. "I'm glad he's doing all right, then," Rowan said. "It was such a one-off accident that got him— we've been at war for four years and that's the only time a scout plane's been hit while getting ready to launch. Such a freak accident." Justin agreed, happy that Riley was happy. Even though it still seemed like there was a lot of war left in the Pacific, with the European war about to end, he expected he'd have a chance to see Riley before the US invaded Japan.

And *that* would be an entirely different affair than this battle, Justin thought. In Okinawa, the Americans had a six-to-one personnel advantage over the enemy. When it came time to invade the home islands, the enemy would have a seventy-to-one advantage over the Americans, which meant that millions of people would die in the preinvasion bombardments, the shelling of ports and landing zones in advance of landing troops, and then the unimaginable toll on both sides as the Americans would have to fight house-to-house to gain control. With the heavy fighting they'd experienced with Japanese infantry on the islands so far, he could only imagine how desperately both civilians and the military would fight to protect their emperor and the homeland. And yet, there was no other way to end the war.

That's why the battle for Okinawa was so important—it put the home islands in range of American fighter aircraft that could accompany the heavy bombers to their drop zones and back, protecting the bomber crews from Japanese fighter retaliation.

"Here we go!" Dan Rowan said, and the next thing Justin knew he was pushed back against the cockpit seat with a force greater than anything he'd ever experienced. It knocked his breath out and slapped his head against the back of the seat. He should have gasped but couldn't help but laugh as he felt the little craft suddenly dip below him, and then he felt the seat push up against him as it gained the airspeed it needed to ascend.

"That was amazing!" he said into the interphone.

"Glad you liked it," said Dan Rowan. "But I'm afraid all the excitement's over. From this point on you're on a sightseeing flight, so sit back and enjoy the show."

And what a show it was! As they gained altitude, Justin looked out over the side of the plane to the vast reaches of the Pacific Ocean stretching out below him. It was fascinating to see how the sun reflected off the surface in a silvery shimmer that made you turn your eyes away. As they reached the apogee of their flight, he was astonished at the number of ships stretching out for miles in every direction—as far as the eye could see. It was one thing to say that there were 1,600 ships lined up for battle, but that could not begin to convey the awesome spectacle of all those ships moving in a tightly choreographed dance in the ocean below—their wakes sometimes crossing each other while the smoke from their funnels smudged the air around them. In his prewar days he could never have imagined such a show of strength. At the beginning of the war the Navy had fewer than 500 ships all told. Now there were 1,600 in a single location!

"Do you see the enemy fighters over there at about five o'clock?" Dan asked, gesturing to his right.

Justin squinted and saw tiny specks in the sky—some of them diving down into the American armada. "Will they come after us?"

"Nah—they have a lot bigger fish to fry than an American observation aircraft. With all those ships to shoot at, it's hard for them to miss." Rowan was quiet for a moment. "I wish I could shoot every single one of them out of the sky myself." Justin nodded. He understood that sentiment all too well.

The flight was short, but Justin had never felt so alive. Freed from the responsibilities of command, up in the sky at a moment of historic significance, the sun bright above him and the water blue below him, Justin smiled.

"All right, sir, I'm afraid your tour is almost over. I'm going to bring us down in the wake of the *Tennessee*, and then they'll swing around and pick us up with their crane. It's an interesting process, so hold tight."

"Got it!" Justin now settled back in fascination as Dan Rowan slowed the single engine aircraft and watched as they settled closer and closer to the water. Off to the left the *Tennessee* grew larger as they drew closer. As big as the *Salt Lake City* was, it was dwarfed by the battleship, which displaced 27,000 tons of water to the *Salt Lake City*'s 10,000 tons.

"Here we go!" Rowan called, and Justin felt the cockpit start to pulse as the propeller slowed, and then there was a strong jolt as the pontoon hit the water, bounced, and then settled again. In what seemed like just a moment the aircraft was down and bobbing in the water. At that point Rowan increased the speed of the propeller and turned the nose into the direction of the waves. "Got to keep some power on, or we'll feel like a cork out here—it will take a little time for them to come about and grab us, so relax."

For his part, Justin couldn't remember the last time he'd been seasick—but there it was in his stomach and head. All the up and down of takeoff and landing added to the motion of the cockpit sitting up above the pontoon provided a very different experience than he felt when traveling by boat between the big ships. But by concentrating he was able to keep his head clear enough to not throw up.

After what seemed a very long time, a great shadow fell over the scout and suddenly Justin felt a jolt as the hook from above grabbed hold of the little aircraft, and then abruptly they were rising in the air, swinging on the cable that had snagged them. Soon, they were on the deck of the great battleship. "There you go, Commander. Safely delivered."

"I'll see you get a little something extra in your rations," Justin said easily into the interphone. Then, when one of the deck crew opened the hatch, he took off his headgear, reached down and grabbed his sea kit and handed it to the man, then allowed himself to be helped out of the plane and onto the platform.

"With respect, sir, the admiral requests your presence in his cabin," a young ensign said. "I'll be glad to show you the way."

Justin turned and saluted Dan Rowan, and then allowed the ensign to carry his bag as he made his way to see his old friend Admiral Bertram Rodgers.

April 1945

Shore leave

"Hey look, a limey just came in," one of Al Jowdy's friends said, pointing at the entrance of the bar where they were enjoying shore leave.

"The British hate us, you know?" Al wasn't sure which one of his pals had said this, but he nodded in agreement. Then he decided that he didn't know that the British hated them.

"Why?" he asked. "Why do they hate us?"

"Because we make nearly twice as much money as they do. And they think we're latecomers to the war who take all the glory—which we do, because we're better equipped, better trained, and just . . . better than them." Everyone laughed at that.

"Plus, they don't bathe very often, so we've been known to call them out for their smell," someone else said.

Al didn't know what to think about all that. He wasn't sure it was a good idea to be saying that about this sailor, who was probably a foot taller than most of his buddies. Even though he was almost eighteen years old now, he still had no desire to drink, so he visited the taverns with his friends just for the company— but it could get dicey when they'd gotten a little drunk.

"I hate the American Navy!" the British fellow said loudly, apparently looking for a fight. He'd obviously already had a few before stumbling into the bar.

"So do we!" one of Al's buddies shouted.

He wandered over to them. "You do?"

"Sure—what have they done for us?"

"Well, I hate FDR!" the British guy said emphatically.

"What's not to hate? All he does is take huge campaign con- tributions to take care of his friends. He doesn't care about guys like us."

"Say," the British sailor said, "you lads are all right."

"You too—why don't you let us buy you a drink?"

"Well, that's downright friendly," the big guy said. "Don't mind if I do."

Al Jowdy couldn't believe what he was hearing. He leaned over to his friend and whispered, "What's going on? I didn't think we liked these guys."

"Oh, just wait and see what they've got planned—I've seen this act before."

"What . . . what do they have planned?"

"Just wait a bit until he's good and drunk and then you'll see."

"They're not going to hurt him, are they?" Al was starting to be concerned.

"No, they're just going to give him a souvenir to remember us by."

As it turned out, when the fellow was so far gone he didn't realize what was happening, they walked him over to a tattoo parlor and paid to have two large American flags crossing each other etched onto his chest, the letters USN directly underneath. Then they rolled him out to the sidewalk, where he promptly fell asleep, having assured them that he thought his tattoo was the greatest idea in the world. But that wouldn't last.

April 1945
At assembly on the ship the next morning

"Attention! Captain Mitchell will now address you!"

"Men—this is Captain McCarthy of the HMS *Argonaut*. You have probably met some of his men in town on shore leave. It seems that some of our men from the *Salt Lake City* played a rather cruel joke on one of their seamen yesterday, and we're here to find out who it was. It seems they got this man drunk and then had his chest tattooed with two American flags." There was a smattering of barely suppressed laughter. Al Jowdy caught a couple of junior officers trying their best not to smile. "The only thing this man remembers about his American pals is that one was short and curly-haired. Stand to attention as we inspect the ranks," the captain barked. He was definitely *not* smiling.

"You look a little green," Alex Mihalka whispered to his short, curly-headed shipmate Al.

"I didn't even do it—I was just there with them."

"Well, try to stand as tall as you can . . ."

As the captains drew nearer, Al unconsciously smoothed his

hair and stretched as much as he possibly could without standing on his tiptoes. The two moved slowly down the line and, to Al's relief, kept moving after reaching him. In addition to stretching, he discovered that he'd been holding his breath, which he now let out as silently as possible.

Suddenly, the British captain stopped and turned back in his direction. Captain Mitchell followed. Once again, Al stretched while simultaneously trying to look as innocent as he could. The British officer looked him up and down but didn't ask any questions.

"Well, captain, I'm not sure about any of this—I suppose it's impossible to make a positive identification. My man admits he was boozed up and doesn't recall much. Still, it's a dreadful way for one ally to treat the other."

"Yes, yes, it is," Captain Mitchell said. "It's terrible that he'll have to go through life with those flags on his chest. Something we'd be proud of, of course, but wrong navy for him." Captain Mitchell betrayed not the slightest hint of a smile, but something in his tone made Al wonder. "Perhaps you could join me for lunch?" Mitchell said amiably.

"A nice offer, captain, but I'll have to pass." The British captain turned and saluted Mitchell smartly, who returned his salute. Then they walked toward the gangplank, where Mitchell could see his Allied counterpart off. At that point the men were dismissed from assembly.

As they made their way toward the fantail, Alex Mihalka said, "Boy, you really got lucky with that one."

"I about had a heart attack right there on the line."

Alex laughed. "Well, the fellow did ask for it." For the first time, Al was relieved enough that he returned the laugh. It was the kind of story that would be told many times in the years to come.

Chapter 17

DEATH AT OKINAWA

April 12, 1945
Honolulu

"What's wrong, Mom?"

Heidi turned her attention to Emery. "Nothing—why do you ask?"

"You're so quiet."

Heidi shook her head. "Sorry about that. I guess I had a bad night's sleep—my dreams were all mixed up and disturbing." She smiled at Emery. "Do you ever have dreams like that?"

He shook his head. "I don't remember my dreams—I used to have nightmares, but not anymore."

She nodded. "I'm glad. When I have bad dreams it always leaves me feeling like something bad happened, even though I know dreams aren't real."

Emery got up from the chair where he'd been reading and came over and gave her a hug. "I love you," he said. For her part, Heidi appreciated that even at fifteen, Emery was still affectionate and caring.

April 12, 1945
On the fantail

Pom pom pom pom pom pom pom pom pom . . .

Al Jowdy put his hands up and over his ears, pressing against the sides of his head to try to relieve the headache. "It's endless! We've been doing this for as long as I can remember! Can't it stop?"

There was no need for Elmer Breeze to answer. They'd both seen American ships damaged or sunk (in fact, at this point more than sixty had), and knew that more sinkings and casualties were certain. Anytime an enemy aircraft approached a ship in their assigned area, they turned their antiaircraft guns at it—and they'd scored a couple of knockdowns. But more often than not, they failed to get a hit and had to watch in frustration as a torpedo was successfully launched at or a kamikaze crashed into a nearby ship. There had been several attacks on the *Salt Lake City*, but they'd all been driven away by their fire. From their vantage point it was almost impossible for them to know where the aircraft came from—that was the job of the spotters and fire control specialists. Their job was to keep discarded shell canisters from jamming up the gun platform, and they were both exhausted.

Pom pom pom pom pom pom pom pom pom . . .

They both knew the guns would have to go silent eventually to allow the barrels to cool down. When the "all-clear" alarm sounded, they stepped back against the bulkhead and took deep gulps of air to steady themselves. "How many more shells *are* there in this old ship?" Jowdy said in amazement. He didn't expect an answer—it just seemed like it was never-ending.

April 12, 1945
Signals department, USS *Tennessee*

After six days on the *Tennessee*, Justin felt like an old hand on the giant ship. He'd been treated swell by everyone he worked with and found that the officers' mess served terrific food. He'd met with several Marine officers agitating for changes in communication protocols, and Justin found that he was able to speak both their language and the language of the Navy in trying to get things right. It certainly felt like he'd made a positive difference. One thing he'd noticed is that the fourteen-inch guns of the battleship created a far greater concussion than the eight-inch guns on the heavy cruiser, so he was grateful that he'd stayed on the *Salt Lake City* during the war. A fourteen-inch armor-piercing shell weighed 1,600 pounds, compared to 260 pounds for an eight-inch shell, and the amount of gunpowder required to throw the larger shell was proportionally that much greater. He wondered how anyone on a battleship could hear anything after a major bombardment.

"We'll miss you, Commander Collier." Justin turned at the sound of Admiral Rodgers's voice. "Your insights into the ground-based attack have been invaluable. We've been receiving reports from both our ships and our shore liaisons that your suggestions have tightened up the supporting fire considerably. It's safe to say that you've saved a lot of American lives."

"Thank you, sir. It's been a pleasure to serve with you again."

Rear Admiral Rodgers, formerly captain of the *Salt Lake City*, had come down to the signals department to personally thank the men in the ad hoc group he'd formed for their work and to declare their efforts a success.

"Well, Collier, I hope you'll give my regards to the other officers of the *Salt Lake City* with whom I served."

"Yes, sir. With pleasure, sir."

The admiral excused himself and Justin turned to the men he'd been collaborating with over the past week, grateful that he'd gotten to work with such a talented group.

As Admiral Rodgers made his way up to the bridge, he glanced over the railing and saw some black spots on the horizon. It was a usual sight by now, so he took no further thought of it.

April 12, 1945
On the bridge of the USS *Salt Lake City*

"Sir! Signals chief sends his regards and transmits this confidential message from Admiral Rodgers."

Captain Mitchell turned to the young signalman and was surprised to see that his face was pale. He reached for the message and said, "Thank you." The young man saluted and exited the bridge in a very subdued fashion. Normally Mitchell would have opened the message on the spot, but in view of the odd behavior of the signalman he moved to his battle cabin at the rear of the bridge where he could open the message in private. It took a moment for it to register, and the captain had to swallow hard to subdue the sharp pain in his throat. He took a moment to collect himself, then stepped back onto the bridge. "If I may have everyone's attention!"

All but the helmsman stopped what they were doing and turned to the captain. Even though he had everyone's attention, the captain hesitated. "I've received a message from fleet." The captain unconsciously bit his lip. "Here's what it says:

To: Captain Edward Mitchell, USS *Salt Lake City*
From: Rear Admiral Bertram Rodgers, 3rd Unit, USS *Tennessee*
Regret to inform you that USS *Tennessee* was struck

by kamikaze attack today, with impact in the signals department where your Commander Justin Collier was stationed. 26 men killed, including Collier. Collier provided invaluable service to the fleet this past week and his loss is deeply felt—he was a friend. My condolences to all of you who served with him. His remains will transfer to the *Salt Lake City* for services.

 RA Rodgers

Mitchell gave the men a moment to absorb the news. He noticed that Worthy Bitler was clenching the railing tightly. Then Captain Mitchell said evenly, "Commander Collier will be missed. He meant a great deal to each of us. I will have more to say at his service." He paused. "Now, let's return to our duty stations."

April 15, 1945

Honolulu, Hawaii

"Mom—someone's come to see us!" Emery yelled.

Heidi Collier looked up from the newspaper she was reading. Not knowing who would be coming to see them at this hour she glanced out the window, where she saw two young officers in uniform stepping out of a navy blue 1939 Ford. Dread flooded through her body. "Oh no!" she gasped, struggling for air. She felt hot tears on her cheeks but gave them no thought. "This can't be—it just can't be! The war's nearly over!" She worked to calm her breathing. "I've got to prepare the children!" She reached down and pulled her apron up to her face to wipe the tears away—there would be plenty of time for crying in the days to come. But right now, she had to protect her children. Moving forcefully toward the door, she motioned for Emery and Verla to come stand with her as she put her arms around each of them.

"What is it, Mama?" Verla asked desperately. She could feel her mother trembling.

"It's bad news, I'm afraid. It's very bad news."

Then there was a knock at the door.

Chapter 18

SOMETHING BLUE

June 15, 1945
Brooklyn, New York

"I don't know you well, Angie, but I thought maybe you've heard the old saying, 'Something old, something new, something borrowed, something blue'?" Heidi Collier said quietly, having found a moment alone with Angie Millburn in the bride's room before the wedding.

"Yes, of course." Angie smiled, aware of the great loss that Heidi had suffered in April. She was grateful that Heidi and her children made the trip to New York to be there for the wedding.

"Well, I don't know if you received all of those yet, but I thought you might like this." Heidi pulled out a blue scarf and held it out to Angie. She started to say something, but choked up before she could speak. Angie reached out and took her hand. Heidi took a few calming breaths, and then continued, "My husband gave this to me on our first anniversary. He thought I'd like having a blue scarf to remind me of the water. Of course, he was the one who loved the water—I often resented it because it took him away from me. But the scarf still meant a great deal to me because it mattered so much to him." She smiled. "I'd like you to have it. Justin loved Riley, and he spoke so highly of you when we visited here last year. I know he'd be honored to have a small part to play in your wedding."

Angie swallowed hard as she took the scarf and pulled it to her face to feel the fabric. "I'm so sorry for your loss—it devastated Riley when he heard the news. It almost sent him back into his depression. He'll be grateful to know I have this."

Heidi nodded. "We'd like to be part of your family—Emery and Verla need Riley right now, so I'm glad you were able to help him through all of his afflictions, including Justin's death."

"Of course—he loves your children, and we'll do whatever we can to support you."

There was a knock on the door. "Is it all right if I come in?" Angie's mother asked. Angie motioned for her to enter.

"I was just leaving," Heidi said. She smiled at Angie. "I'll see you after the ceremony."

"Thank you so much—I'll treasure my 'something blue' gift forever."

As she walked down the hall, she spotted Riley, who motioned for her to join him. "Were you talking with Angie?"

"I was—she's a wonderful person. I'm so happy for you."

Riley's eyes darted. "She's the best."

"Are you *nervous*, Riley?" The thought made Heidi smile.

"Nervous about being married? No. Nervous about *getting* married? Yes. I wanted to elope, but that wasn't going to happen, so here we are with all these people, and I'm likely to trip over my artificial leg and make a fool of myself. Or worse—I'll blubber when it's time for me to speak."

Heidi laughed. "You won't fall, and you won't blubber. And people will only like you more if you *do* show a little emotion— it's an important day. It's going to be all right, whatever happens."

"Thanks." He turned and looked at her earnestly. "We haven't had time to talk, and there isn't time now, but I really want to talk to you about Justin." His voice caught. "I honestly can't imagine the world without him."

Heidi took his hand and rubbed it. "This has happened to thousands of other people, but somehow that doesn't help." They stood silently for a time, and she touched his face to look at her. "Thank you for asking Emery to be your best man—I don't know how often it's a young man's honor to serve, but it means the world to him."

Riley nodded. "There's no one I love more—and it's the closest I could come to having Justin, who should be here." Again there was silence. But the remarkable part was that it wasn't an uncomfortable silence—just two people who cared for each other who had suffered the ultimate loss.

"Well," Heidi said, "I think it's almost time. Let's move to the chapel so Emery can walk you up the aisle. He's been practicing ever since you asked him."

Riley smiled. "Thanks."

"Thanks?"

"For coming, for loving me and making me part of your family."

"He does look handsome in his full-dress uniform," Heidi whispered to Verla.

"He looks happy." Verla, who was mature beyond her years, had captured the real reason he looked so handsome.

"And Emery looks handsome too." This was said with a mother's pride, and Verla took Heidi's hand in hers.

The music stopped, and the minister stepped forward and said, "Would the audience please rise!" Then the organist started the stirring introduction to Mendelssohn's Wedding March, which had been sending brides down the aisle for more than a hundred years. Naturally, everyone turned to see the bride. Only a handful, including Heidi, were prepared for what they saw, and the gasps from the others were audible as Angie Millburn, on the arm of her father, stepped into the aisle wearing a dazzling white aviator's jumpsuit instead of a wedding gown. Heidi turned to look at Riley, whose eyes looked like they were going to pop right out of his head. When he noticed Heidi looking at him, they both burst out laughing—which somehow enabled the rest of the audience to laugh and clap as well. For her part, Angie simply beamed as she and her father made their way up the aisle, where Emery shook Riley's hand, presented him with the ring, then stepped away to join his mother and sister on the front row.

At first, Heidi wanted to skip the reception and dance that followed the wedding, but Verla and Emery prevailed on her. She found a table in the corner, where her parents and Justin's parents joined her. Her father-in-law asked tentatively, "So do you think you'll stay in Hawaii, or will you move back here?" Then, worried that he'd offended her, quickly added, "Or maybe it's too soon to think about it."

Heidi shook her head. "No, it's not too soon. I had thought we'd stay—it's the only life Emery's ever known, after all. But now that we're here, with all of you, the thought of going back, particularly while the war is on, seems overwhelming. Plus, I'd like Emery to have some men in his life—his grandfathers and Riley."

"Well," her mother said, "we'd love to have you close by. We've missed you all these years."

Justin's mother looked away and wiped her cheek. "We'd like it too, if it works out."

Heidi smiled. Justin had been away at sea so much of the time that the thought of being alone with the children didn't frighten her. But she'd always looked forward to his return—now that hope was gone. Here she felt supported. Somehow she knew that it would all work out in the end.

EPILOGUE

The USS *Salt Lake City* continued its service in the western Pacific by supporting beach landings and protecting the aircraft carriers that would be essential for the expected invasion of Japan. Then, on August 6, 1945, the United States dropped an atomic bomb on the Japanese city of Hiroshima. Three days later, when Japan had still not surrendered, a second bomb was dropped on the city of Nagasaki. Together, these two bombs killed between 129,000 and 226,000 (the exact number is unknown) Japanese subjects—mostly civilians. The shock of these actions, along with a declaration of war from the Allied nation of Russia on August 9, forced the military government of Japan, at the urging of the emperor, to surrender unconditionally. The necessity for invasion was averted, with an estimate of more than one million Allied lives saved by this early end to the war.

Each of the battles depicted in this book are authentic, as are the stories of being named the "One-Ship Fleet" and the fouling of the fuel tank with salt water during the battle in the Aleutians. The USS *Salt Lake City* served with distinction right up until the end, having returned to Okinawa after repairs at Leyte following the Battle of Okinawa. Once back on site, the *Salt Lake City* assisted in minesweeping activities and general patrol as part of Task Force 95 in the East China Sea. On August 31, 1945, the *Salt Lake City* was en route to the Aleutian Islands when she was diverted to Honshu, Japan, to assist in the occupation of the Ominato naval base.

In reviewing the ship's record—which is really the record of the people who served on board—the assault on Okinawa provides an insight into the kind of actions that the *Salt Lake City* encountered throughout the war. In that battle the *Salt Lake City* fired 9,070 rounds of eight-inch shells; 14,225 rounds of five-inch shells; 5,770 rounds of forty-mm shells; and 1,711 rounds of twenty-mm shells for a total of 30,776 shots. In addition, the ship's antiaircraft batteries assisted in downing hostile enemy aircraft and repulsing several kamikaze attacks.

Following the war, the *Salt Lake City* helped return veterans of the Pacific theater back to the United States.

On November 14, 1945, the *Salt Lake City* was scheduled for deactivation and was added to the list of warships to be used as test vessels for "Operation Crossroads," the atomic bomb experiments at Bikini Atoll. With her crew removed, the *Salt Lake City* was anchored near the atoll during an aerial atomic bomb explosion on July 1, 1946, and again during an underwater explosion on July 25. Remarkably, the *Salt Lake City* survived both of these blasts, though the hull was now radioactive and unfit for human habitation. The ship was towed to a decommissioning site on August 29, 1946, and mothballed until May 25, 1948, when the *Salt Lake City* was used as target practice and sunk off the coast of Southern California. A list of her distinguished accomplishments follows in the author's notes.

AUTHOR'S NOTE

The USS *Salt Lake City*'s distinguished combat record includes:

- Four enemy warships as well as eleven enemy transport and cargo ships sunk.
- Twelve confirmed enemy aircraft destroyed.
- Forty island beach landings supported with heavy shore fire.
- Multiple aircraft carriers protected as part of escort groups throughout the war.
- Eleven battle stars as well as a Navy unit commendation won.

As one of the few ships to serve the entire duration of the war, the *Salt Lake City* and its crew was the inspiration for popular books and movies. The 1962 bestselling book *In Harm's Way* was written by a veteran of the *Salt Lake City*, Captain James Bassett. The 1965 film *The Old Swayback* was based on the *Salt Lake City*, whose nickname was the "Swayback Maru," and starred several preeminent actors of the day, including John Wayne, Kirk Douglas, and Henry Fonda.

In 1973, nearly thirty years after the war, a reunion was

organized for the veterans of the *Salt Lake City* that was attended by hundreds of veterans and their families. There have been many reunions since. In 2022, just two veterans who served on the ship in World War II attended the reunion in Alexandria, Virginia: Gunner's Mate Al Jowdy, and Stores Assistant Sandy Oppenheimer. I had the good fortune to meet Al and Sandy at the 2022 reunion, as well as Walter Freysinger, who served on the *Salt Lake City* after the war. It was inspiring to learn of the pride they feel for their service on the ship and the camaraderie that has kept them coming to the reunions, even at ninety-six (Sandy) and ninety-five years of age (Al). They welcomed me with open arms, and it was a distinct honor to join them with their families for that experience.

Al Jowdy and his wife, Louise, have reviewed the manuscript for corrections and suggestions, particularly those chapters that discuss Al's service on the ship, as have Sandy Oppenheimer and his son Randy Oppenheimer.

With Al's and Sandy's permission I have created scenes in which they interact with other characters in the book, including fictional characters. While the settings for these scenes are based on Al's and Sandy's actual experiences in the war, such as their duty assignments and battle stations, the dialogue was invented to support the story line.

I appreciate their time and their friendship. Their firsthand knowledge of the ship provides authenticity to this story.

The USS *Salt Lake City (CA-25)* Association has been diligent in capturing the personal histories of many who served, and their stories are available at https://ussslcca25.com. I encourage you to visit the site and scroll through the hundreds of reminiscences captured by website curator Sandy Eskew, who has devoted countless hours to recording the history of the *Salt Lake City* and the men who served aboard it. I also want to recognize the tireless efforts of Mike Asea, who has collected memorabilia and photos that he brings to the reunions, and to Randy Oppenheimer, current president of the USS *Salt Lake City (CA-25)* Association, who helped me at every turn, including editing the manuscript.

After announcing to the group that I intended to write a book about the USS *Salt Lake City*, the people at the reunion—veterans and family members of men who served—adopted me into their circle and have helped this project move forward. I am deeply grateful.

CHARACTERS IN THIS BOOK

This novel is based on historical events. The battles and timelines are authentic, but in order to tell the remarkable story of the USS *Salt Lake City* most effectively, I mixed authentic characters who served during World War II with fictional characters. A list of which characters are historical and which are fictional precedes the first chapter.

Primary Historical Characters Who Served on the USS *Salt Lake City*

Al Jowdy of Houston, Texas. Al joined the Navy at age fifteen by writing down an incorrect birth year—at the time, seventeen was the minimum acceptable age. He served as a gunner's mate in the fantail of the ship (at the stern, directly above the propellers). Except for his trip to the bridge to be chastised by the captain and his assignment to move ammunition from the forward magazines to the stern, Al spent all his time in the fantail because enlisted men did not travel freely throughout the ship. His specific assignment was maintaining and assisting in the firing of the five-inch antiaircraft artillery guns on the fantail.

In 2022, Al Jowdy was an outgoing and friendly ninety-five-year-old who shared dozens of stories of his experiences on the *Salt Lake City* and other ships, as well as answering all the questions asked of him. I was captivated and have included many of these experiences in the book with his permission. I appreciate Al and his wife, Louise, for reading the manuscript and encouraging me through the writing.

It's important to note that *all* the stories in the book that feature Al Jowdy are based on his real-life experiences on the ship—and remarkable stories they are.

Al Jowdy

Sandy Oppenheimer of Langhorne, Pennsylvania. Sandy was ninety-six at the reunion, and is a thoughtful and considerate man. Sandy was a storekeeper on the ship and was proud to point to a photo of him and twenty-two other storekeepers taken during the war. It's believed that Sandy is the only one of this group who is still alive. Storekeepers ordered supplies and provisioning for the ship and manned the commissary, snack bar, and ice cream stand.

Sandy is a former president of the *Salt Lake City* association and organized many reunions. He befriended me and talked about the close association that existed among the men who served on the ship, even after the war.

Sandy Oppenheimer

Alex Mihalka and Elmer Breeze—Alex served as a bosun's mate, responsible for maintaining order on the deck, and Elmer was a gunner's mate working on the fantail. Both were friends of and at various times supervised Al Jowdy. Since Al was just fifteen years old when he started service on the *Salt Lake City*, Alex and Elmer watched out for him.

Walter Freysinger—Walter served on the *Salt Lake City* immediately after the end of World War II. I was pleased to meet him at the reunion. Walt worked to maintain the fresh-water evaporator/condensers that provided drinking water for the crew and fresh water for the steam turbines. I included him in Chapter 12, anachronistically, but as a way to explain the vital role that he and other technicians would play in meeting the needs of a crew of more than 1,000.

Captains of the USS *Salt Lake City* during the war. The following men served as commanding officers of the ship during the war. None are alive today, so any dialogue I attribute to a captain is a product of my imagination:

Captain **Ellis Zacharias** served from November 1940 to May 1942. Captain Zacharias was born in Jacksonville, Florida, and graduated in 1912 from the United States Naval Academy in Annapolis, Maryland. His first cruise was aboard the battleship USS *Arkansas* (BB-33) when it escorted President William Howard Taft to Panama to inspect the Panama Canal before water was turned into it. From 1913 to 1915, Zacharias served aboard the USS *Virginia* and was then stationed on the survey ship USS *Hannibal*. During World War I, he served aboard the USS *Pittsburgh*. Prior to commanding the USS *Salt Lake City*, Zacharias served as a naval attaché to Japan, which gave him unique insights into the culture of his future enemy. He predicted that Japan's initial attack on the United States would occur at

Pearl Harbor on a Sunday, which is exactly what happened on December 7, 1941. During the war, he remained at the rank of captain. After commanding the *Salt Lake City*, he conducted radio psychological warfare against the Japanese high command.

Captain **Ernest G. Small** served from May 1942 to January 2, 1943. Small was born in Waltham, Massachusetts, on November 5, 1888. He graduated from the USNA, receiving his commission in 1912. From 1940 to 1942 he headed the ordnance and gunnery department at the Naval Academy. He assumed command of the *Salt Lake City* in 1942 and was awarded the Navy Cross for extraordinary heroism for his conning of the *Salt Lake City* against enemy combatants at Savo Island in October 1942 in the Battle of Cape Esperance. After his service on the ship, Small served as a war plans officer on the staff of the Pacific fleet's commander-in-chief. He was then promoted to commander of Cruiser Division 5. He died a rear admiral in Brooklyn, New York, in 1944.

Captain **Bertram J. Rodgers** served from January 2, 1943, to September 1943. Rodgers was born March 19, 1894, in Knoxville, Pennsylvania. He graduated from the USNA in 1916. He was assigned to the battleship USS *South Carolina* and served in the Atlantic during World War I. He received a Navy Cross as the captain of the USS *Salt Lake City* during the Aleutian Islands campaign. He subsequently commanded the submarines USS *H-8* and USS *R-8* and also served as an engineer and repair officer at the submarine base Coco Solo in the Panama Canal Zone. He was eventually promoted to vice admiral. I met his granddaughters Cece Casey and Casey Quinlan at the 2022 reunion and appreciated their insights.

Captain **Leroy W. Busbey** served from September 5, 1943, to October 25, 1944. He was born March 7, 1897, in Washington,

DC. He graduated from the USNA in 1917, and served as executive officer or commander of several submarines and destroyers before being advanced to the rank of captain and given command of the USS *Salt Lake City*. As captain of the *Salt Lake City*, he was awarded the Silver Star during the occupation of the Gilbert Islands in November 1943, and the Legion of Merit with Combat "V" during the Marshall Islands campaign in January and February of 1944. He was a rear admiral and the general inspector of the 12th Naval District when he retired in 1949. He died in San Francisco, California, on February 27, 1952.

Captain **Edward A. Mitchell** served from October 1944 to September 1945. Biographical information on Captain Mitchell is incomplete, but under his command, the *Salt Lake City* participated actively in the final year of battles in World War II, including offensive action against the Volcano Islands to protect B-29 airfields on Saipan, Tinian, and Guam. The ship bombarded Iwo Jima on multiple occasions to support the landing of troops there. While doing so, the ship came under attack by kamikaze bombers but shot down two of these aircraft and evaded others. During this time the ship lost a scout observation plane and two officers to enemy gunfire. Following Iwo Jima, the *Salt Lake City* moved on to support the assault on Okinawa. In August 1945, the *Salt Lake City* was assigned to cover the Allied occupation of the Ominato naval base in northern Honshu, Japan, after the cessation of hostilities and Japan's unconditional surrender.

CHAPTER NOTES

Chapter 1

The Pearl Harbor attack came in two waves. The first wave of Japanese aircraft arrived in Oahu at 7:40 a.m. Hawaii time and came from the northwest; the second wave came from the northeast and about a third of its planes attacked the naval air station at Kaneohe first, then flew over the eastern mountains to attack Pearl Harbor. Three US Navy ships were a complete loss: the USS *Arizona*, the USS *Oklahoma*, and the USS *Utah*. Sixteen other US ships were damaged but later repaired or rebuilt.

The Japanese air assault was comprised of 353 aircraft supported by sixty-seven ships; of those ships, only one survived through the end of World War II. Twenty-nine of the aircraft were lost in the attack.

There were 2,404 US citizens killed in the attack: sixty-eight civilians and 1,227 military personnel, of which 1,177 were sailors aboard the USS *Arizona* when it exploded. Of the military survivors, fifteen were given the Medal of Honor and fifty-one the Navy Cross for their actions during the attack. All military veterans of the attack were given the Pearl Harbor Commemorative Medal.

See https://cdn.britannica.com/40/230940-050-4DE23CD8
/infographic-Pearl-Harbor-attack-World-War-II-1941.jpg.

Chapter 2

Casualties from the Pearl Harbor attack were sent initially to
aid stations set up on shore or to the hospital ship USS *Solace*.
From there, many were sent to the Pearl Harbor Naval Hospital
and the Aeia Plantation Hospital. See https://www.history.navy
.mil/research/library/online-reading-room/title-list-alphabetically
/p/pearl-harbor-navy-medical-activities.html.

Chapter 3

The Kingfisher SOCs were powered by an air-cooled Pratt
and Whitney 450-horsepower rotary engine, but rarely could ex-
ceed a top speed of about 166 miles per hour. While that was
advantageous for a search and reconnaissance plane, it also meant
that the Kingfisher pilots needed to be aware and resourceful in
the middle of hostilities. "A crafty pilot could, however, work
the Kingfisher's slow speed to his advantage. Joe McGuinness
was flying a Kingfisher from the light cruiser USS *Birmingham*
over Japanese-occupied Wake Island when a Zero jumped him.
McGuinness immediately reduced his speed to just above stall
speed. 'We were almost falling out of the sky,' recalls the retired
naval aviator. He turned the Kingfisher toward the oncoming
Japanese fighter to give his gunner a good shot at the enemy pilot.
'He [the Zero] was going too fast, and just skidded right over us.
My gunner was shooting at him, but we didn't stick around to see
if we hit him or his airplane'" (James L. Noles Jr., "Old Slow and
Ugly," *Air and Space*, February/March 2005, 68).

Chapter 4

Officially, no one underage served in the United States military during World War II—the regulations were that you could enlist at eighteen, or seventeen with a parent's permission. That didn't stop US teenagers (and even younger) from misrepresenting their ages and joining under false pretenses. More than 50,000 underage soldiers and sailors were identified during the war, and many were discharged from the service. One estimate is that up to 200,000 US troops were underage. The youngest of those caught was Calvin Graham, who escaped an abusive home situation and enlisted in the Navy in 1942 at the age of twelve. He was discovered, discharged, and stripped of his medals in 1943, but rejoined the military (the Marines this time) at seventeen. He left the Marines when he broke his back in 1951. He had most of his medals returned and was given an honorable discharge from the Navy by President Jimmy Carter in 1978; his Purple Heart (and disability benefits) were returned to his widow posthumously in 1988. See Joshua Pollarine, "Children at War: Underage Americans Illegally Fighting the Second World War" (master's thesis, University of Montana, 2008; available at https://scholarworks.umt.edu/cgi/viewcontent.cgi?article=1210&contex=etd); see also en.wikipedia.org/wiki/Calvin_Graham.

Chapter 5

The wreck of the USS *Wasp* was discovered in 2019 by the expedition vessel RV *Petrel*. See https://www.history.com/news/wwii-shipwreck-uss-wasp-discovery.

Chapter 6

While the nickname the "One-Ship Fleet" was given to the USS *Salt Lake City* after the Battle of Cape Esperance, she was nicknamed the "Swayback Maru" by the war correspondent Robert J. Casey and was also known by her crew as the "Old Swayback." See, for example, "USS *Salt Lake City*," *University of Utah Athletics*; available at https://ussslc.utah.edu/history/.

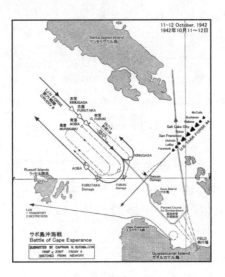

Chapter 7

The USS *Salt Lake City* spent four months in dry dock at Pearl Harbor after the Battle of Cape Esperance, sailing in March 1943 for the Aleutian Islands.

Chapter 8

For their service during the Battle of the Komandorski Islands, two of the USS *Salt Lake City*'s officer corps were awarded the Silver Star and seven other sailors (two officers and five enlisted) were awarded letters of commendation, of which SF1/C Vito Bommarito was one.

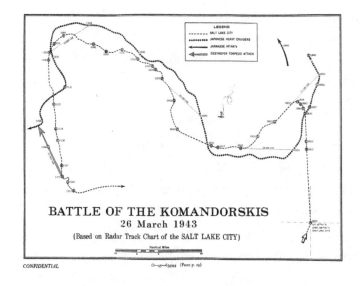

BATTLE OF THE KOMANDORSKIS
26 March 1943
(Based on Radar Track Chart of the SALT LAKE CITY)

CONFIDENTIAL

Chapter 9

For more information about Marlene Dietrich's involvement in the USO during World War II, see Danielle DeSimone, "Why Marlene Dietrich Was One of the Most Patriotic Women in World War II," *USO.org*; available at https://www .uso.org/stories/2414-marlene-dietrich-most-patriotic-women -in-world-war-ii; see also Maria Riva, *Marlene Dietrich: The Life* (New York: Knopf, 1993), and Karin Wieland, *Dietrich and Riefenstahl: Hollywood, Berlin, and a Century in Two Lives* (New York: Liveright, 2016).

Chapter 10

While most chaplains' duties include the kind of service Al Jowdy encountered, there is a long history of heroism among the chaplain corps as well. See, for example, "US Navy Chaplain Corps," *Naval History and Heritage Command* (website); available at https://www.history.navy.mil/browse-by-topic/communities

/chaplain-corps.html; as well as Steven T. Collis, *The Immortals: The World War II Story of Five Fearless Heroes, the Sinking of the* Dorchester, *and an Awe-Inspiring Rescue* (Salt Lake City: Shadow Mountain, 2021).

Chapter 11

Riley Bracken (and to a lesser extent, Justin Collier) suffered from what we today call PTSD—post-traumatic stress disorder. But this condition has been recognized as far back as the Assyrian dynasty in Mesopotamia (ca. 1300–609 BCE).

"The battles were over, but the soldiers still fought. Flashbacks, nightmares, and depression plagued them. Some slurred their speech. Others couldn't concentrate. Haunted and fearful, the soldiers struggled with the ghosts of war.

"Which war? If you guessed Vietnam, the U.S. Civil War, or even World War I, you'd be wrong. These soldiers' symptoms were recorded not on paper charts, but on cuneiform tablets inscribed in Mesopotamia more than 3,000 years ago. . . .

"WWI introduced terrifying new combat technology on a previously unimaginable scale, and soldiers left the front shattered. Seemingly overnight, the field of war psychiatry emerged and a new term—shell shock—appeared to describe a range of mental injuries, from facial tics to an inability to speak. Hundreds of thousands of men on both sides left World War I with what would now be called PTSD. . . .

"By World War II, psychiatrists increasingly recognized that combat would have mental health ramifications—and concluded that too many men who were prone to anxiety or 'neurotic tendencies' had been selected to serve in the previous war. But though six times as many American men were screened and rejected for service in the lead-up to World War II, military service still took its toll. About twice as many American soldiers showed symptoms of PTSD during World War II than in World War I. This time their condition was called 'psychiatric collapse,' 'combat fatigue,' or 'war neurosis'" (Erin Blakemore, "How PTSD went from 'shell shock' to a recognized medical diagnosis," *NationalGeographic. com* (website); available at https://www.nationalgeographic.com /history/article/ptsd-shell-shock-to-recognized-medical-diagnosis).

Chapter 12

The guns pictured here are the forty-mm "Bofors" guns for which Al Jowdy was part of the gun crew. Note the spent shells against the bulkhead at the bottom right of the picture.

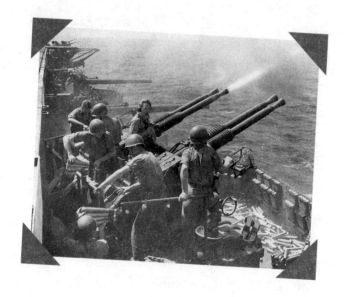

Chapter 13

Years before the Collier family's cross-country trip, the *City of San Francisco* train was the target of intentional sabotage, derailed in Nevada along the Humboldt River. See, for instance,

Jerry Borrowman, *Catastrophes and Heroes: True Stories of Man-Made Disasters* (Salt Lake City: Shadow Mountain, 2020), 121–41. The picture here is from the initial trial run of the *City of San Francisco* in 1936.

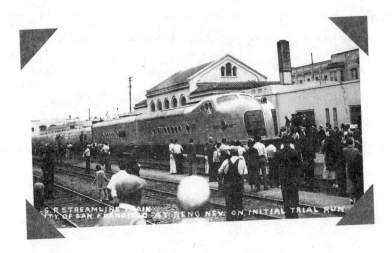

Chapter 14

Al Jowdy's experience with smuggled rations in the brig was exceptional by naval standards. It wasn't until January 1, 2019, that a punishment of confinement with bread and water rations was discontinued in the US Navy (by then, it had been standardized to "only" three days punishment and "only" for the three lowest pay grades of enlisted sailors). See John Ismay, "The End of the Navy's Bread-and-Water Punishment," *New York Times Magazine*, January 4, 2019.

Chapter 15

For a good overview of the WASPs in World War II, see Caroline Johnson, "Women with Wings: The Legacy of the WASP,"

National Air and Space Museum (website); available at https://airandspace.si.edu/stories/editorial/women-wings-legacy-wasp. See also "WASP History," *Women Airforce Service Pilots Official Archive* (website); available at https://twu.edu/library/womans-collection/collections/women-airforce-service-pilots-official-archive/history/.

Chapter 16

For more information about the Navy's bombardment and the Marines' subsequent invasion of Okinawa, see "Battle of Okinawa," *The National WWII Museum* (website); available at https://www.nationalww2museum.org/war/topics/battle-of-okinawa.